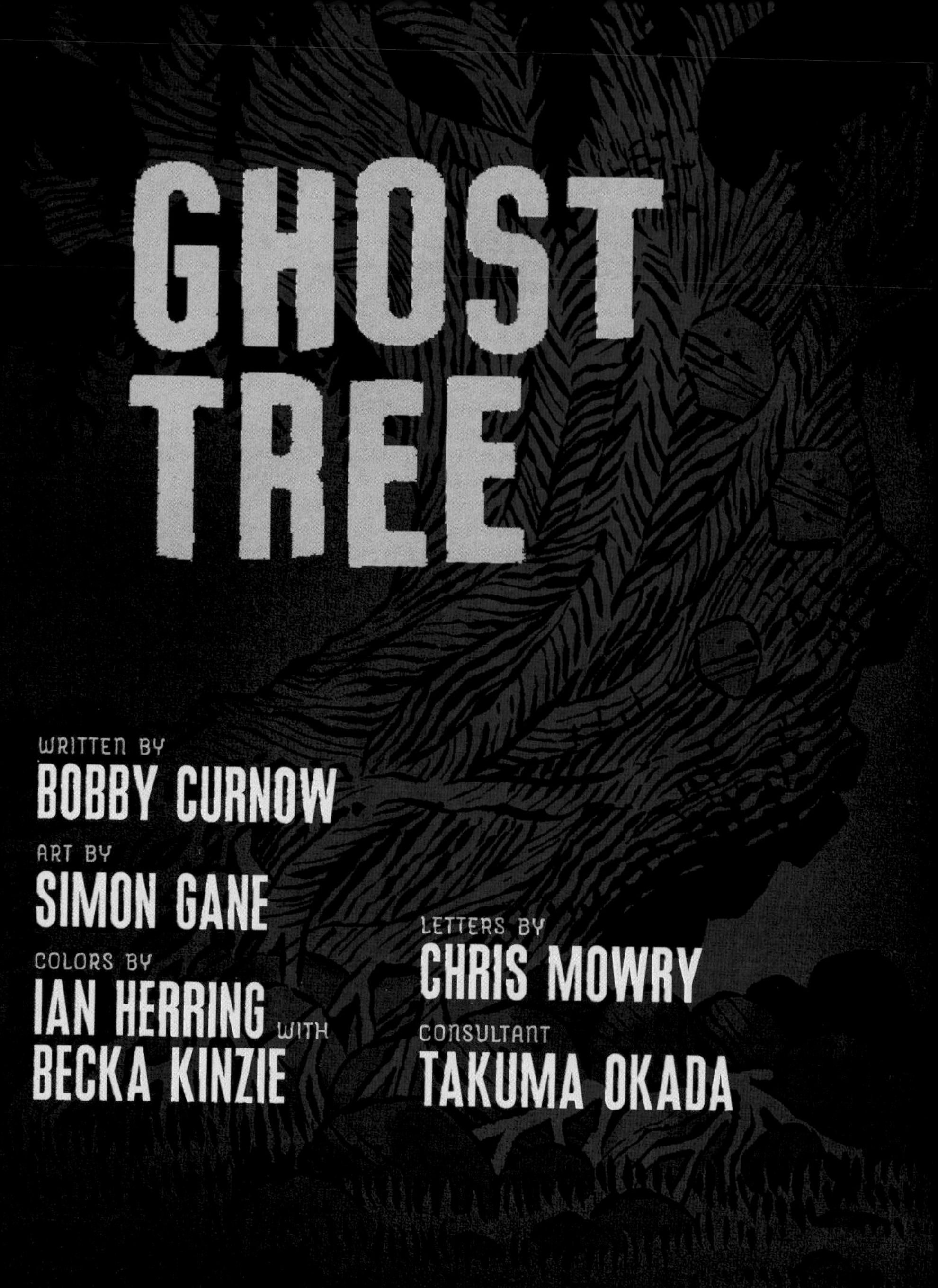

GHOST TREE

WRITTEN BY
BOBBY CURNOW

ART BY
SIMON GANE

COLORS BY
IAN HERRING WITH
BECKA KINZIE

LETTERS BY
CHRIS MOWRY

CONSULTANT
TAKUMA OKADA

COVER ART BY
MON GANE

COLLECTION EDITS BY
JSTIN EISINGER
ND ALONZO SIMON

COLLECTION DESIGN BY
FF POWELL

ebsite: facebook.com/idwpublishing
tter: @idwpublishing
Tube: voutu /idwpublishing

ISBN: 978-1-68405-599-9   22 21 20 19   1 2 3 4

GHOST TREE. NOVEMBER 2019. FIRST PRINTING. © CURNOW, GANE, HERRING
© 2019 Idea and Design Works, LLC. The IDW logo is registered in the U.S.
Patent and Trademark Office. IDW Publishing, a division of Idea and Design
Works, LLC. Editorial offices: 2765 Truxtun Road, San Diego, CA 92106. Any
similarities to persons living or dead are purely coincidental. With the exception
of artwork used for review purposes, none of the contents of this publication
may be reprinted without the permission of Idea and Design Works, LLC. Printed
in Korea.

Chris Ryall, President, Publisher, & CCO

John Barber, Editor-In-Chief

Cara Morrison, Chief Financial Officer

Matt Ruzicka, Chief Accounting Officer

David Hedgecock, Associate Publisher

Jerry Bennington, VP of New Product Development

Lorelei Bunjes, VP of Digital Services

Justin Eisinger, Editorial Director, Graphic Novels & Collections

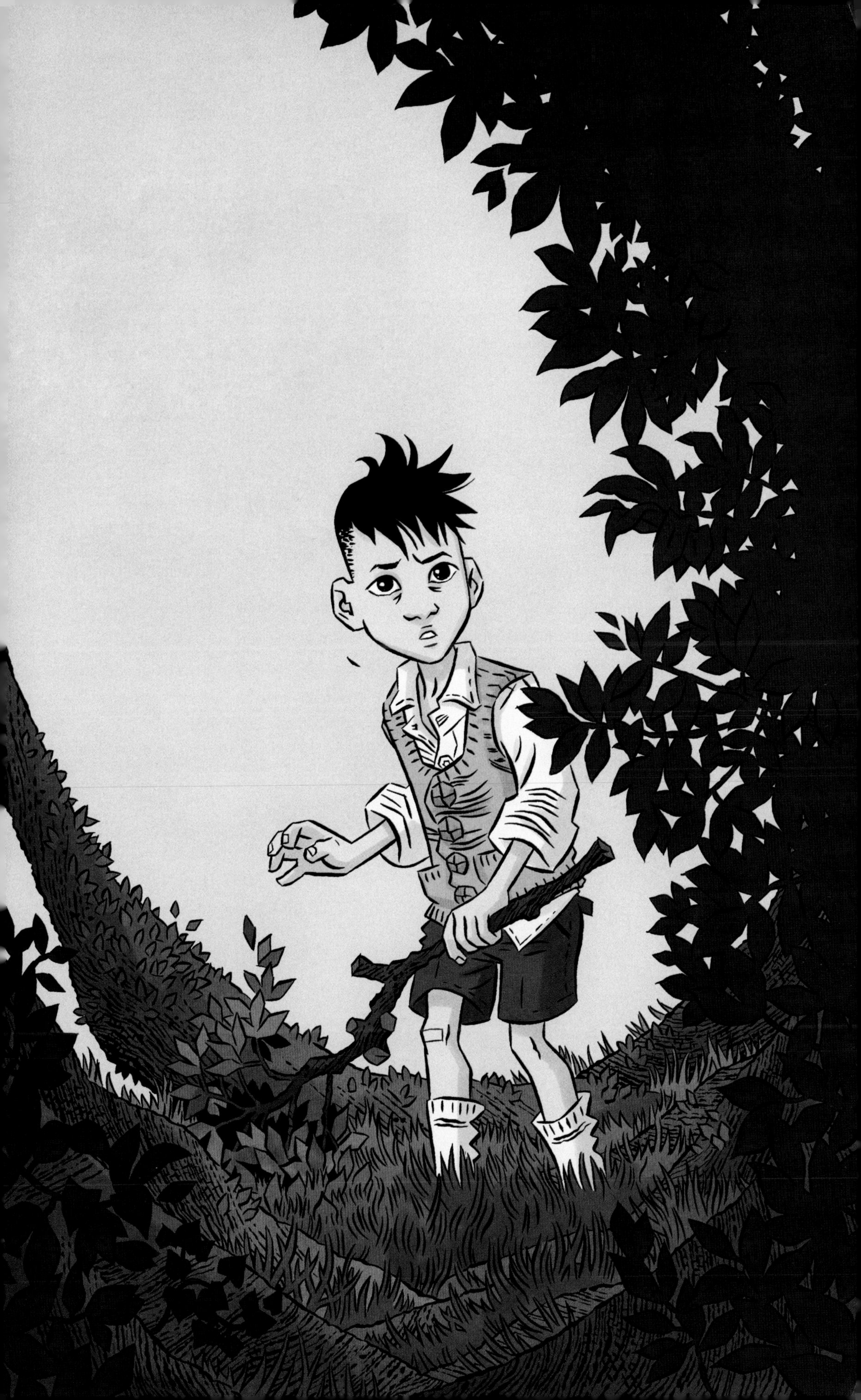

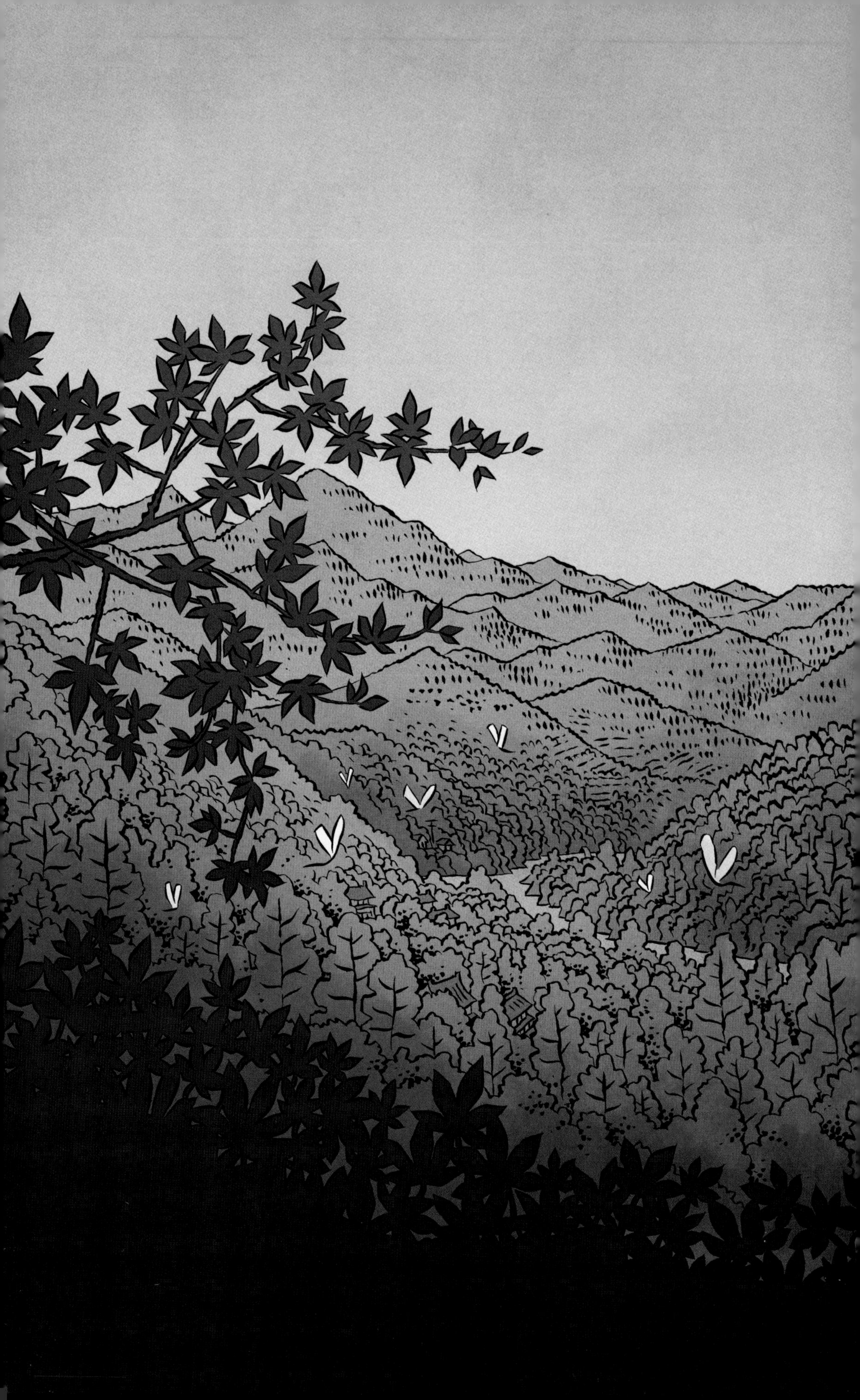

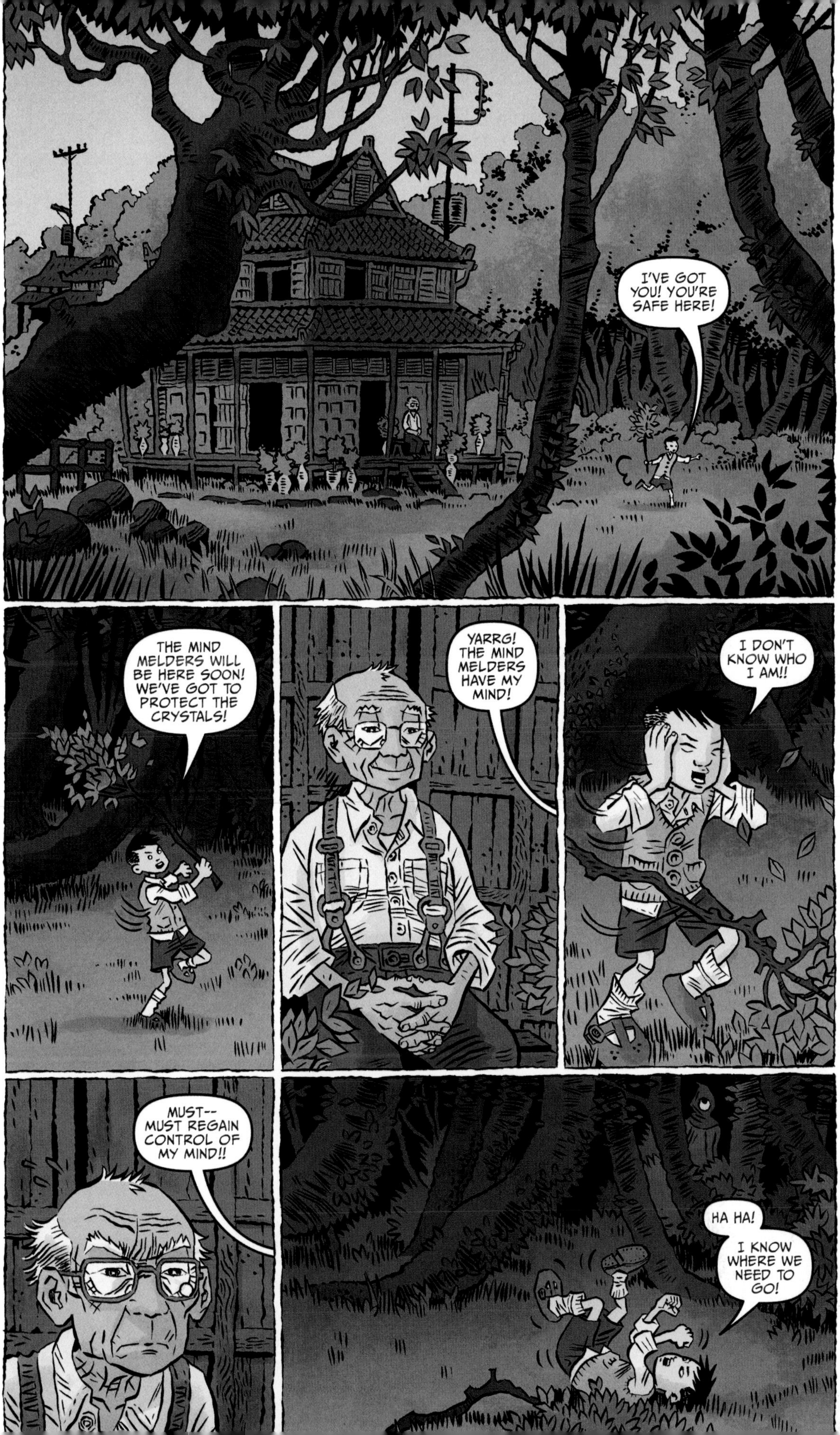
I'VE GOT YOU! YOU'RE SAFE HERE!
THE MIND MELDERS WILL BE HERE SOON! WE'VE GOT TO PROTECT THE CRYSTALS!
YARRG! THE MIND MELDERS HAVE MY MIND!
I DON'T KNOW WHO I AM!!
MUST-- MUST REGAIN CONTROL OF MY MIND!!
HA HA!
I KNOW WHERE WE NEED TO GO!

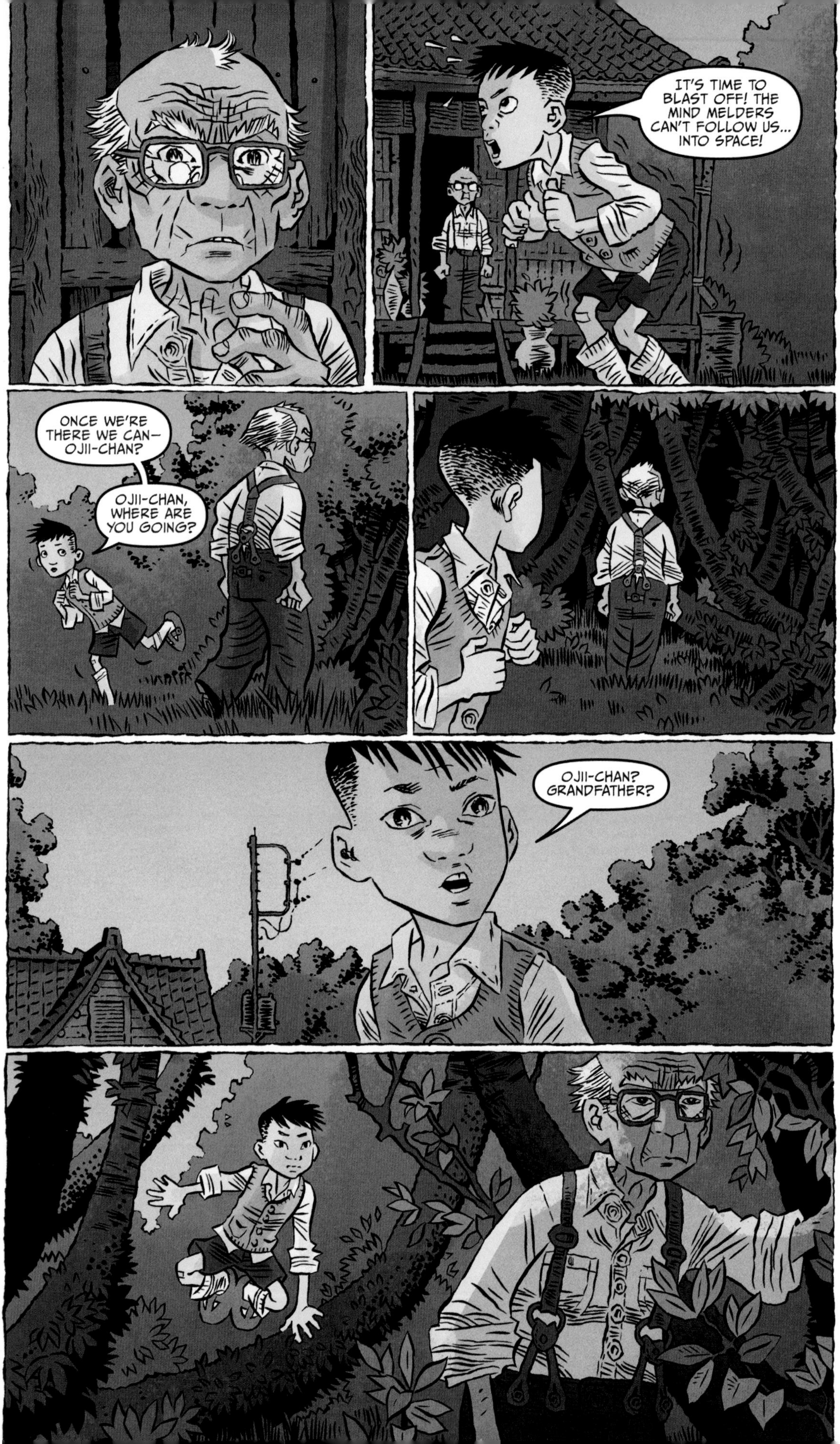
IT'S TIME TO BLAST OFF! THE MIND MELDERS CAN'T FOLLOW US... INTO SPACE!
ONCE WE'RE THERE WE CAN— OJII-CHAN?
OJII-CHAN, WHERE ARE YOU GOING?
OJII-CHAN? GRANDFATHER?

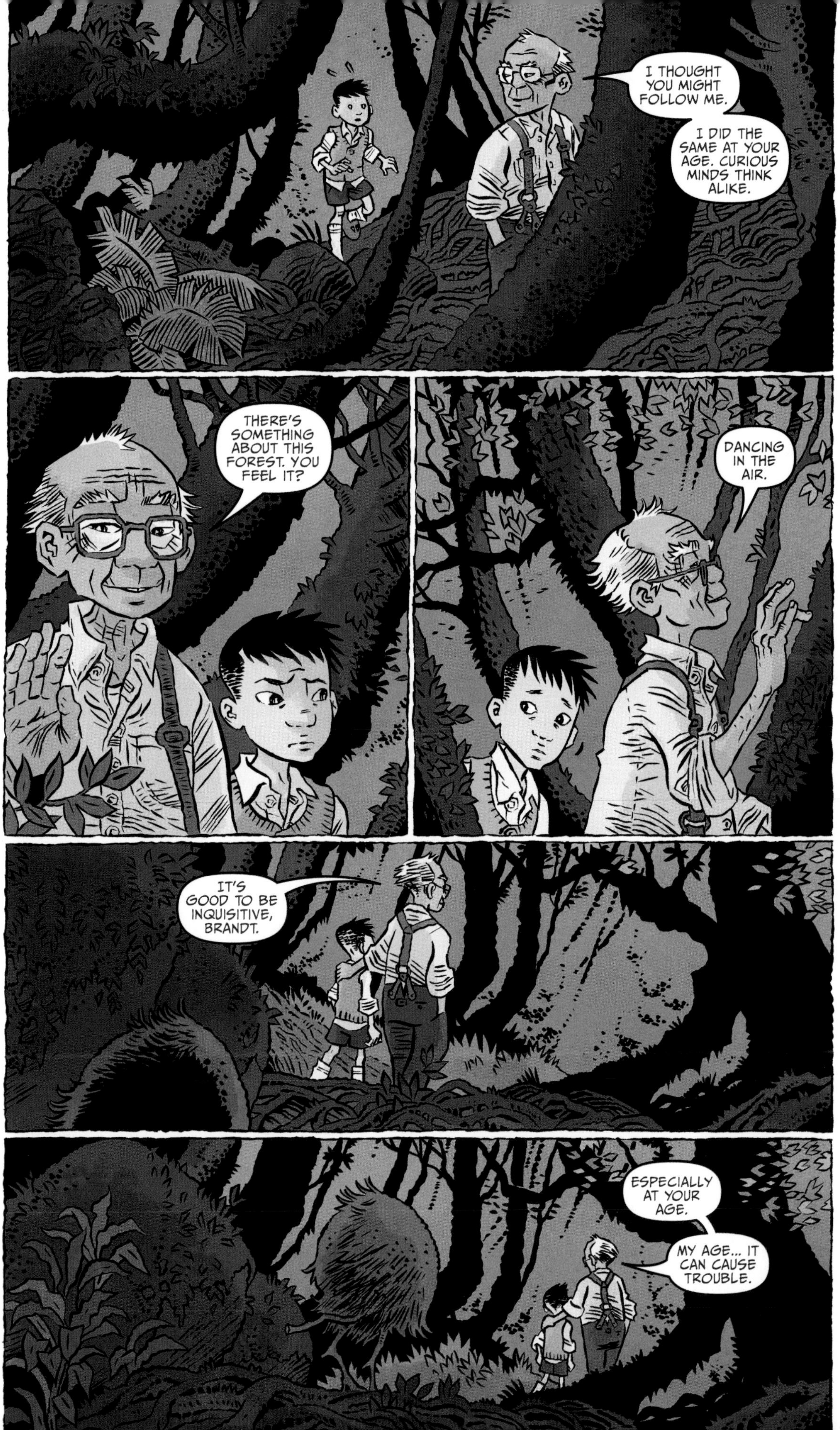
I THOUGHT YOU MIGHT FOLLOW ME.
I DID THE SAME AT YOUR AGE. CURIOUS MINDS THINK ALIKE.
THERE'S SOMETHING ABOUT THIS FOREST. YOU FEEL IT?
DANCING IN THE AIR.
IT'S GOOD TO BE INQUISITIVE, BRANDT.
ESPECIALLY AT YOUR AGE.
MY AGE... IT CAN CAUSE TROUBLE.

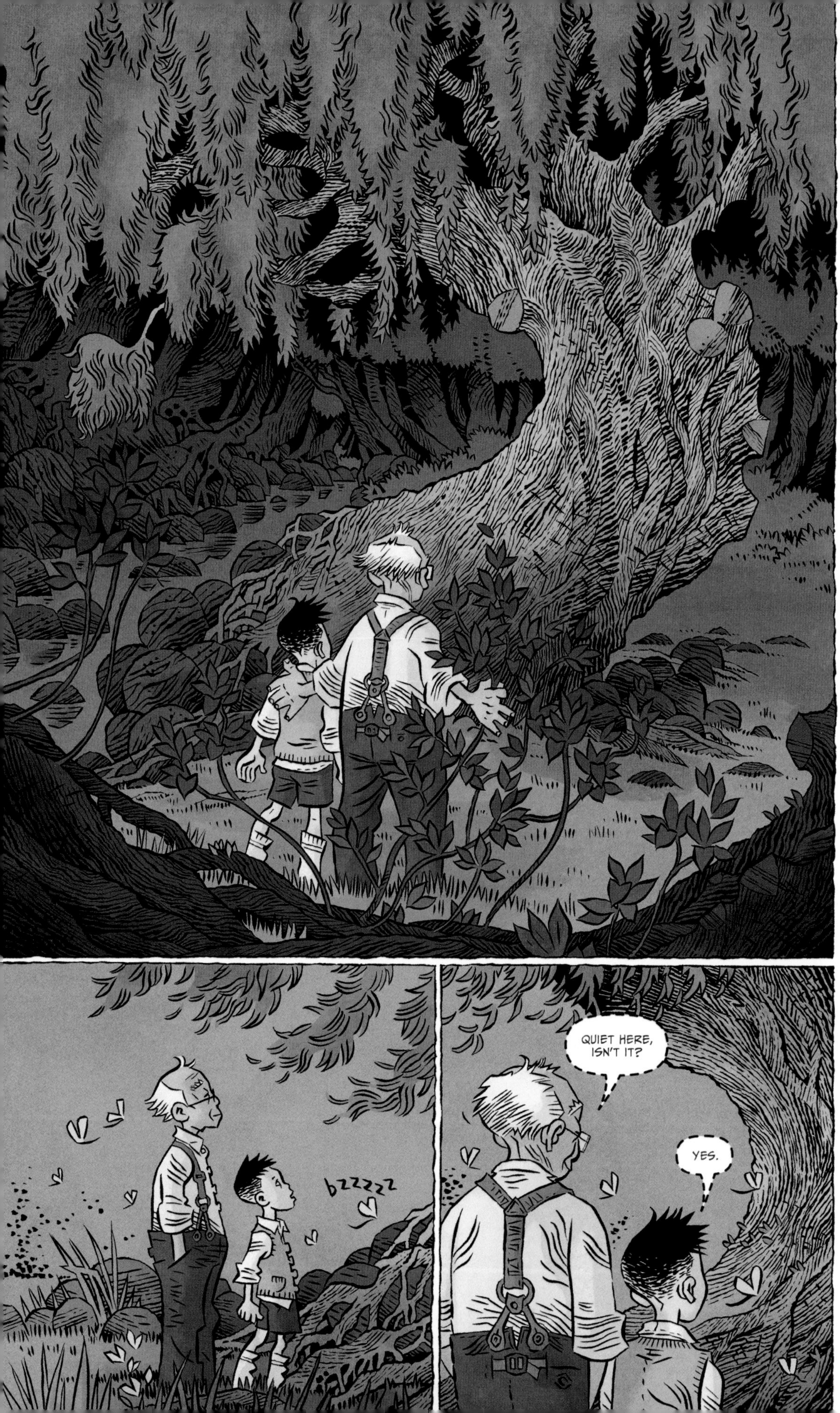
bzzzzz
QUIET HERE, ISN'T IT?
YES.

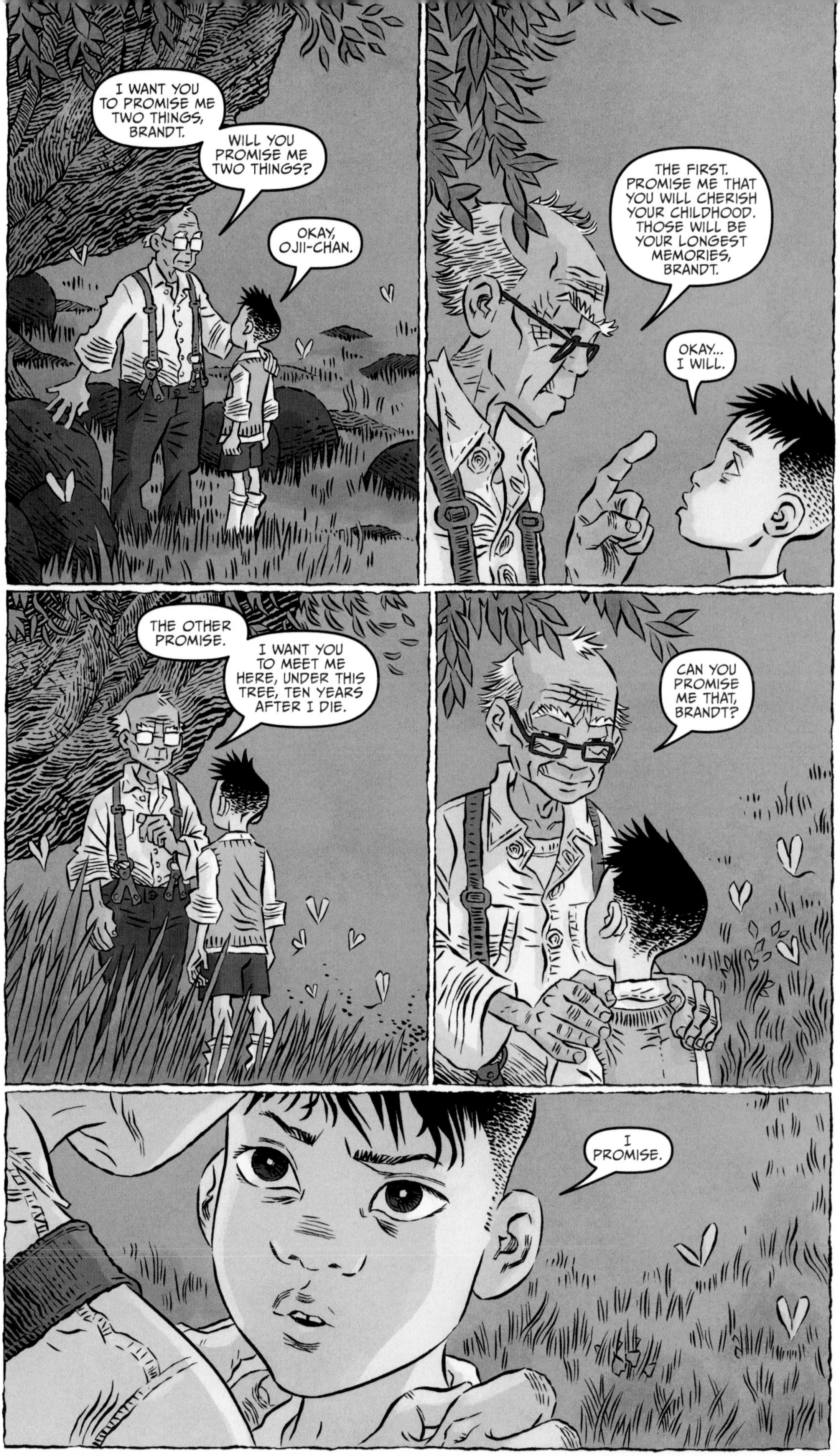
I WANT YOU TO PROMISE ME TWO THINGS, BRANDT.
WILL YOU PROMISE ME TWO THINGS?
OKAY, OJII-CHAN.
THE FIRST. PROMISE ME THAT YOU WILL CHERISH YOUR CHILDHOOD. THOSE WILL BE YOUR LONGEST MEMORIES, BRANDT.
OKAY... I WILL.
THE OTHER PROMISE.
I WANT YOU TO MEET ME HERE, UNDER THIS TREE, TEN YEARS AFTER I DIE.
CAN YOU PROMISE ME THAT, BRANDT?
I PROMISE.

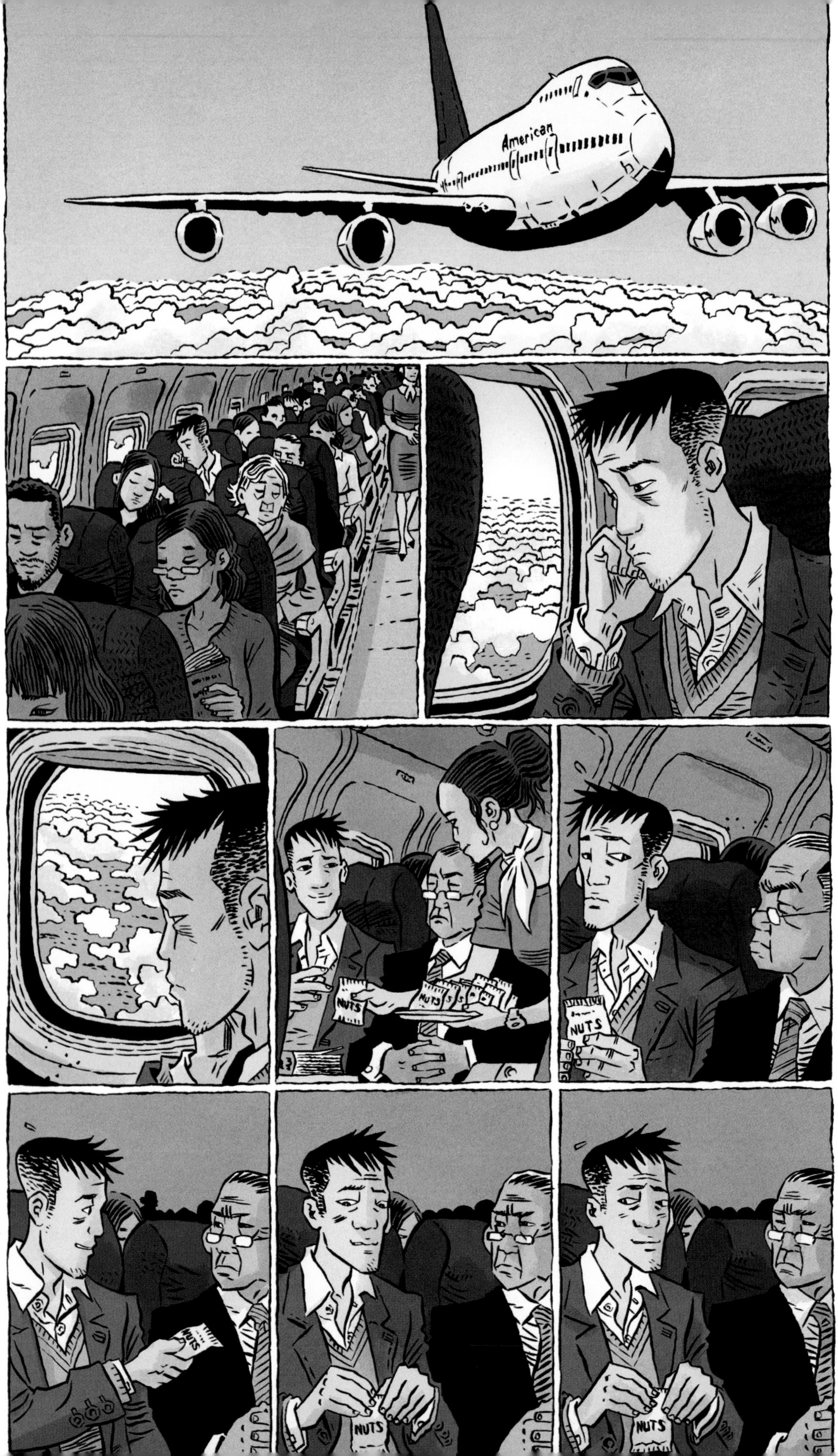
American
NUTS
NUTS
NUTS
NUTS
NUTS

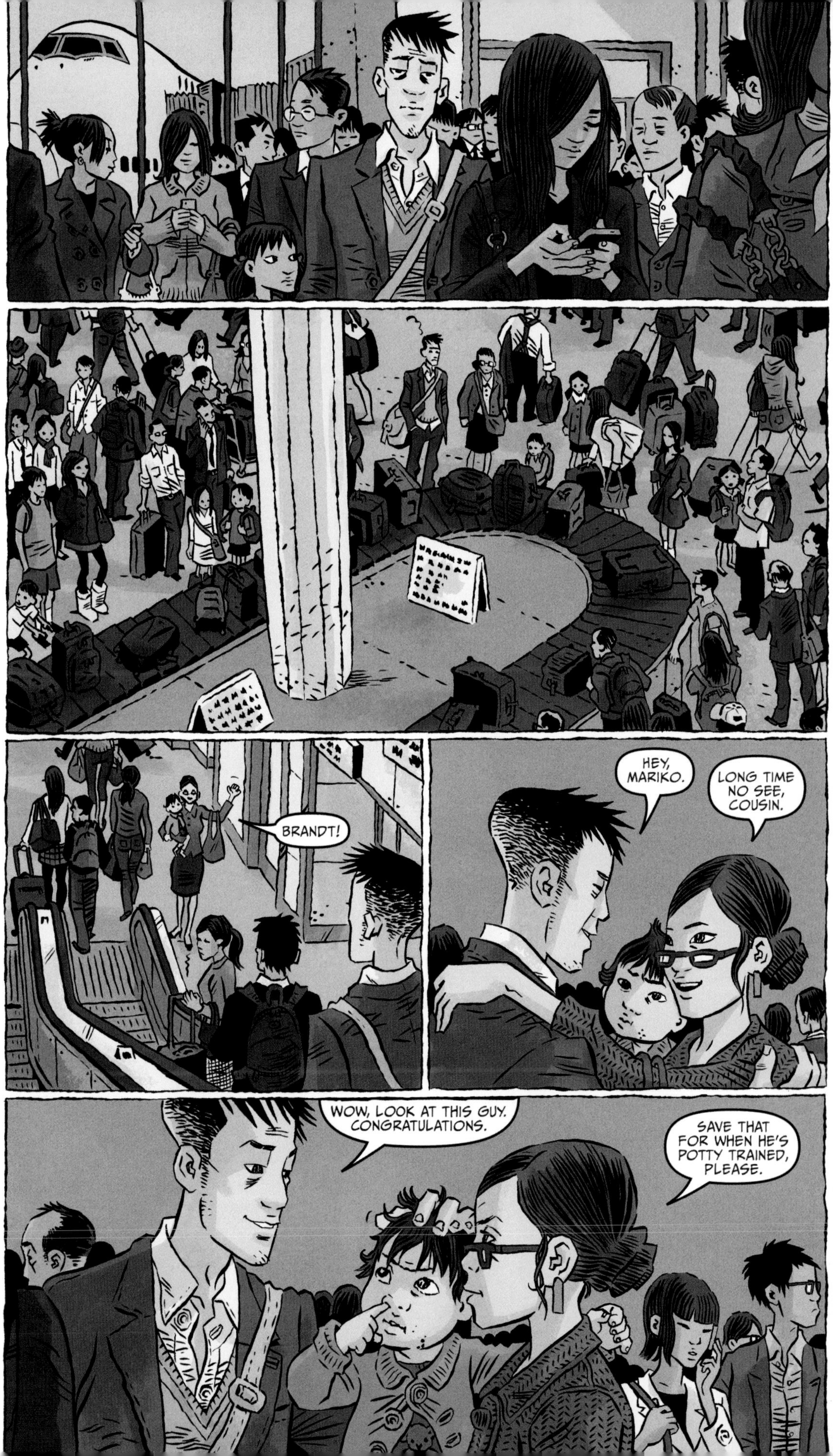
BRANDT!
HEY, MARIKO.
LONG TIME NO SEE, COUSIN.
WOW, LOOK AT THIS GUY. CONGRATULATIONS.
SAVE THAT FOR WHEN HE'S POTTY TRAINED, PLEASE.

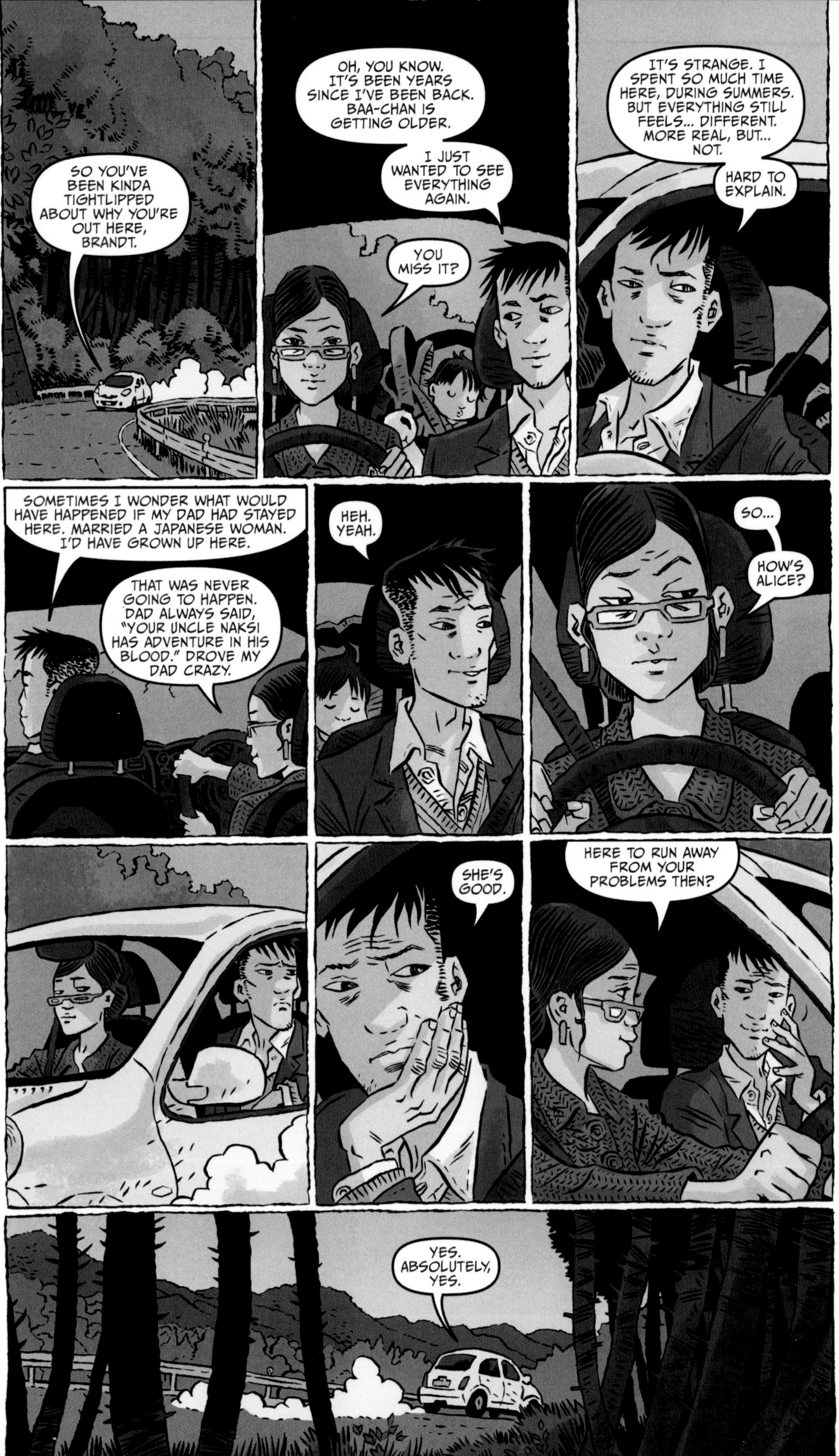
SO YOU'VE BEEN KINDA TIGHTLIPPED ABOUT WHY YOU'RE OUT HERE, BRANDT.
OH, YOU KNOW. IT'S BEEN YEARS SINCE I'VE BEEN BACK. BAA-CHAN IS GETTING OLDER.
I JUST WANTED TO SEE EVERYTHING AGAIN.
YOU MISS IT?
IT'S STRANGE. I SPENT SO MUCH TIME HERE, DURING SUMMERS. BUT EVERYTHING STILL FEELS... DIFFERENT. MORE REAL, BUT... NOT.
HARD TO EXPLAIN.
SOMETIMES I WONDER WHAT WOULD HAVE HAPPENED IF MY DAD HAD STAYED HERE. MARRIED A JAPANESE WOMAN. I'D HAVE GROWN UP HERE.
THAT WAS NEVER GOING TO HAPPEN. DAD ALWAYS SAID, "YOUR UNCLE NAKSI HAS ADVENTURE IN HIS BLOOD." DROVE MY DAD CRAZY.
HEH. YEAH.
SO...
HOW'S ALICE?
SHE'S GOOD.
HERE TO RUN AWAY FROM YOUR PROBLEMS THEN?
YES. ABSOLUTELY, YES.

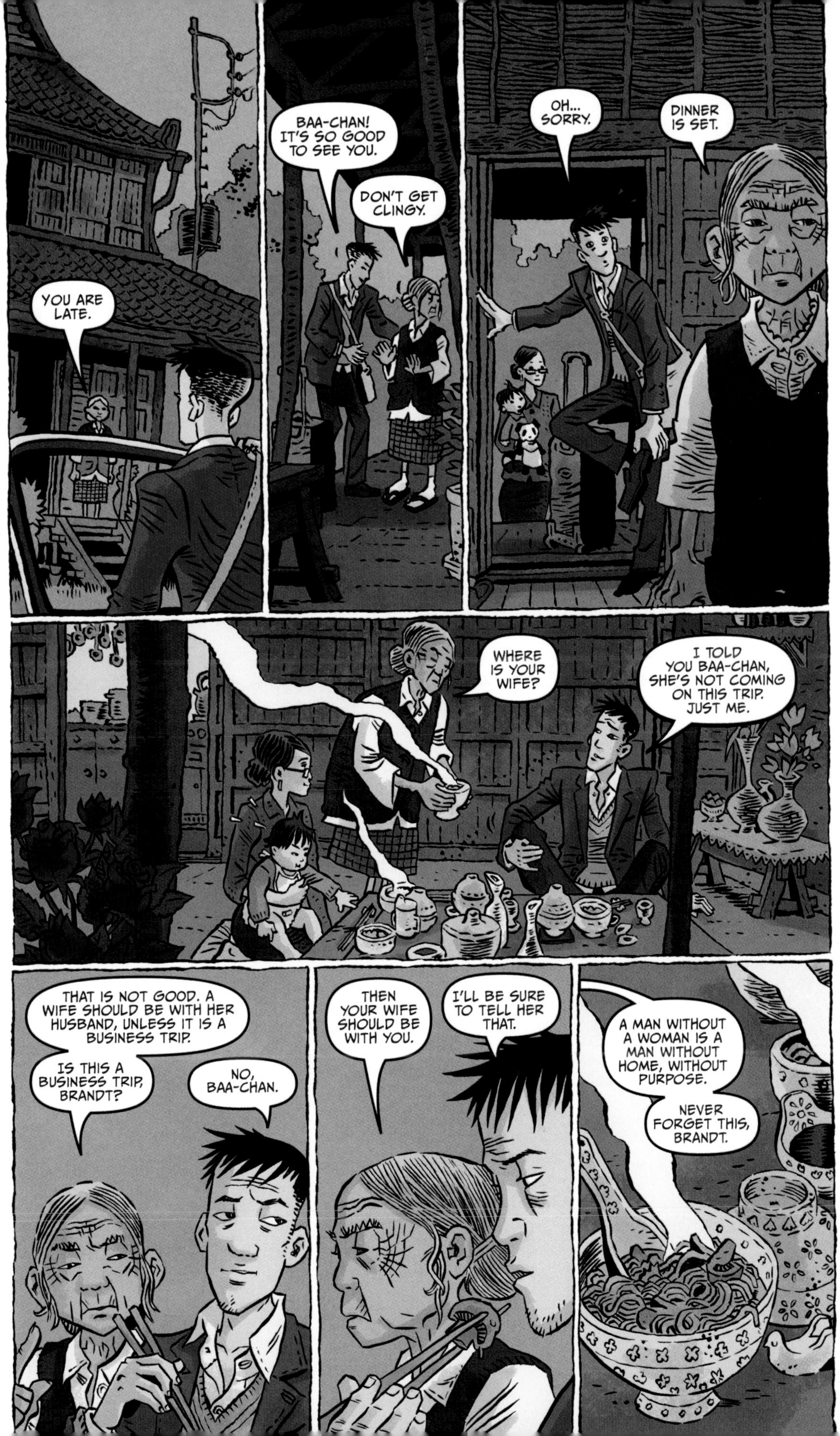
YOU ARE LATE.
BAA-CHAN! IT'S SO GOOD TO SEE YOU.
DON'T GET CLINGY.
OH... SORRY.
DINNER IS SET.
WHERE IS YOUR WIFE?
I TOLD YOU BAA-CHAN, SHE'S NOT COMING ON THIS TRIP. JUST ME.
THAT IS NOT GOOD. A WIFE SHOULD BE WITH HER HUSBAND, UNLESS IT IS A BUSINESS TRIP.
IS THIS A BUSINESS TRIP, BRANDT?
NO, BAA-CHAN.
THEN YOUR WIFE SHOULD BE WITH YOU.
I'LL BE SURE TO TELL HER THAT.
A MAN WITHOUT A WOMAN IS A MAN WITHOUT HOME, WITHOUT PURPOSE.
NEVER FORGET THIS, BRANDT.

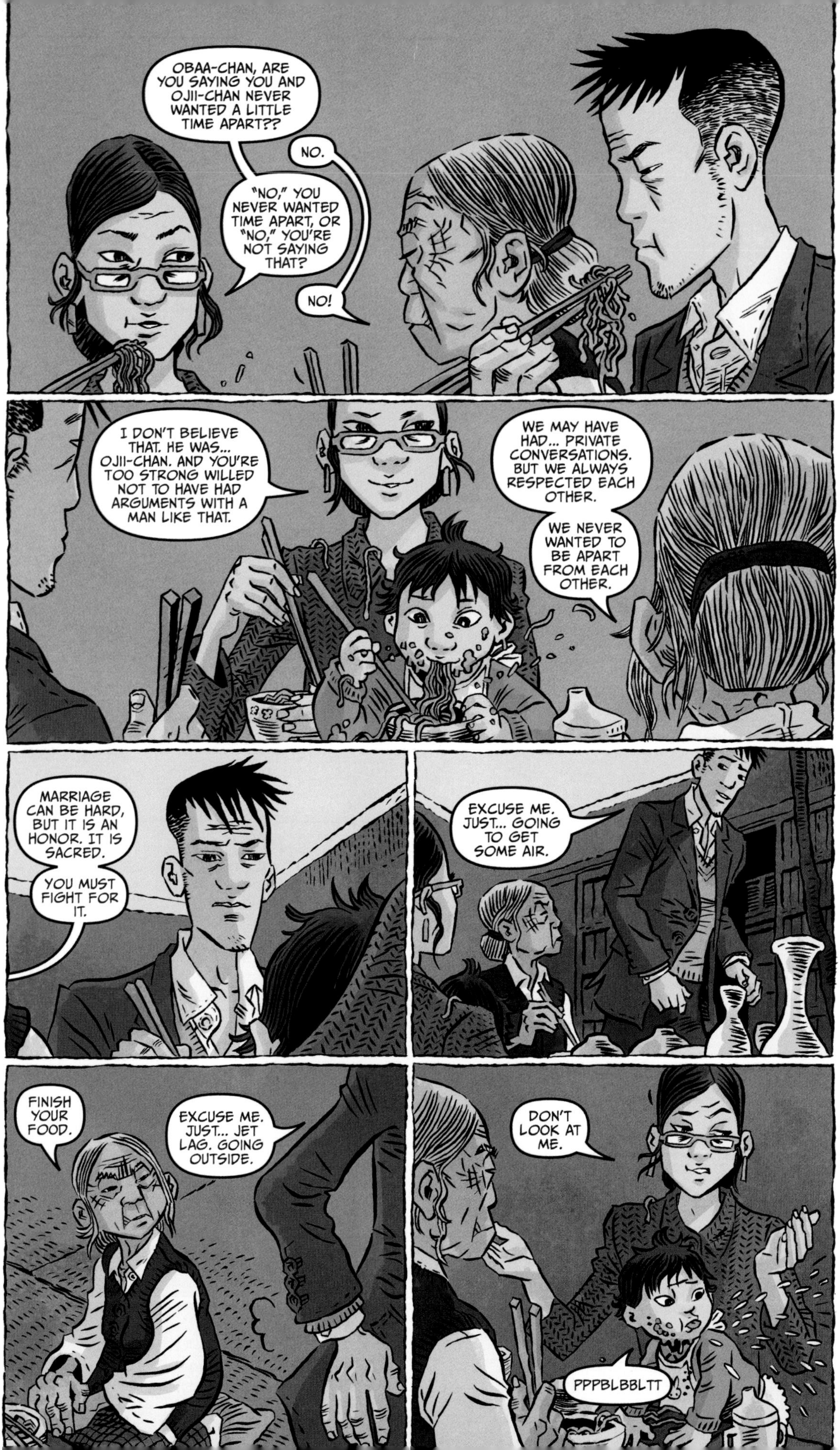
OBAA-CHAN, ARE YOU SAYING YOU AND OJII-CHAN NEVER WANTED A LITTLE TIME APART??
NO.
"NO," YOU NEVER WANTED TIME APART, OR "NO," YOU'RE NOT SAYING THAT?
NO!
I DON'T BELIEVE THAT. HE WAS... OJII-CHAN. AND YOU'RE TOO STRONG WILLED NOT TO HAVE HAD ARGUMENTS WITH A MAN LIKE THAT.
WE MAY HAVE HAD... PRIVATE CONVERSATIONS. BUT WE ALWAYS RESPECTED EACH OTHER.
WE NEVER WANTED TO BE APART FROM EACH OTHER.
MARRIAGE CAN BE HARD, BUT IT IS AN HONOR. IT IS SACRED.
YOU MUST FIGHT FOR IT.
EXCUSE ME. JUST... GOING TO GET SOME AIR.
FINISH YOUR FOOD.
EXCUSE ME. JUST... JET LAG. GOING OUTSIDE.
DON'T LOOK AT ME.
PPPBLBBLTT

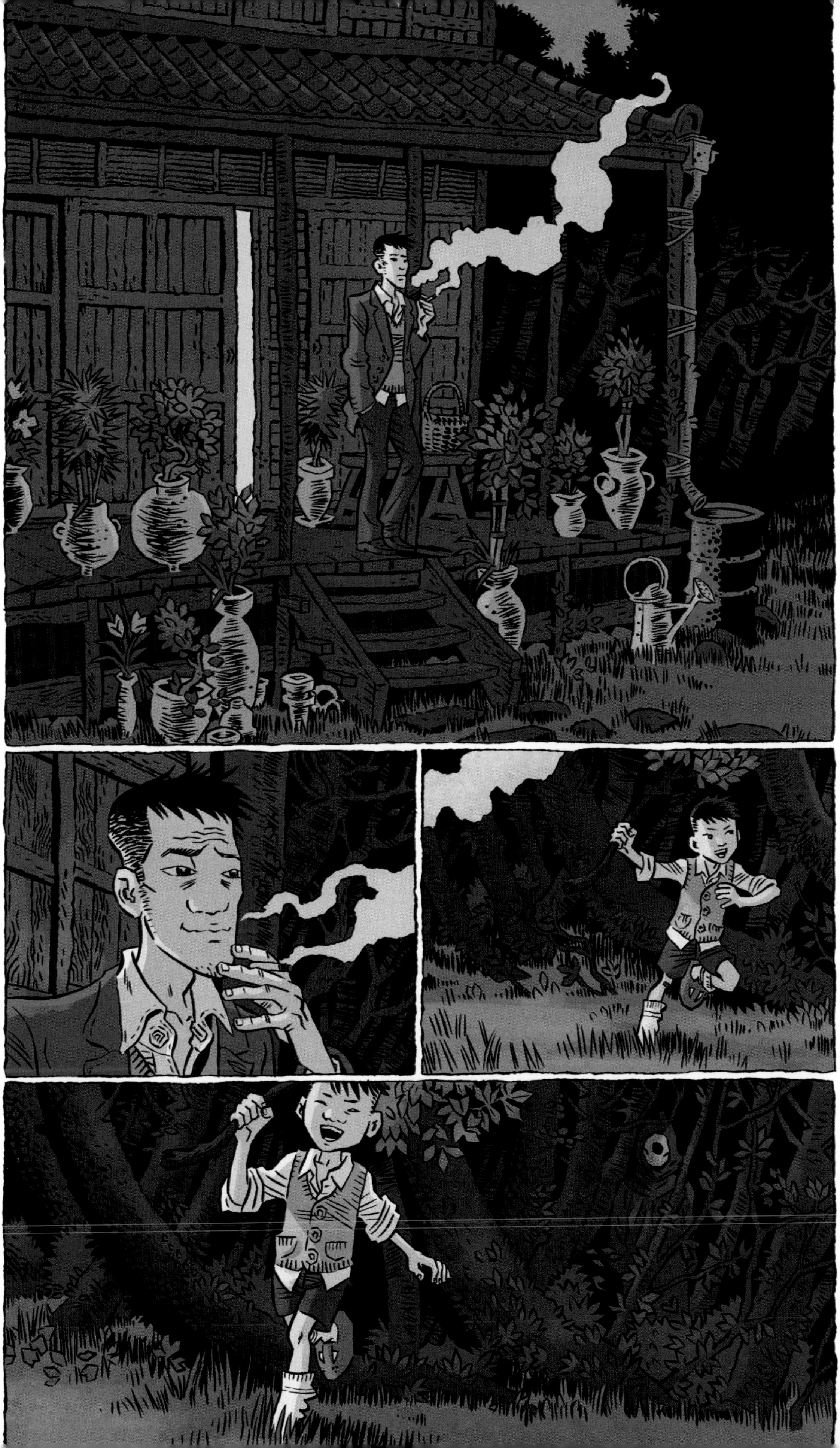

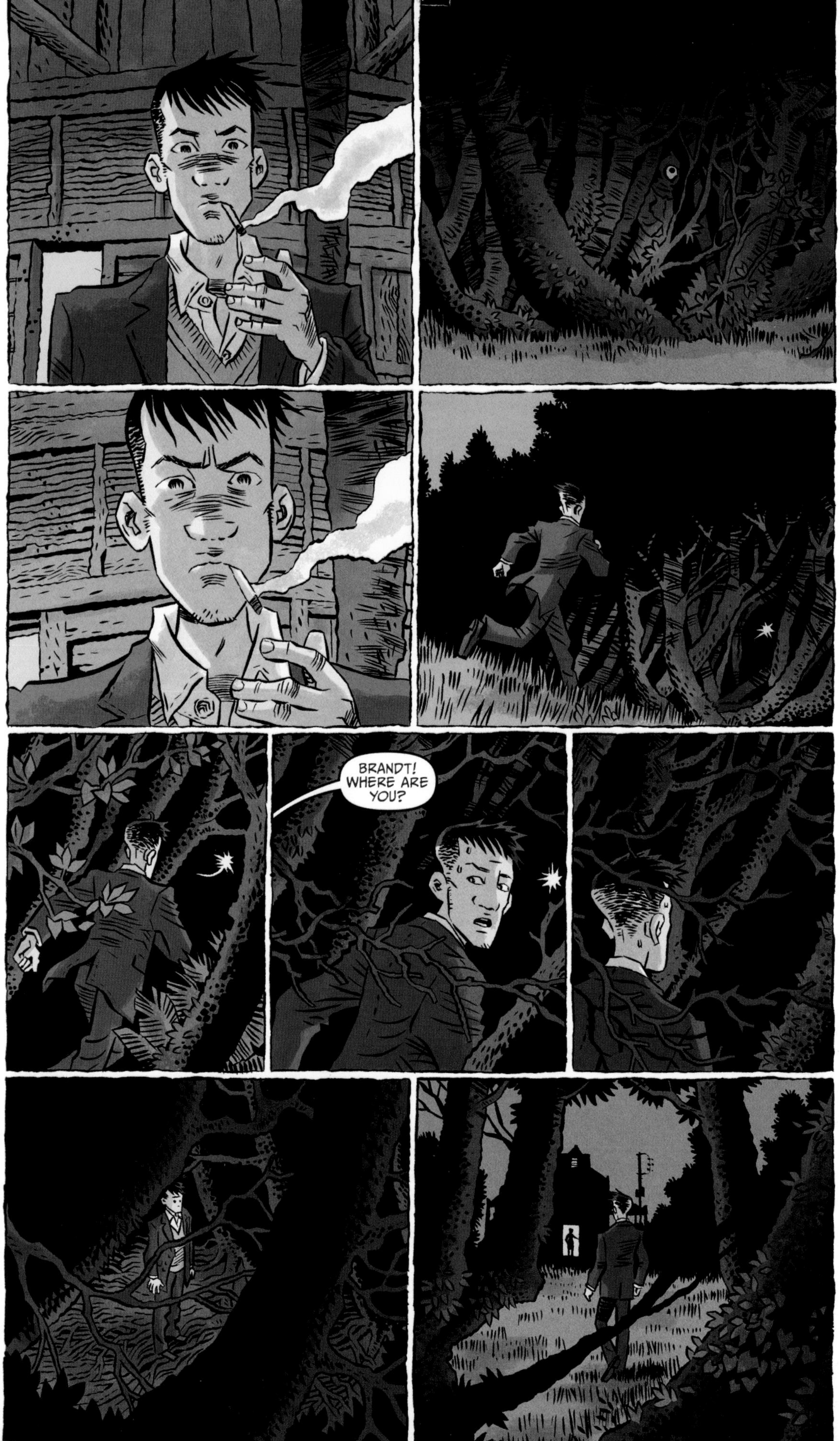
BRANDT! WHERE ARE YOU?

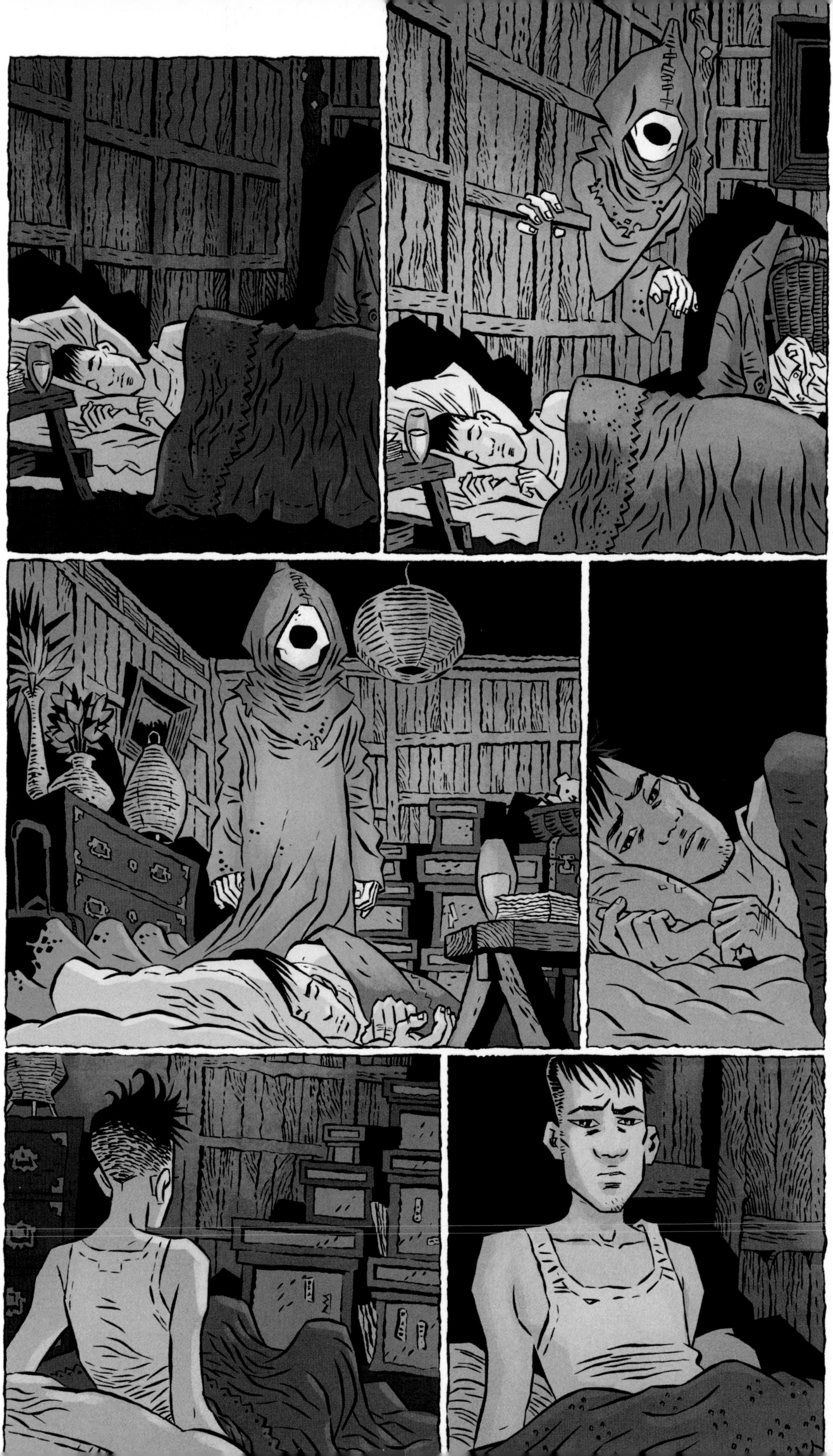

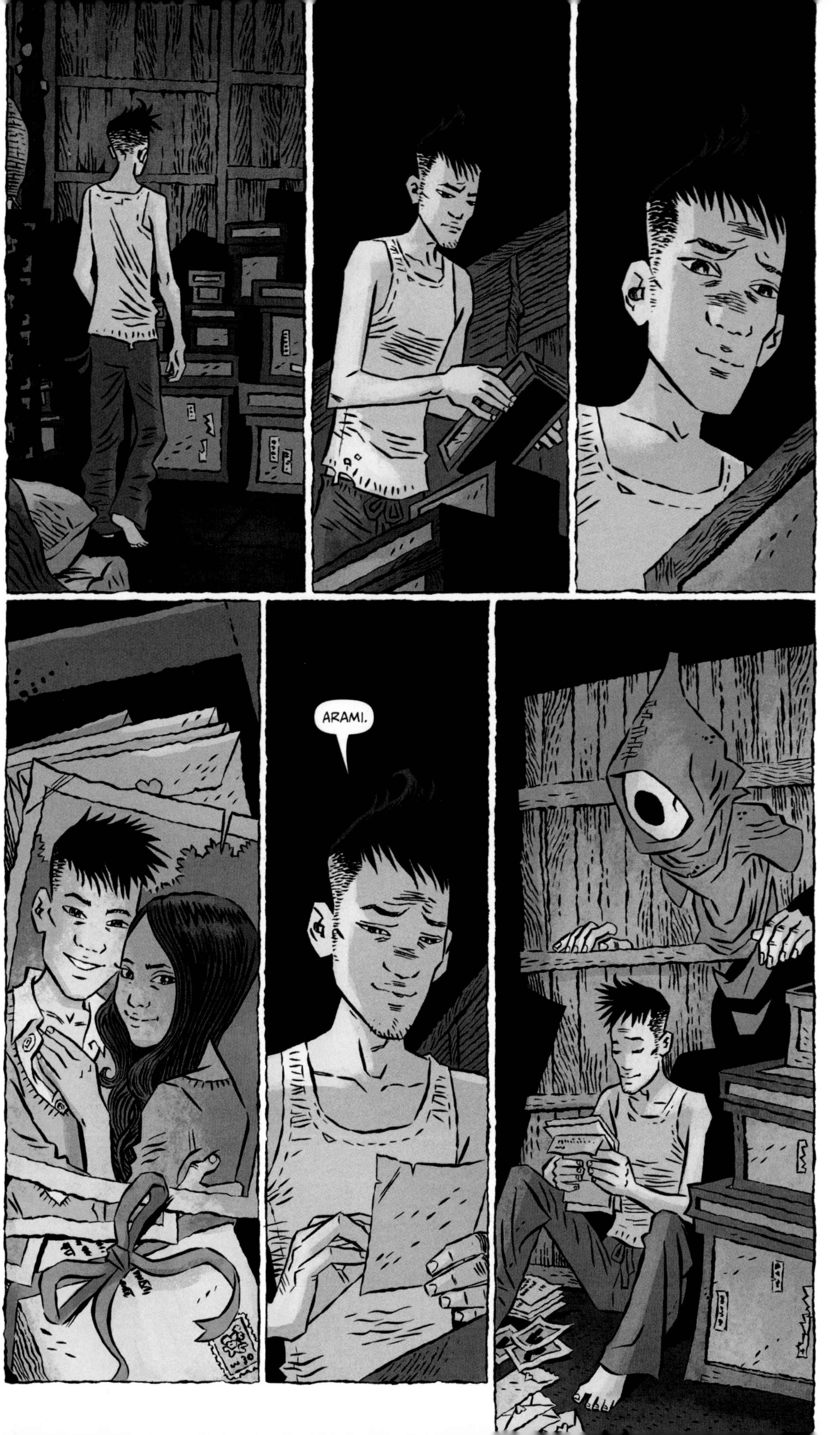
ARAMI.

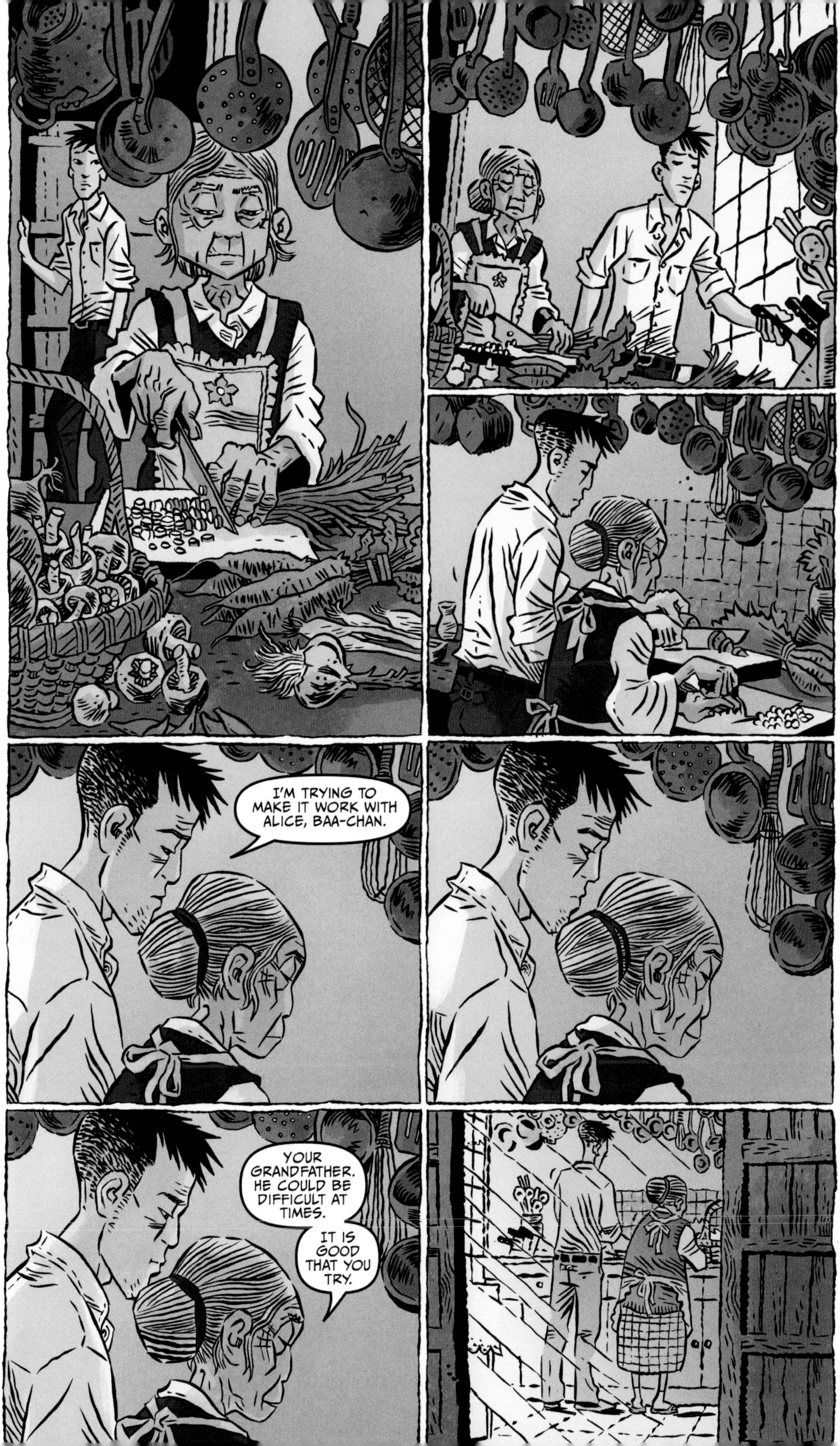
I'M TRYING TO MAKE IT WORK WITH ALICE, BAA-CHAN.
YOUR GRANDFATHER. HE COULD BE DIFFICULT AT TIMES.
IT IS GOOD THAT YOU TRY.

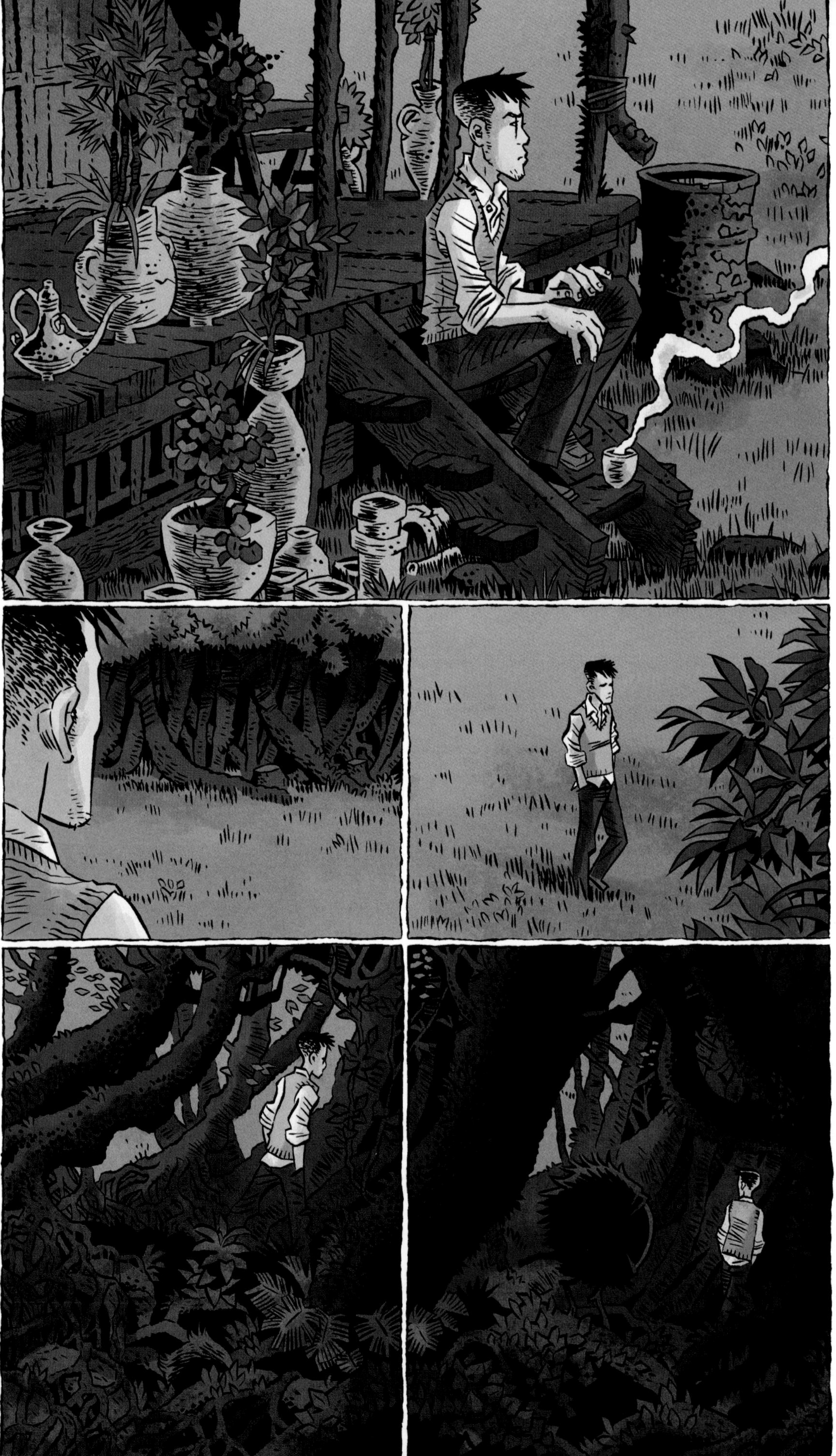

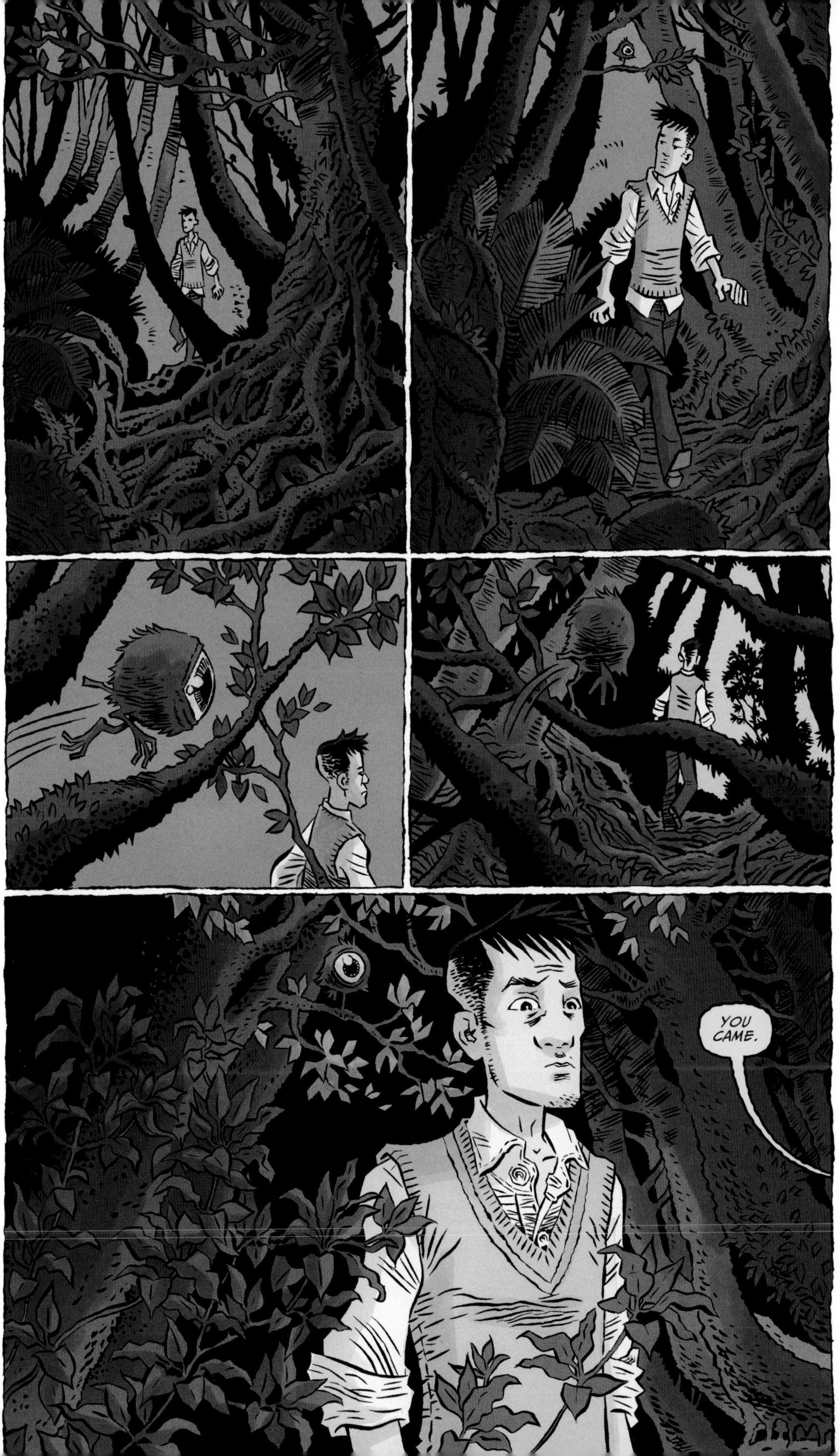
YOU CAME.

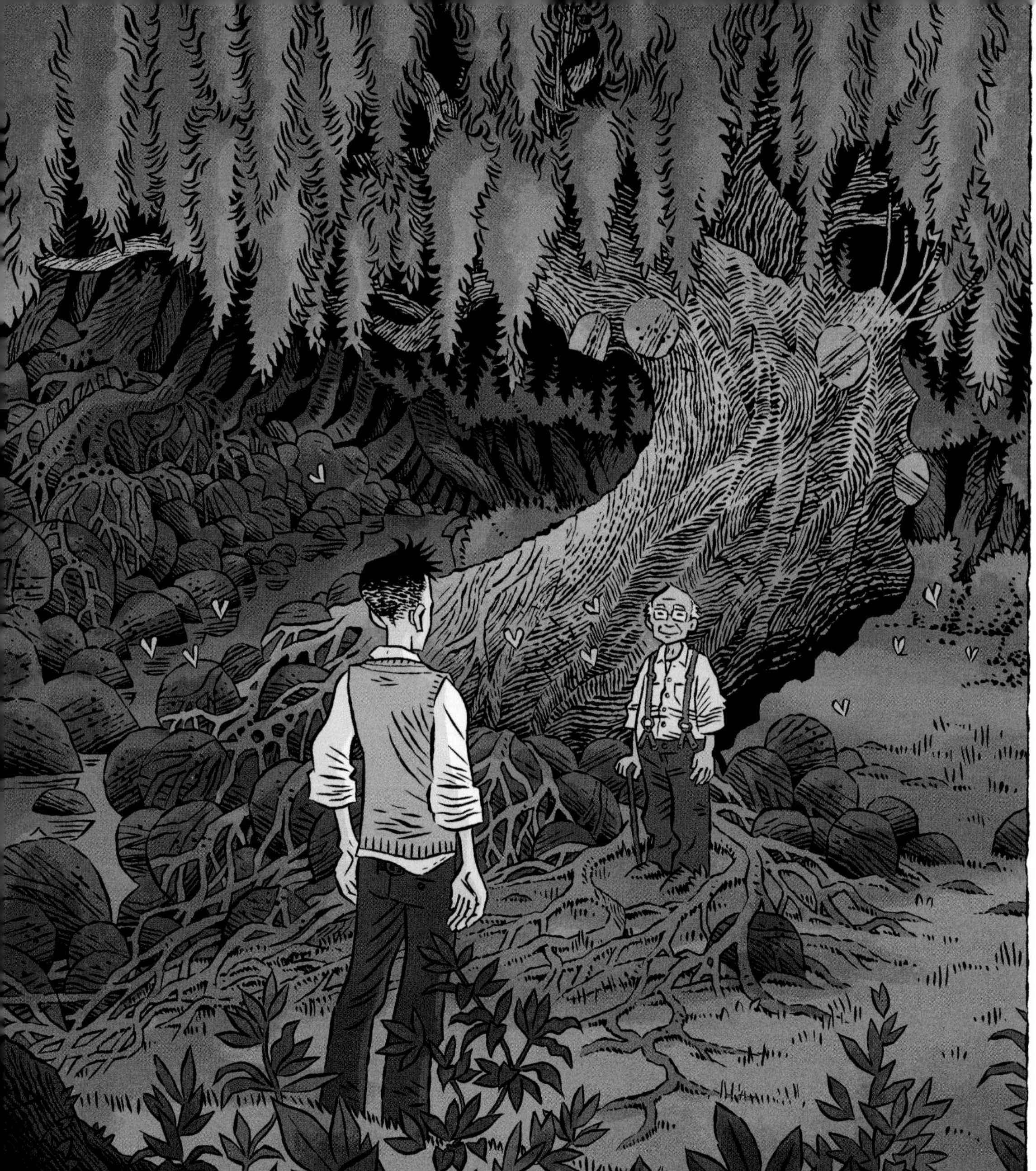

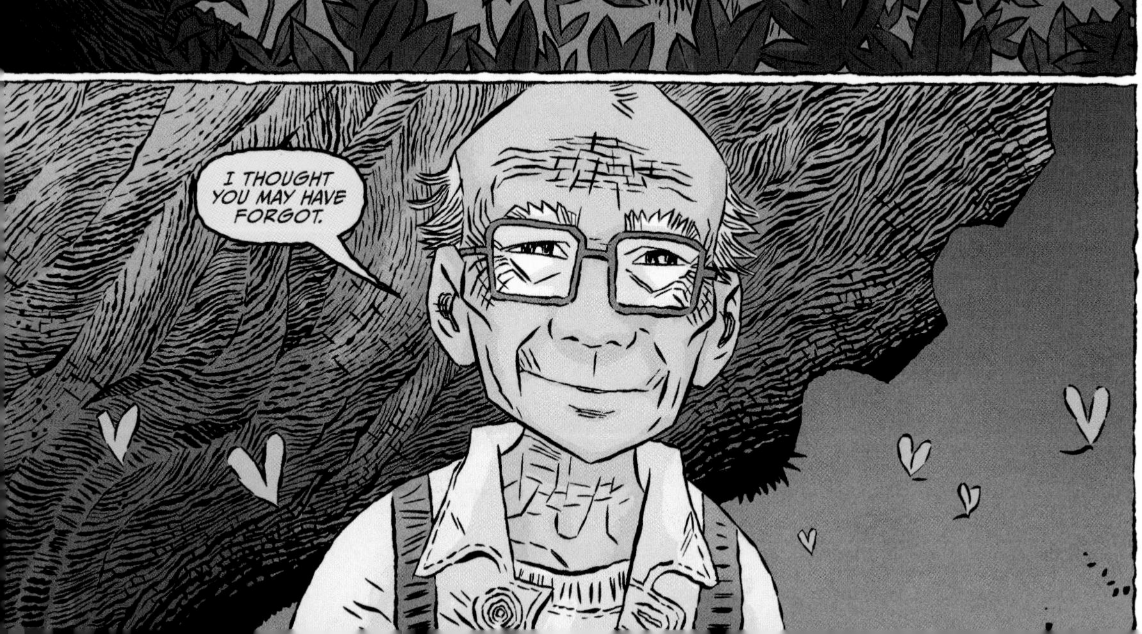
I THOUGHT YOU MAY HAVE FORGOT.

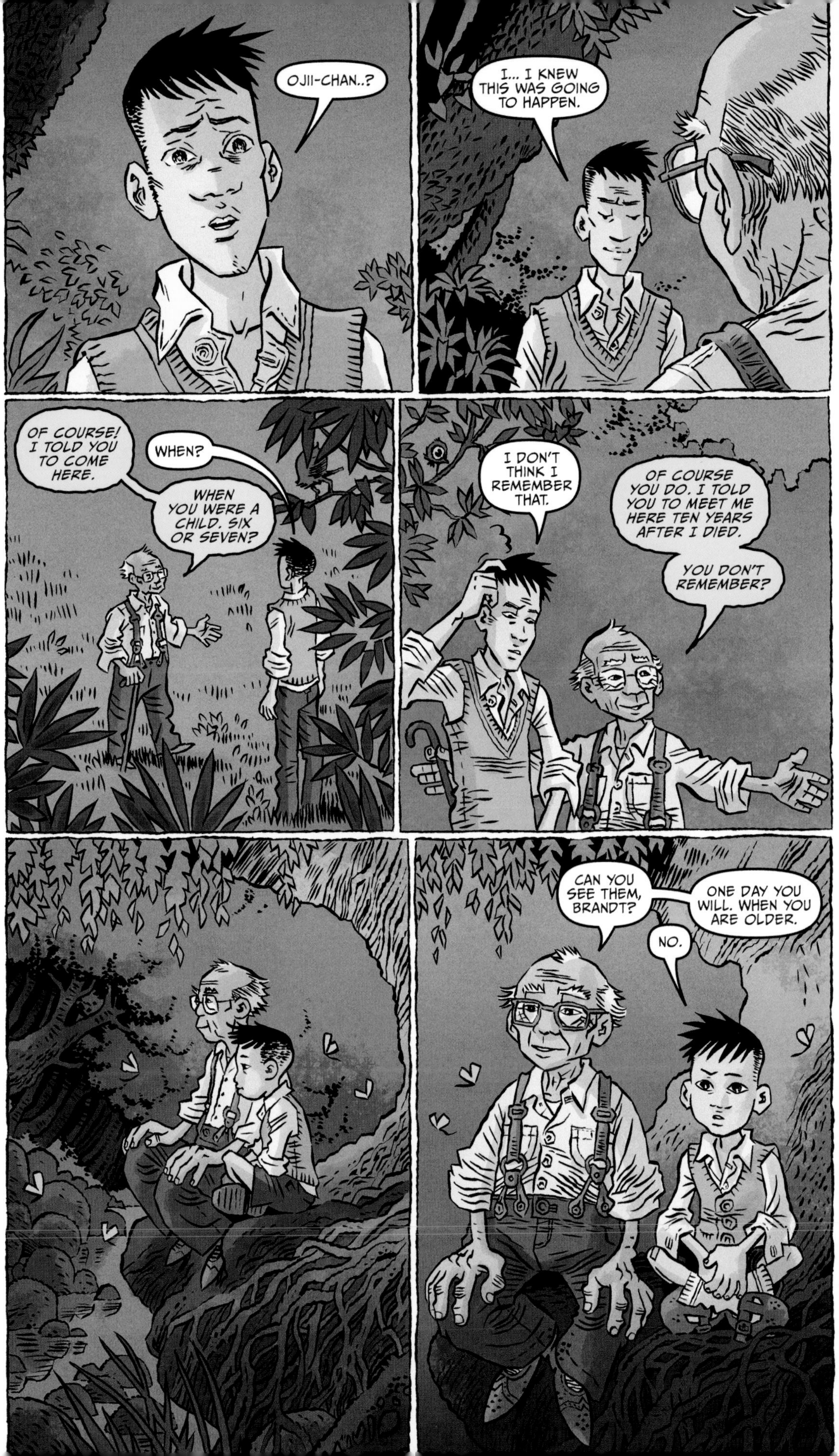
OJII-CHAN..?
I... I KNEW THIS WAS GOING TO HAPPEN.
OF COURSE! I TOLD YOU TO COME HERE.
WHEN?
WHEN YOU WERE A CHILD. SIX OR SEVEN?
I DON'T THINK I REMEMBER THAT.
OF COURSE YOU DO. I TOLD YOU TO MEET ME HERE TEN YEARS AFTER I DIED.
YOU DON'T REMEMBER?
CAN YOU SEE THEM, BRANDT?
NO.
ONE DAY YOU WILL. WHEN YOU ARE OLDER.

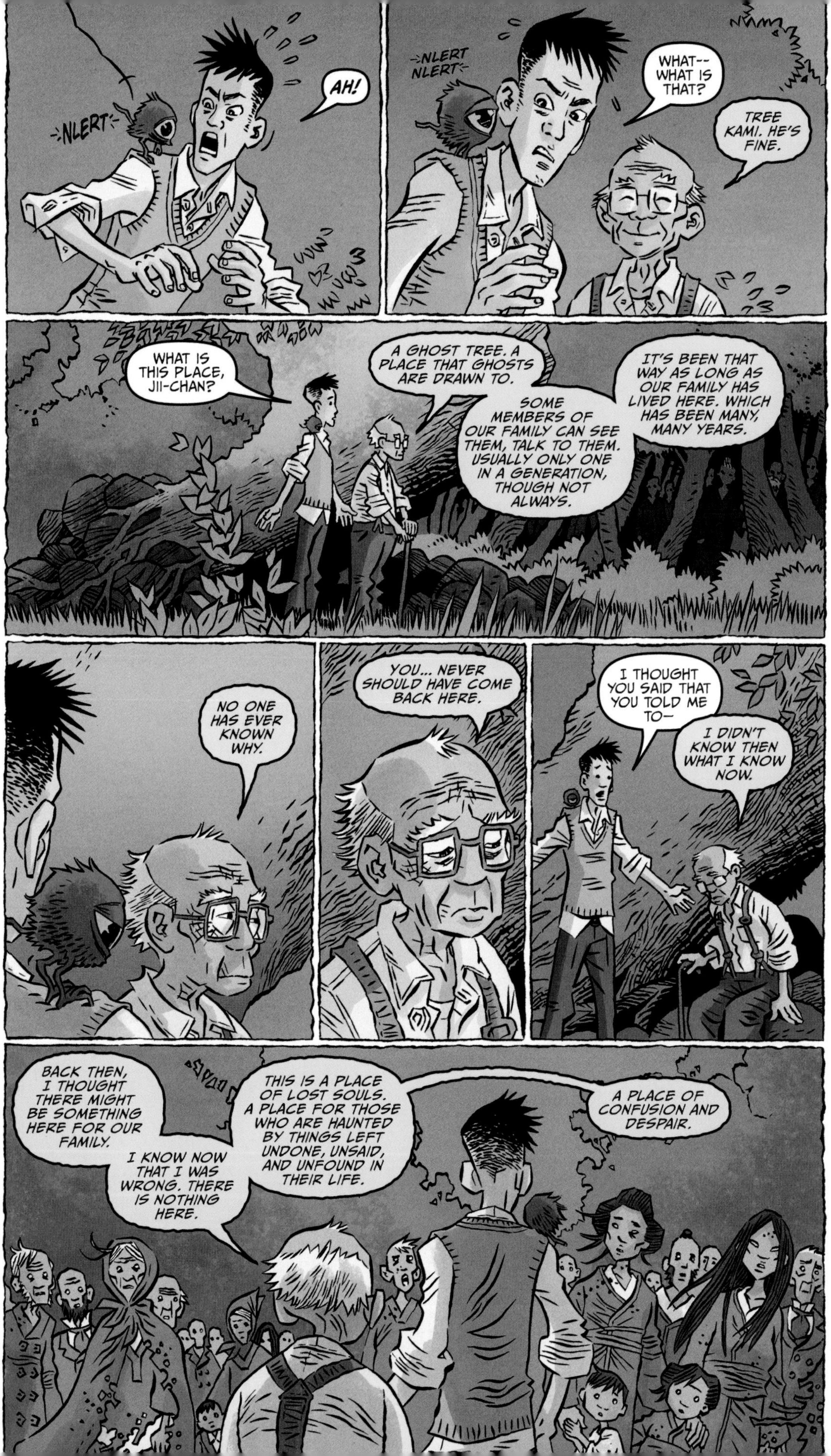
NLERT
AH!
NLERT NLERT
WHAT-- WHAT IS THAT?
TREE KAMI. HE'S FINE.
WHAT IS THIS PLACE, JII-CHAN?
A GHOST TREE. A PLACE THAT GHOSTS ARE DRAWN TO.
SOME MEMBERS OF OUR FAMILY CAN SEE THEM, TALK TO THEM. USUALLY ONLY ONE IN A GENERATION, THOUGH NOT ALWAYS.
IT'S BEEN THAT WAY AS LONG AS OUR FAMILY HAS LIVED HERE. WHICH HAS BEEN MANY, MANY YEARS.
NO ONE HAS EVER KNOWN WHY.
YOU... NEVER SHOULD HAVE COME BACK HERE.
I THOUGHT YOU SAID THAT YOU TOLD ME TO—
I DIDN'T KNOW THEN WHAT I KNOW NOW.
BACK THEN, I THOUGHT THERE MIGHT BE SOMETHING HERE FOR OUR FAMILY.
I KNOW NOW THAT I WAS WRONG. THERE IS NOTHING HERE.
THIS IS A PLACE OF LOST SOULS. A PLACE FOR THOSE WHO ARE HAUNTED BY THINGS LEFT UNDONE, UNSAID, AND UNFOUND IN THEIR LIFE.
A PLACE OF CONFUSION AND DESPAIR.

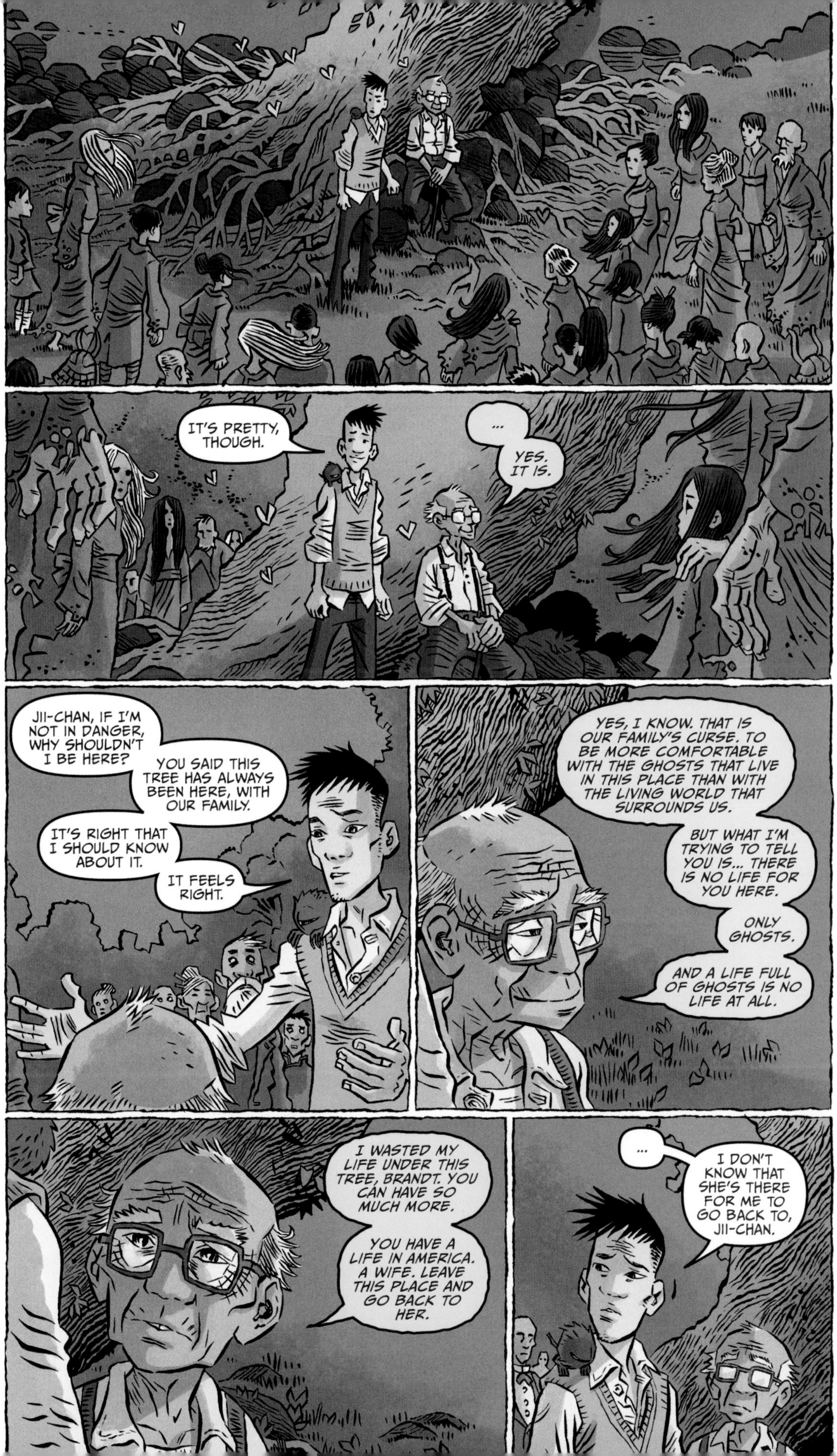
IT'S PRETTY, THOUGH.
...
YES. IT IS.
JII-CHAN, IF I'M NOT IN DANGER, WHY SHOULDN'T I BE HERE?
YOU SAID THIS TREE HAS ALWAYS BEEN HERE, WITH OUR FAMILY.
IT'S RIGHT THAT I SHOULD KNOW ABOUT IT.
IT FEELS RIGHT.
YES, I KNOW. THAT IS OUR FAMILY'S CURSE. TO BE MORE COMFORTABLE WITH THE GHOSTS THAT LIVE IN THIS PLACE THAN WITH THE LIVING WORLD THAT SURROUNDS US.
BUT WHAT I'M TRYING TO TELL YOU IS... THERE IS NO LIFE FOR YOU HERE.
ONLY GHOSTS.
AND A LIFE FULL OF GHOSTS IS NO LIFE AT ALL.
I WASTED MY LIFE UNDER THIS TREE, BRANDT. YOU CAN HAVE SO MUCH MORE.
YOU HAVE A LIFE IN AMERICA. A WIFE. LEAVE THIS PLACE AND GO BACK TO HER.
...
I DON'T KNOW THAT SHE'S THERE FOR ME TO GO BACK TO, JII-CHAN.

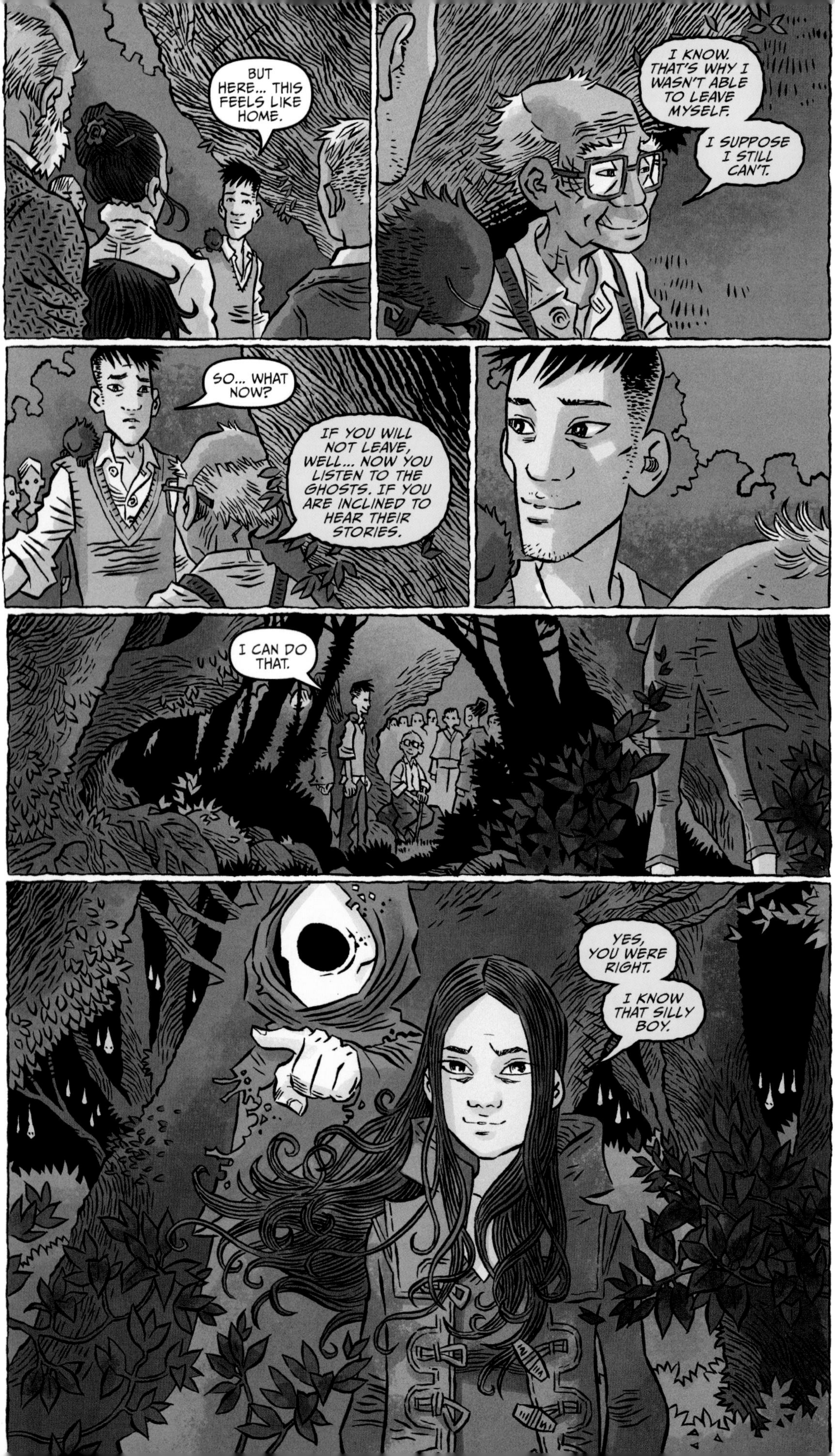
BUT HERE... THIS FEELS LIKE HOME.
I KNOW. THAT'S WHY I WASN'T ABLE TO LEAVE MYSELF.
I SUPPOSE I STILL CAN'T.
SO... WHAT NOW?
IF YOU WILL NOT LEAVE, WELL... NOW YOU LISTEN TO THE GHOSTS. IF YOU ARE INCLINED TO HEAR THEIR STORIES.
I CAN DO THAT.
YES, YOU WERE RIGHT.
I KNOW THAT SILLY BOY.

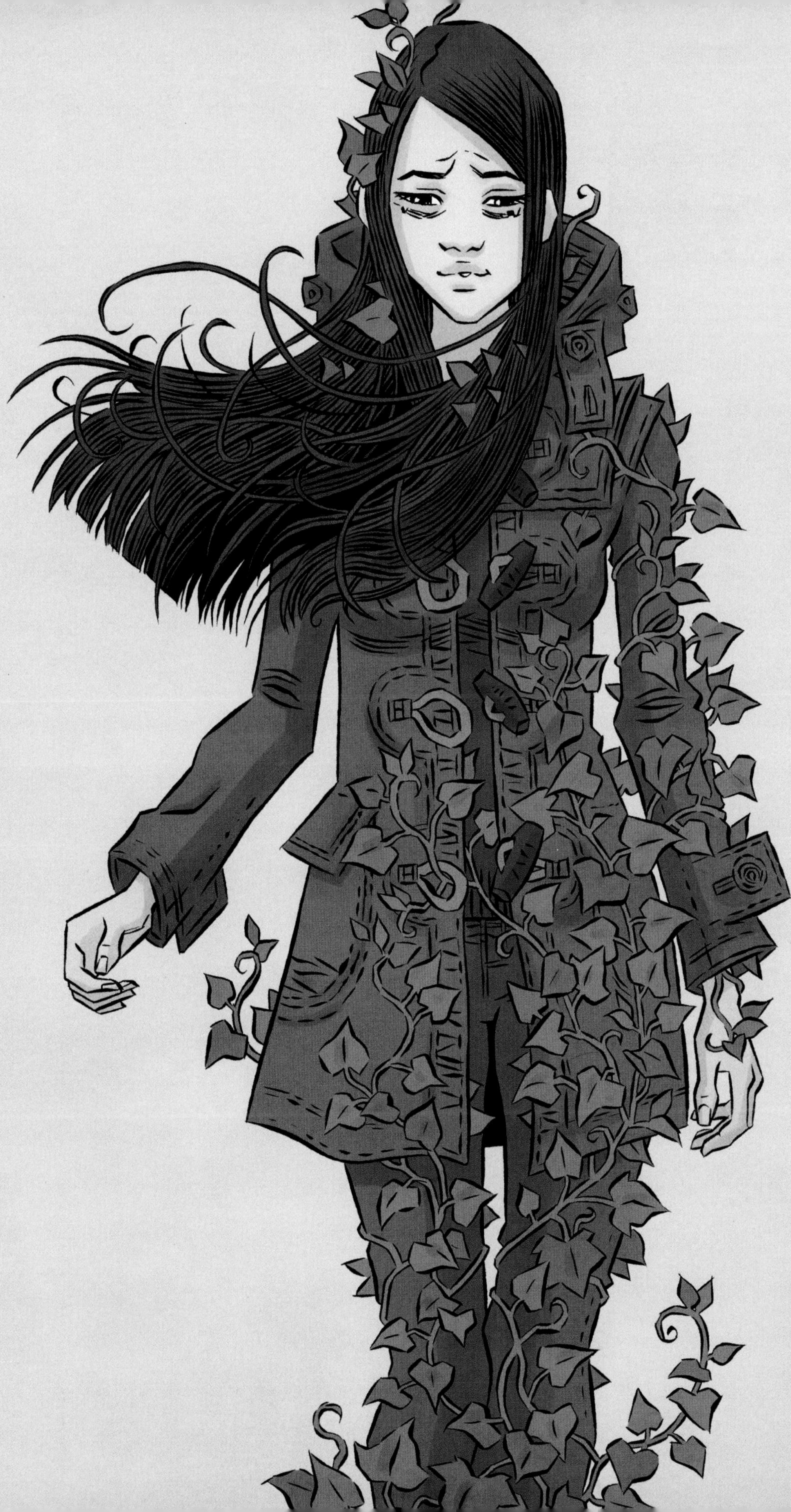

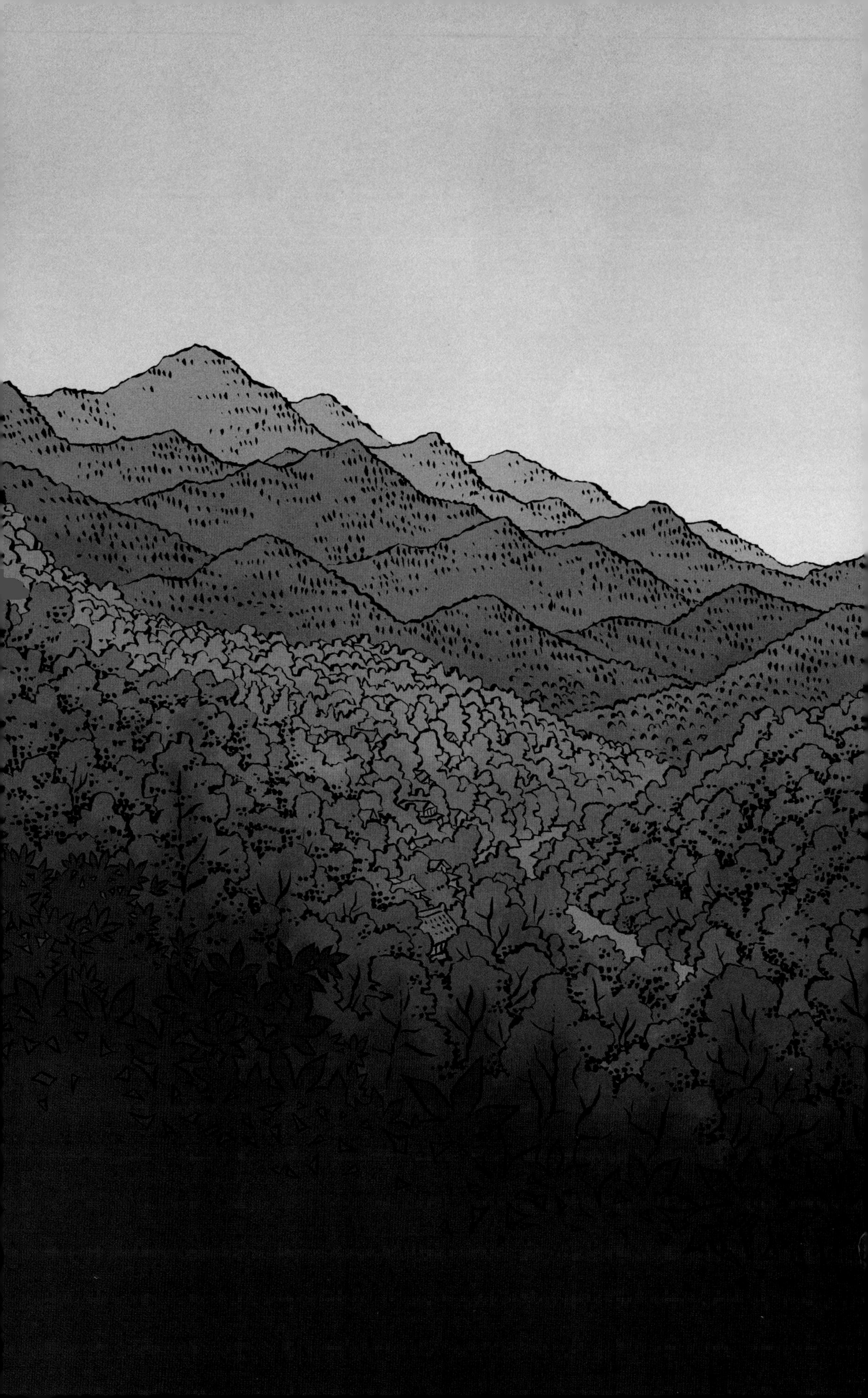

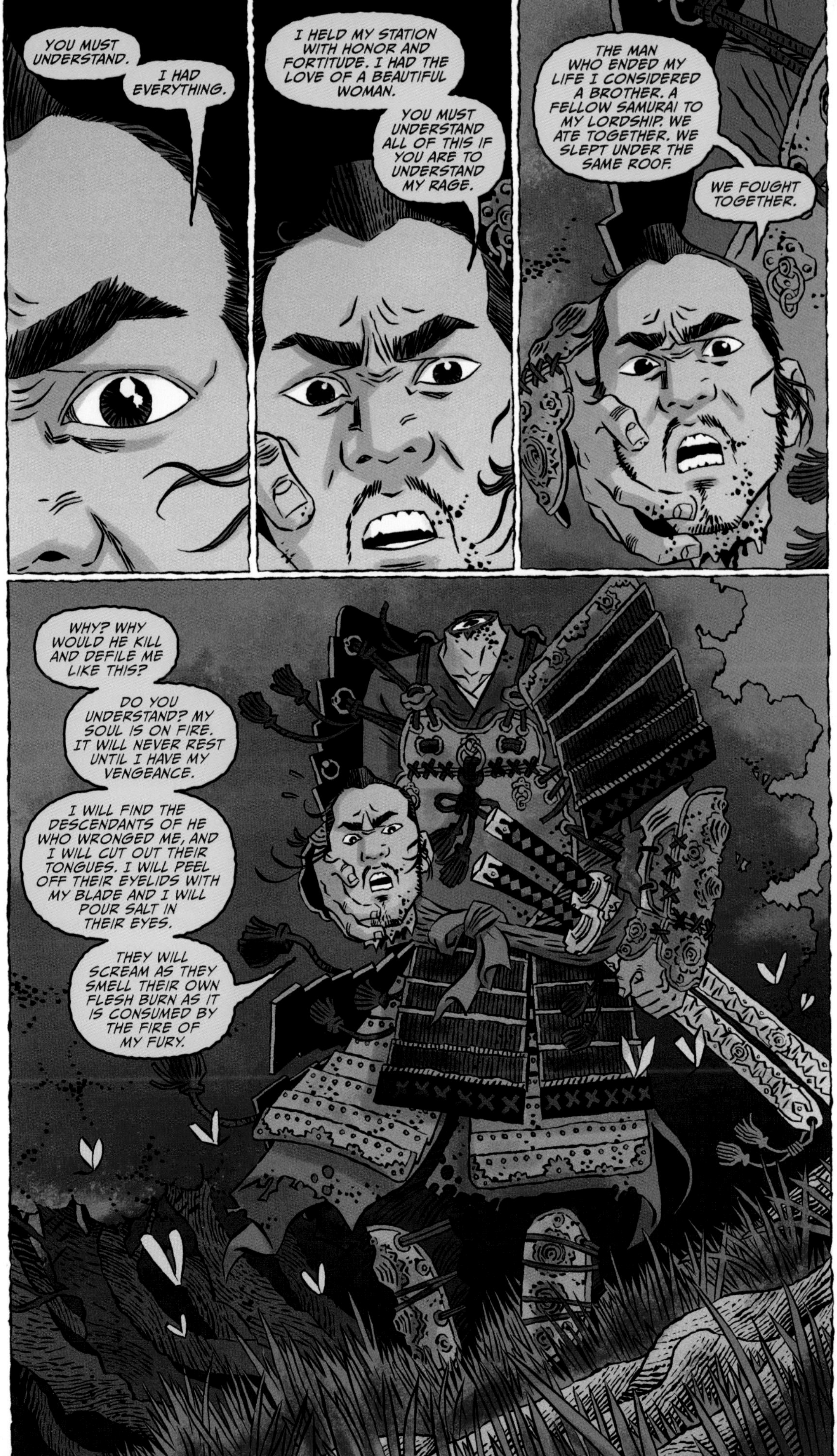
YOU MUST UNDERSTAND.
I HAD EVERYTHING.
I HELD MY STATION WITH HONOR AND FORTITUDE. I HAD THE LOVE OF A BEAUTIFUL WOMAN.
YOU MUST UNDERSTAND ALL OF THIS IF YOU ARE TO UNDERSTAND MY RAGE.
THE MAN WHO ENDED MY LIFE I CONSIDERED A BROTHER. A FELLOW SAMURAI TO MY LORDSHIP. WE ATE TOGETHER. WE SLEPT UNDER THE SAME ROOF.
WE FOUGHT TOGETHER.
WHY? WHY WOULD HE KILL AND DEFILE ME LIKE THIS?
DO YOU UNDERSTAND? MY SOUL IS ON FIRE. IT WILL NEVER REST UNTIL I HAVE MY VENGEANCE.
I WILL FIND THE DESCENDANTS OF HE WHO WRONGED ME, AND I WILL CUT OUT THEIR TONGUES. I WILL PEEL OFF THEIR EYELIDS WITH MY BLADE AND I WILL POUR SALT IN THEIR EYES.
THEY WILL SCREAM AS THEY SMELL THEIR OWN FLESH BURN AS IT IS CONSUMED BY THE FIRE OF MY FURY.

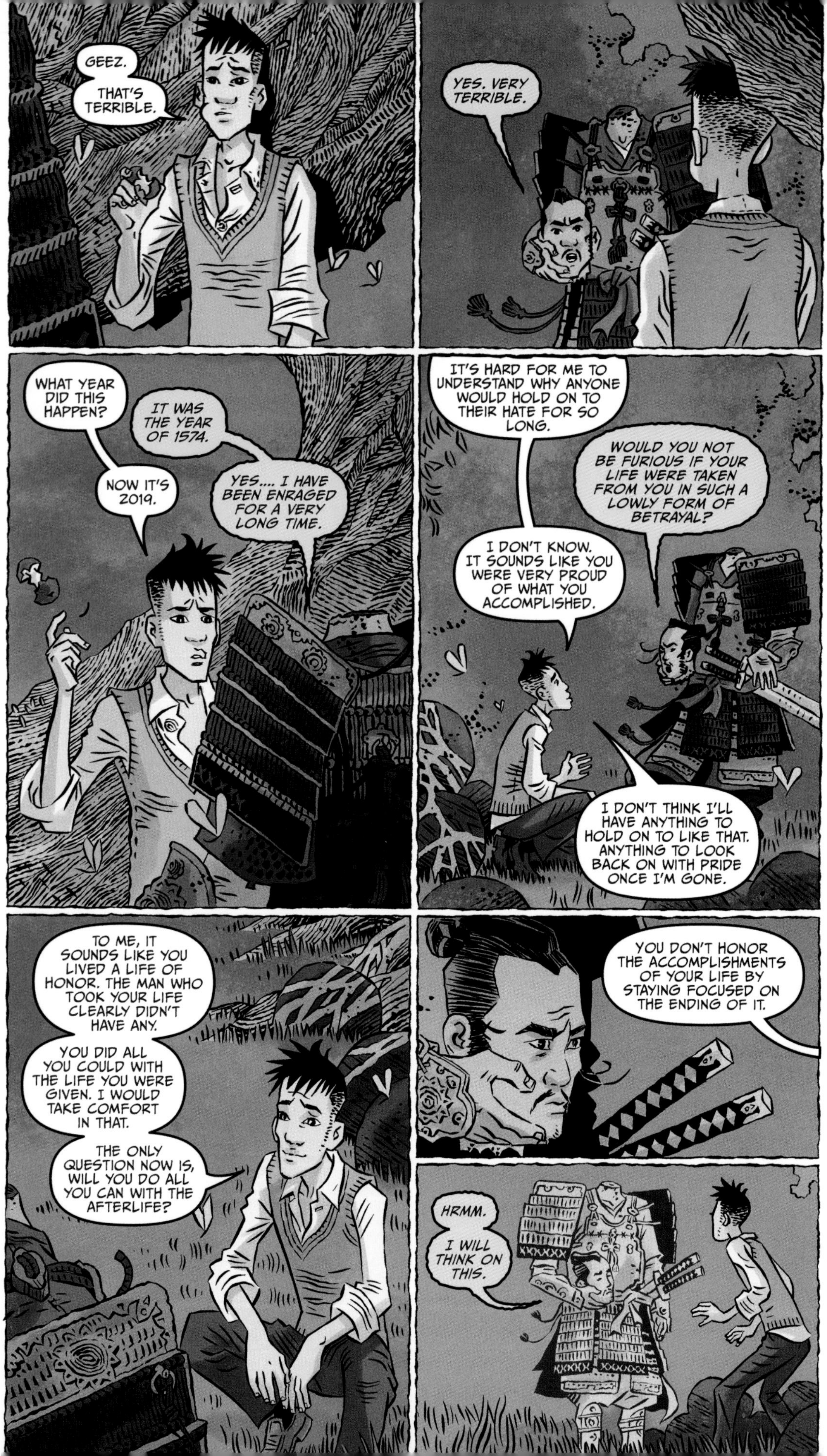
GEEZ.
THAT'S TERRIBLE.
YES. VERY TERRIBLE.
WHAT YEAR DID THIS HAPPEN?
IT WAS THE YEAR OF 1574.
NOW IT'S 2019.
YES.... I HAVE BEEN ENRAGED FOR A VERY LONG TIME.
IT'S HARD FOR ME TO UNDERSTAND WHY ANYONE WOULD HOLD ON TO THEIR HATE FOR SO LONG.
WOULD YOU NOT BE FURIOUS IF YOUR LIFE WERE TAKEN FROM YOU IN SUCH A LOWLY FORM OF BETRAYAL?
I DON'T KNOW. IT SOUNDS LIKE YOU WERE VERY PROUD OF WHAT YOU ACCOMPLISHED.
I DON'T THINK I'LL HAVE ANYTHING TO HOLD ON TO LIKE THAT. ANYTHING TO LOOK BACK ON WITH PRIDE ONCE I'M GONE.
TO ME, IT SOUNDS LIKE YOU LIVED A LIFE OF HONOR. THE MAN WHO TOOK YOUR LIFE CLEARLY DIDN'T HAVE ANY.
YOU DID ALL YOU COULD WITH THE LIFE YOU WERE GIVEN. I WOULD TAKE COMFORT IN THAT.
THE ONLY QUESTION NOW IS, WILL YOU DO ALL YOU CAN WITH THE AFTERLIFE?
YOU DON'T HONOR THE ACCOMPLISHMENTS OF YOUR LIFE BY STAYING FOCUSED ON THE ENDING OF IT.
HRMM.
I WILL THINK ON THIS.

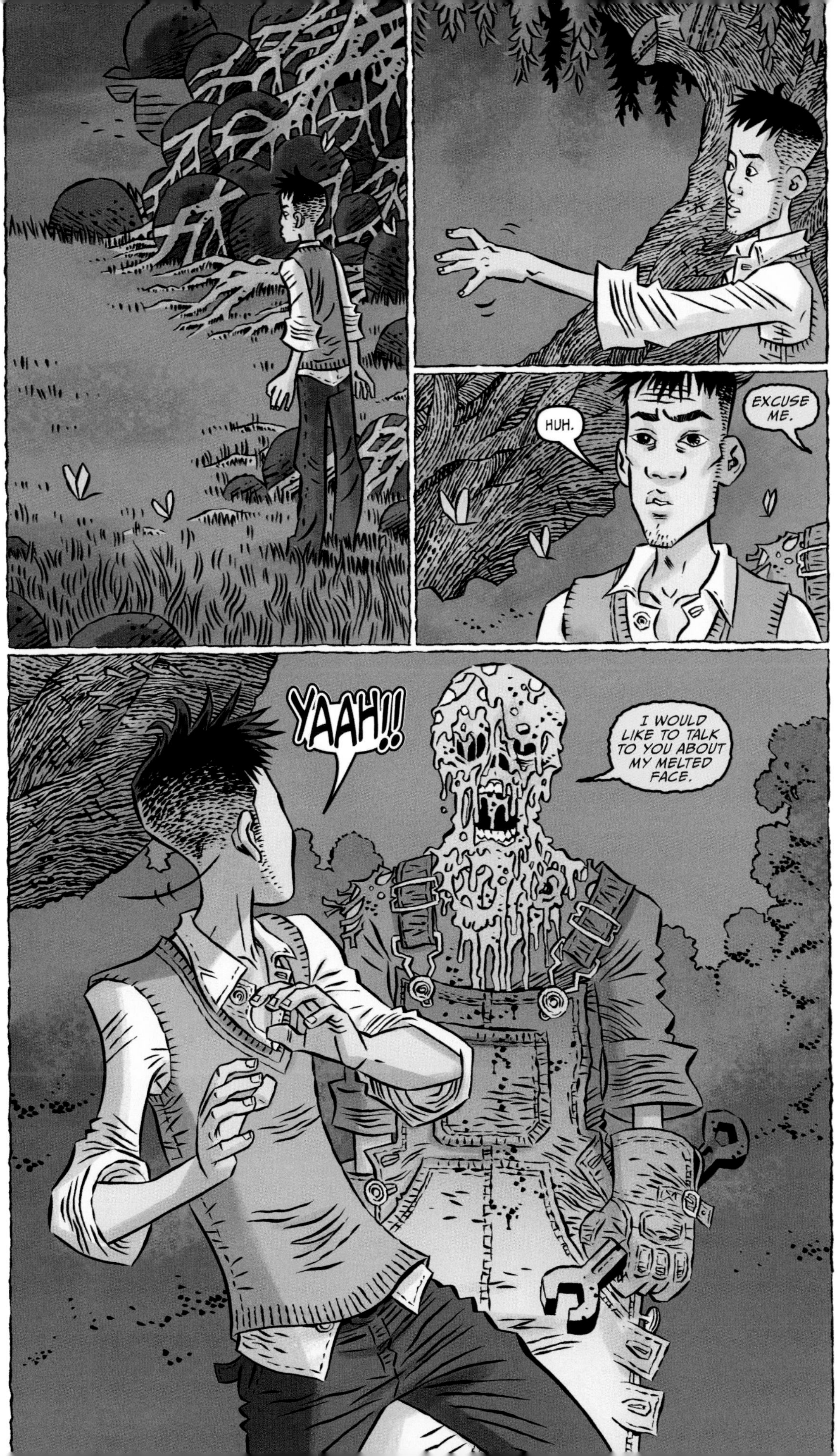
HUH.
EXCUSE ME.
YAAH!!
I WOULD LIKE TO TALK TO YOU ABOUT MY MELTED FACE.

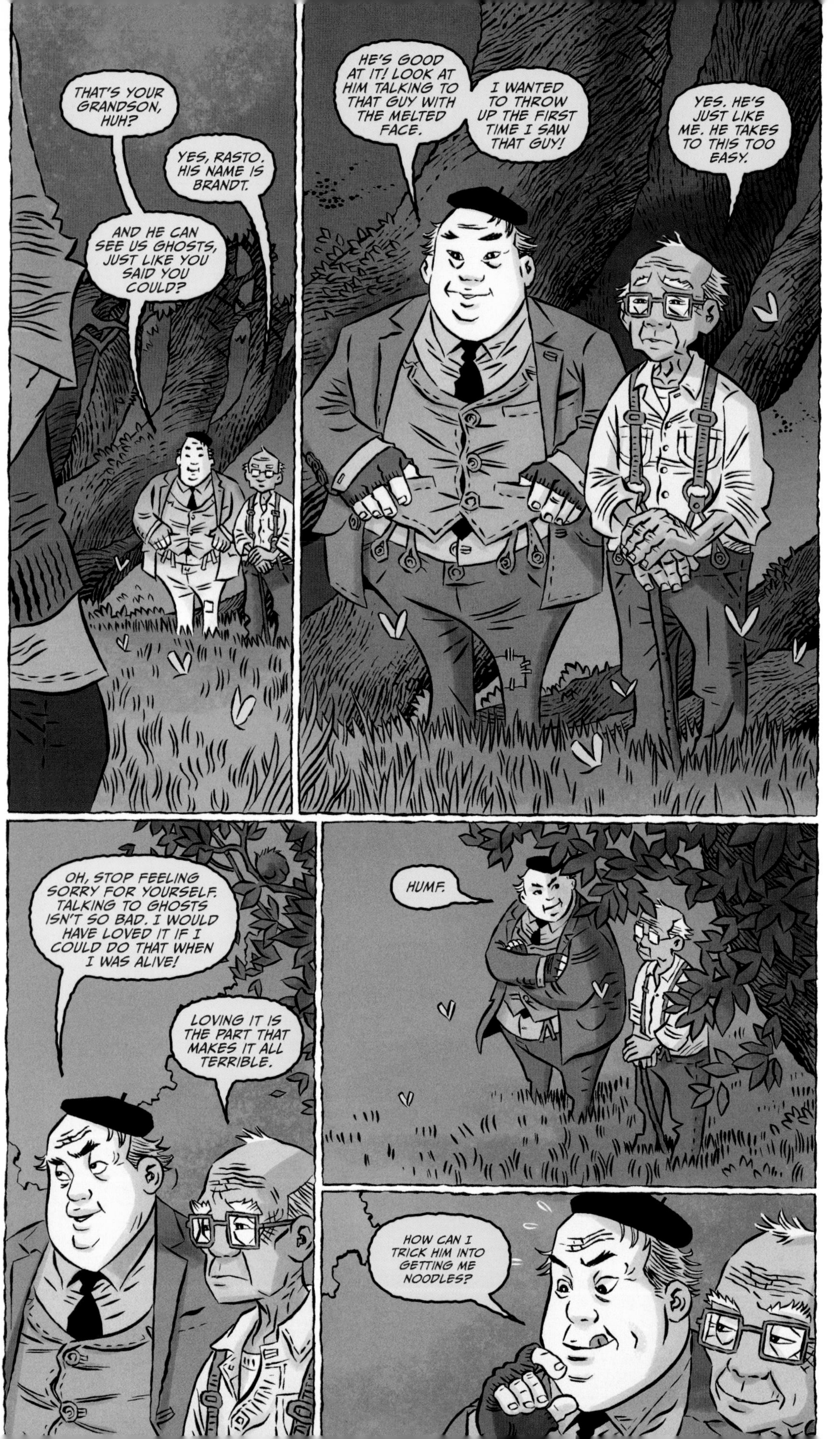

THAT'S YOUR GRANDSON, HUH?
YES, RASTO. HIS NAME IS BRANDT.
AND HE CAN SEE US GHOSTS, JUST LIKE YOU SAID YOU COULD?
HE'S GOOD AT IT! LOOK AT HIM TALKING TO THAT GUY WITH THE MELTED FACE.
I WANTED TO THROW UP THE FIRST TIME I SAW THAT GUY!
YES. HE'S JUST LIKE ME. HE TAKES TO THIS TOO EASY.
OH, STOP FEELING SORRY FOR YOURSELF. TALKING TO GHOSTS ISN'T SO BAD. I WOULD HAVE LOVED IT IF I COULD DO THAT WHEN I WAS ALIVE!
LOVING IT IS THE PART THAT MAKES IT ALL TERRIBLE.
HUMF.
HOW CAN I TRICK HIM INTO GETTING ME NOODLES?

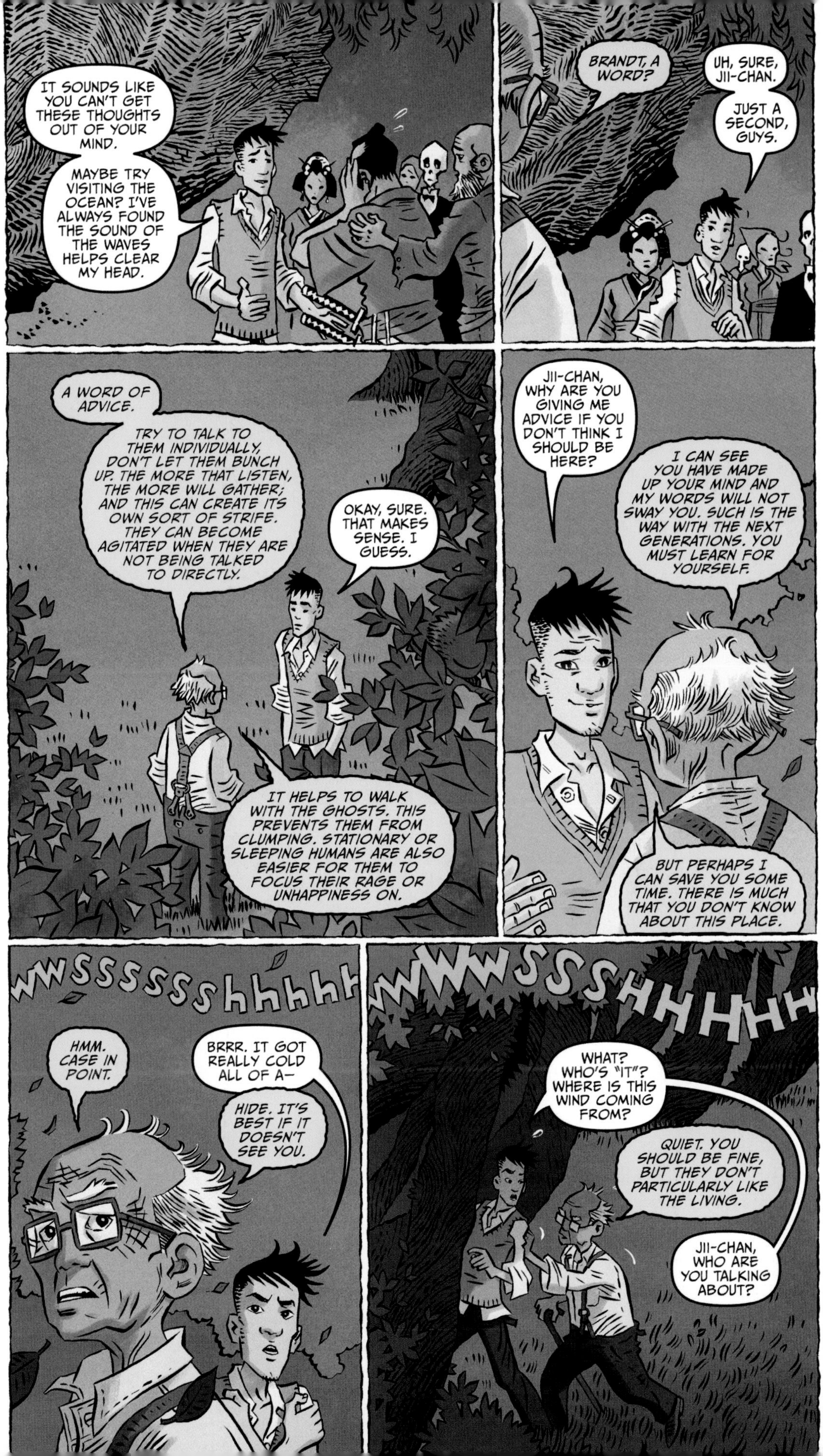
IT SOUNDS LIKE YOU CAN'T GET THESE THOUGHTS OUT OF YOUR MIND.
MAYBE TRY VISITING THE OCEAN? I'VE ALWAYS FOUND THE SOUND OF THE WAVES HELPS CLEAR MY HEAD.
BRANDT, A WORD?
UH, SURE, JII-CHAN.
JUST A SECOND, GUYS.
A WORD OF ADVICE.
TRY TO TALK TO THEM INDIVIDUALLY, DON'T LET THEM BUNCH UP. THE MORE THAT LISTEN, THE MORE WILL GATHER; AND THIS CAN CREATE ITS OWN SORT OF STRIFE. THEY CAN BECOME AGITATED WHEN THEY ARE NOT BEING TALKED TO DIRECTLY.
OKAY, SURE. THAT MAKES SENSE. I GUESS.
IT HELPS TO WALK WITH THE GHOSTS. THIS PREVENTS THEM FROM CLUMPING. STATIONARY OR SLEEPING HUMANS ARE ALSO EASIER FOR THEM TO FOCUS THEIR RAGE OR UNHAPPINESS ON.
JII-CHAN, WHY ARE YOU GIVING ME ADVICE IF YOU DON'T THINK I SHOULD BE HERE?
I CAN SEE YOU HAVE MADE UP YOUR MIND AND MY WORDS WILL NOT SWAY YOU. SUCH IS THE WAY WITH THE NEXT GENERATIONS. YOU MUST LEARN FOR YOURSELF.
BUT PERHAPS I CAN SAVE YOU SOME TIME. THERE IS MUCH THAT YOU DON'T KNOW ABOUT THIS PLACE.
WWSSSSSShhhhh
HMM. CASE IN POINT.
BRRR. IT GOT REALLY COLD ALL OF A—
HIDE. IT'S BEST IF IT DOESN'T SEE YOU.
WWWSSSHHHHH
WHAT? WHO'S "IT"? WHERE IS THIS WIND COMING FROM?
QUIET. YOU SHOULD BE FINE, BUT THEY DON'T PARTICULARLY LIKE THE LIVING.
JII-CHAN, WHO ARE YOU TALKING ABOUT?

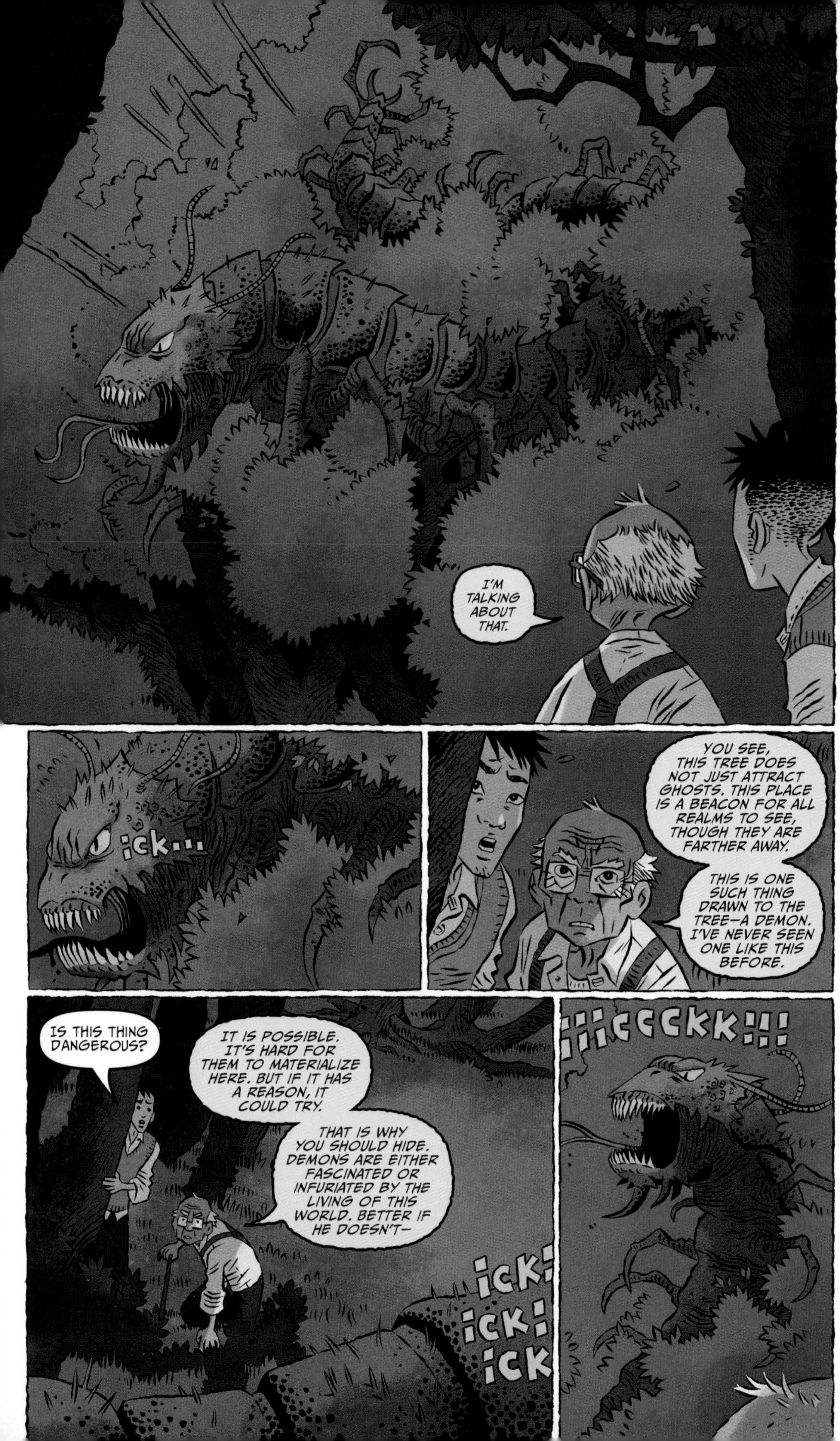
I'M TALKING ABOUT THAT.
ICK...
YOU SEE, THIS TREE DOES NOT JUST ATTRACT GHOSTS. THIS PLACE IS A BEACON FOR ALL REALMS TO SEE, THOUGH THEY ARE FARTHER AWAY.
THIS IS ONE SUCH THING DRAWN TO THE TREE—A DEMON. I'VE NEVER SEEN ONE LIKE THIS BEFORE.
IS THIS THING DANGEROUS?
IT IS POSSIBLE. IT'S HARD FOR THEM TO MATERIALIZE HERE. BUT IF IT HAS A REASON, IT COULD TRY.
THAT IS WHY YOU SHOULD HIDE. DEMONS ARE EITHER FASCINATED OR INFURIATED BY THE LIVING OF THIS WORLD. BETTER IF HE DOESN'T—
ICK! ICK! ICK
IIICCCKK!!!

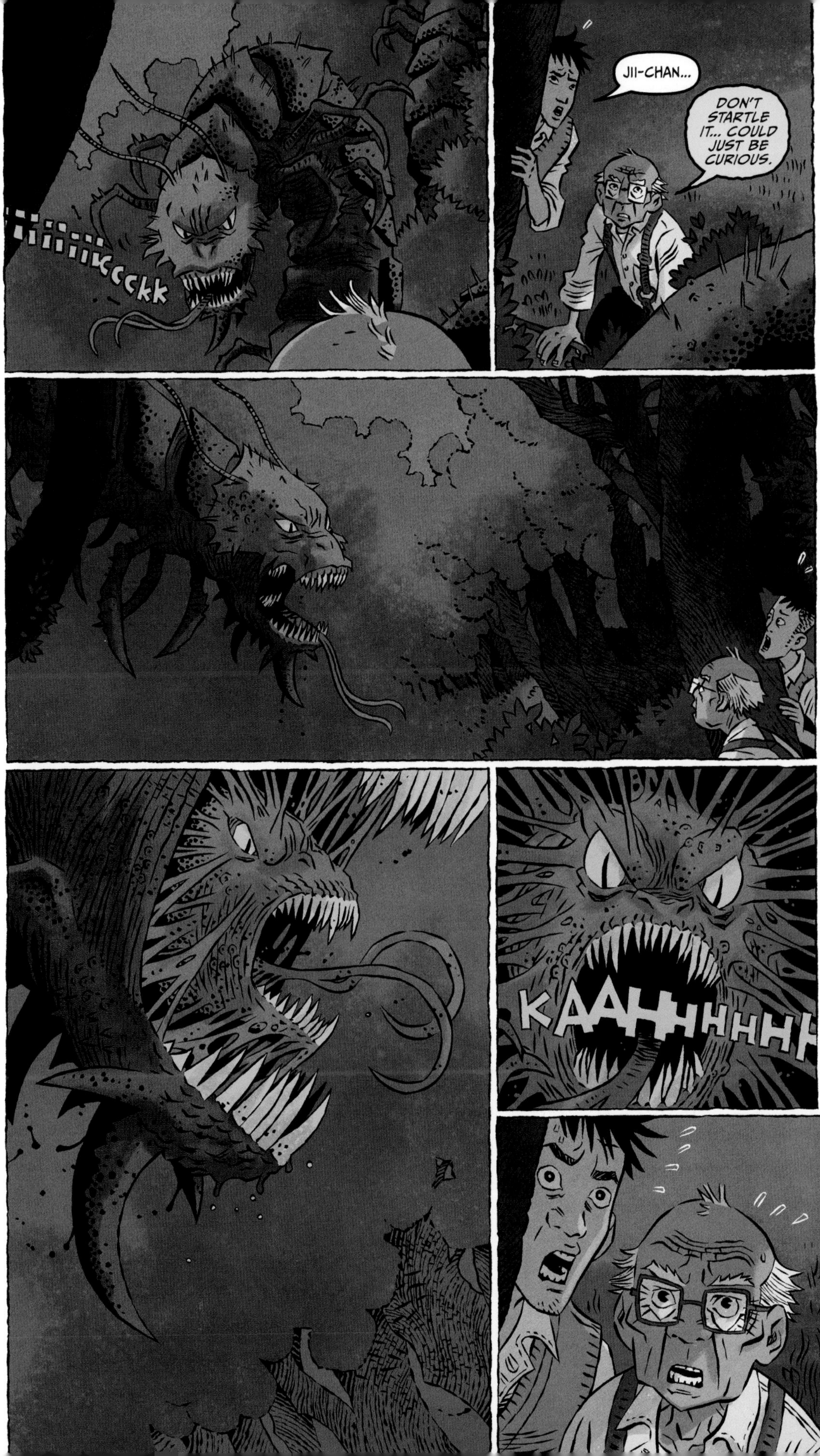

Tiiiiickckk
JII-CHAN...
DON'T STARTLE IT... COULD JUST BE CURIOUS.
KAAHHHHHH

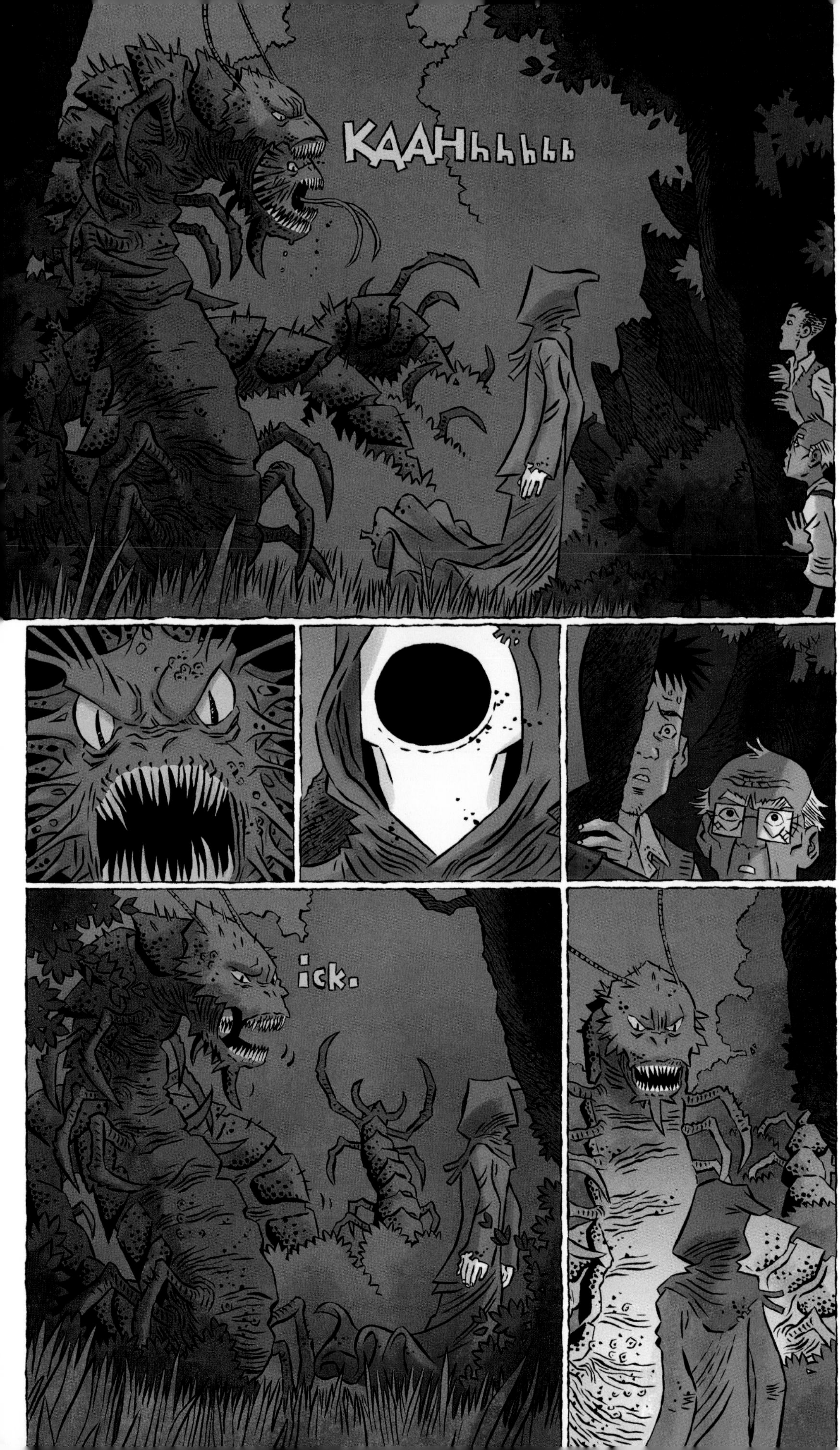
KAAHhhhhh
ick.

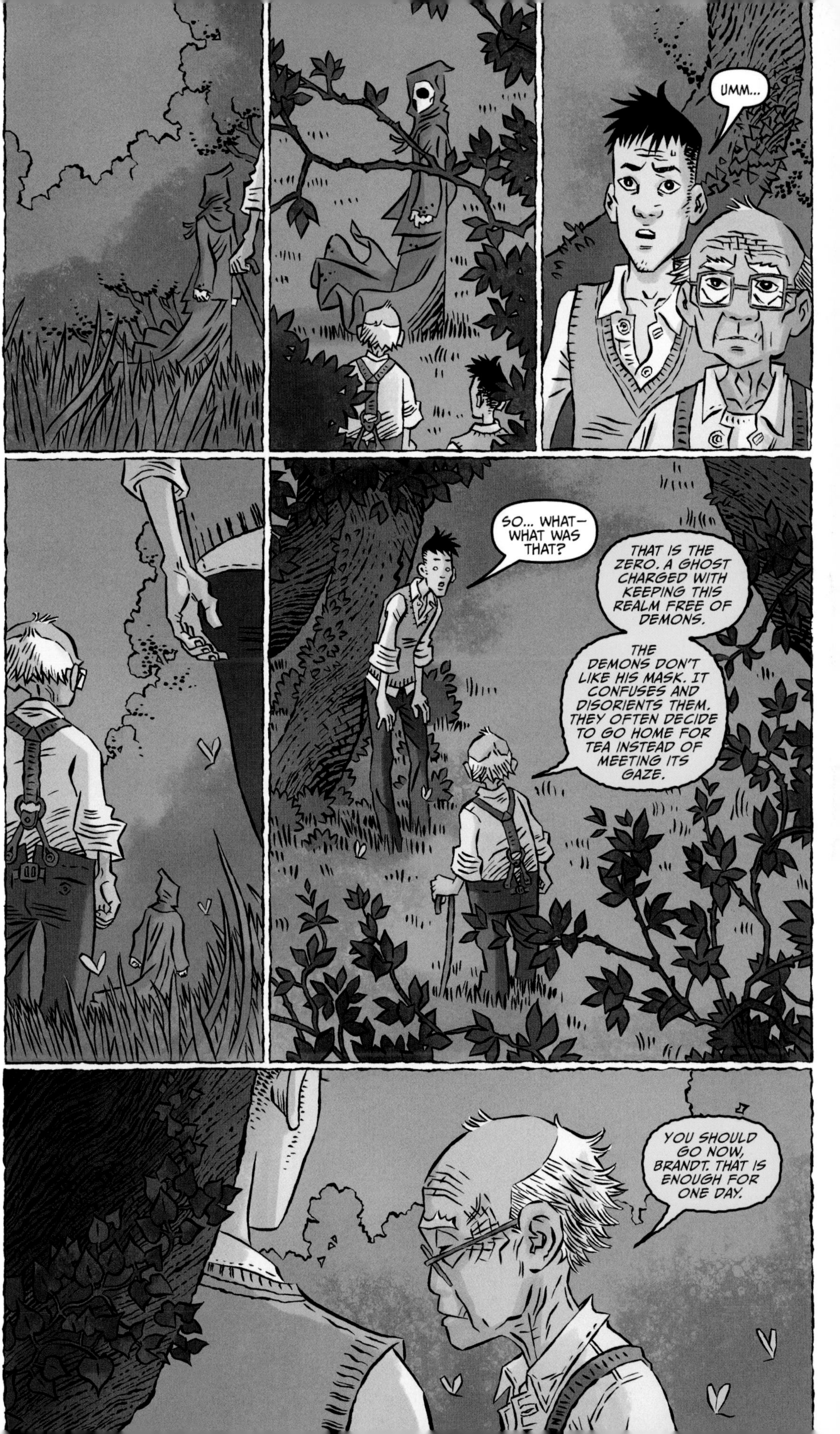
UMM...
SO... WHAT—WHAT WAS THAT?
THAT IS THE ZERO. A GHOST CHARGED WITH KEEPING THIS REALM FREE OF DEMONS.
THE DEMONS DON'T LIKE HIS MASK. IT CONFUSES AND DISORIENTS THEM. THEY OFTEN DECIDE TO GO HOME FOR TEA INSTEAD OF MEETING ITS GAZE.
YOU SHOULD GO NOW, BRANDT. THAT IS ENOUGH FOR ONE DAY.

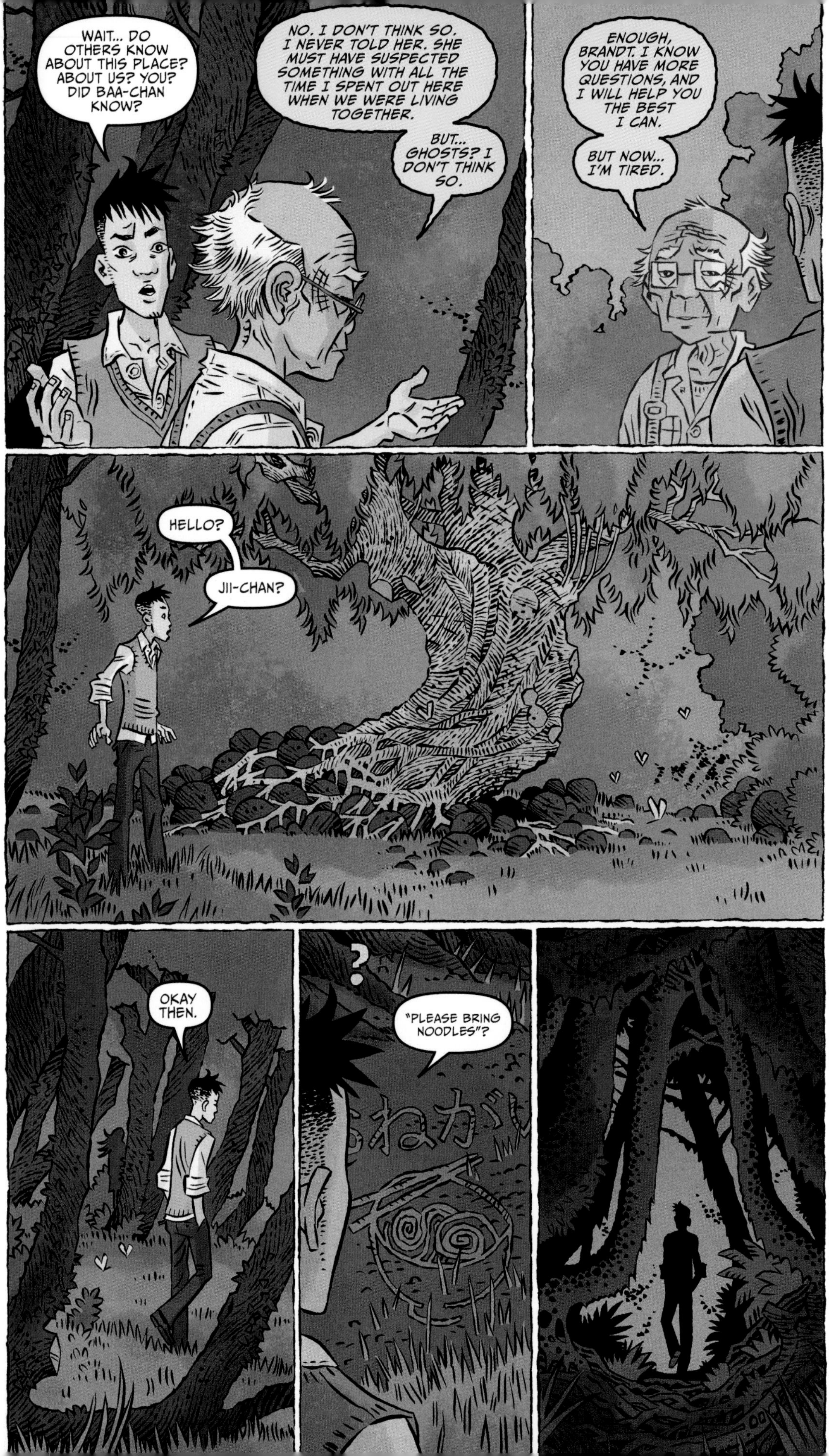
WAIT... DO OTHERS KNOW ABOUT THIS PLACE? ABOUT US? YOU? DID BAA-CHAN KNOW?
NO. I DON'T THINK SO. I NEVER TOLD HER. SHE MUST HAVE SUSPECTED SOMETHING WITH ALL THE TIME I SPENT OUT HERE WHEN WE WERE LIVING TOGETHER.
BUT... GHOSTS? I DON'T THINK SO.
ENOUGH, BRANDT. I KNOW YOU HAVE MORE QUESTIONS, AND I WILL HELP YOU THE BEST I CAN.
BUT NOW... I'M TIRED.
HELLO?
JII-CHAN?
OKAY THEN.
?
"PLEASE BRING NOODLES"?

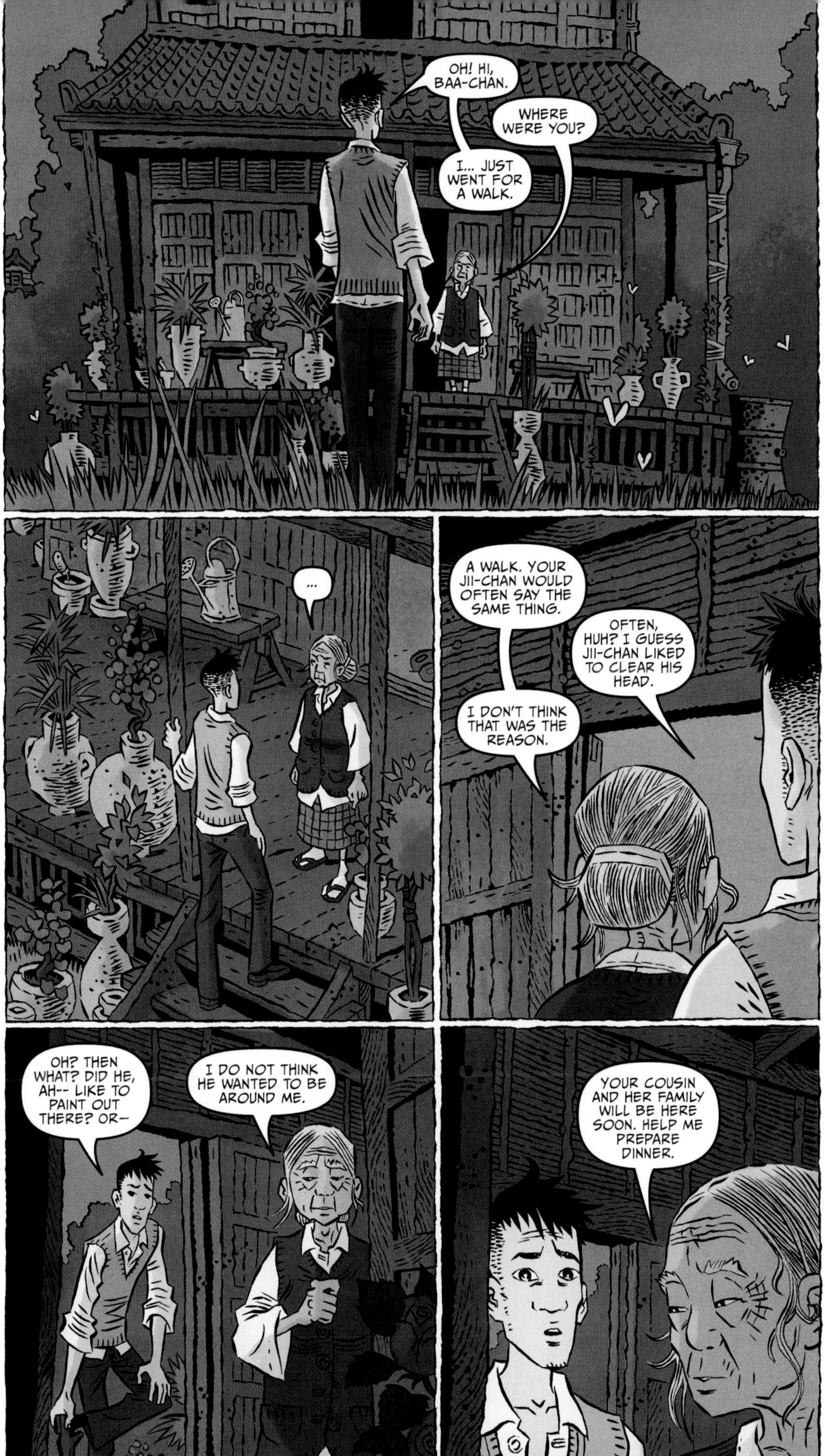
OH! HI, BAA-CHAN.
WHERE WERE YOU?
I... JUST WENT FOR A WALK.
...
A WALK. YOUR JII-CHAN WOULD OFTEN SAY THE SAME THING.
OFTEN, HUH? I GUESS JII-CHAN LIKED TO CLEAR HIS HEAD.
I DON'T THINK THAT WAS THE REASON.
OH? THEN WHAT? DID HE, AH-- LIKE TO PAINT OUT THERE? OR--
I DO NOT THINK HE WANTED TO BE AROUND ME.
YOUR COUSIN AND HER FAMILY WILL BE HERE SOON. HELP ME PREPARE DINNER.

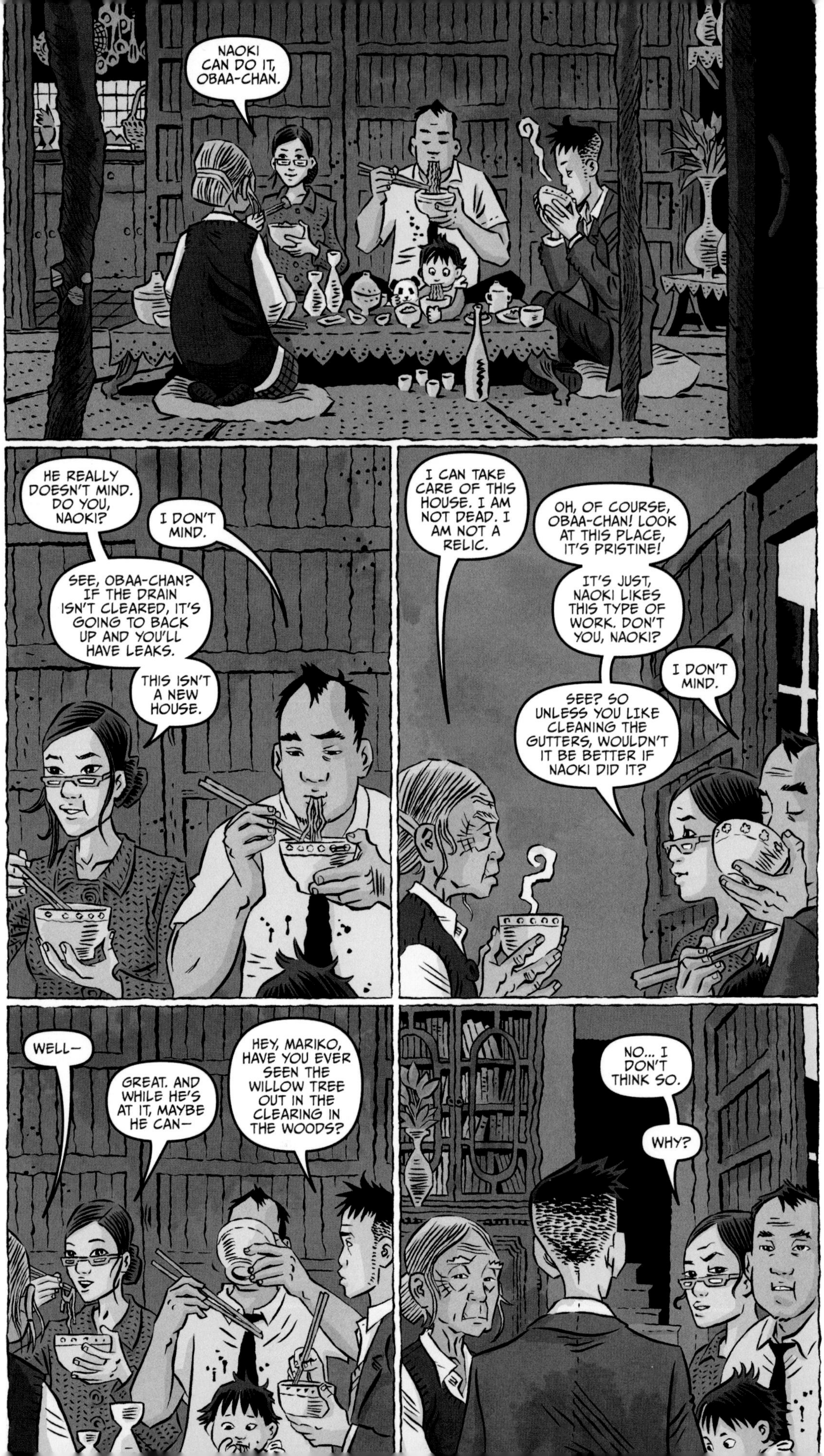
NAOKI CAN DO IT, OBAA-CHAN.
HE REALLY DOESN'T MIND. DO YOU, NAOKI?
I DON'T MIND.
SEE, OBAA-CHAN? IF THE DRAIN ISN'T CLEARED, IT'S GOING TO BACK UP AND YOU'LL HAVE LEAKS.
THIS ISN'T A NEW HOUSE.
I CAN TAKE CARE OF THIS HOUSE. I AM NOT DEAD. I AM NOT A RELIC.
OH, OF COURSE, OBAA-CHAN! LOOK AT THIS PLACE, IT'S PRISTINE!
IT'S JUST, NAOKI LIKES THIS TYPE OF WORK. DON'T YOU, NAOKI?
I DON'T MIND.
SEE? SO UNLESS YOU LIKE CLEANING THE GUTTERS, WOULDN'T IT BE BETTER IF NAOKI DID IT?
WELL—
GREAT. AND WHILE HE'S AT IT, MAYBE HE CAN—
HEY, MARIKO, HAVE YOU EVER SEEN THE WILLOW TREE OUT IN THE CLEARING IN THE WOODS?
NO... I DON'T THINK SO.
WHY?

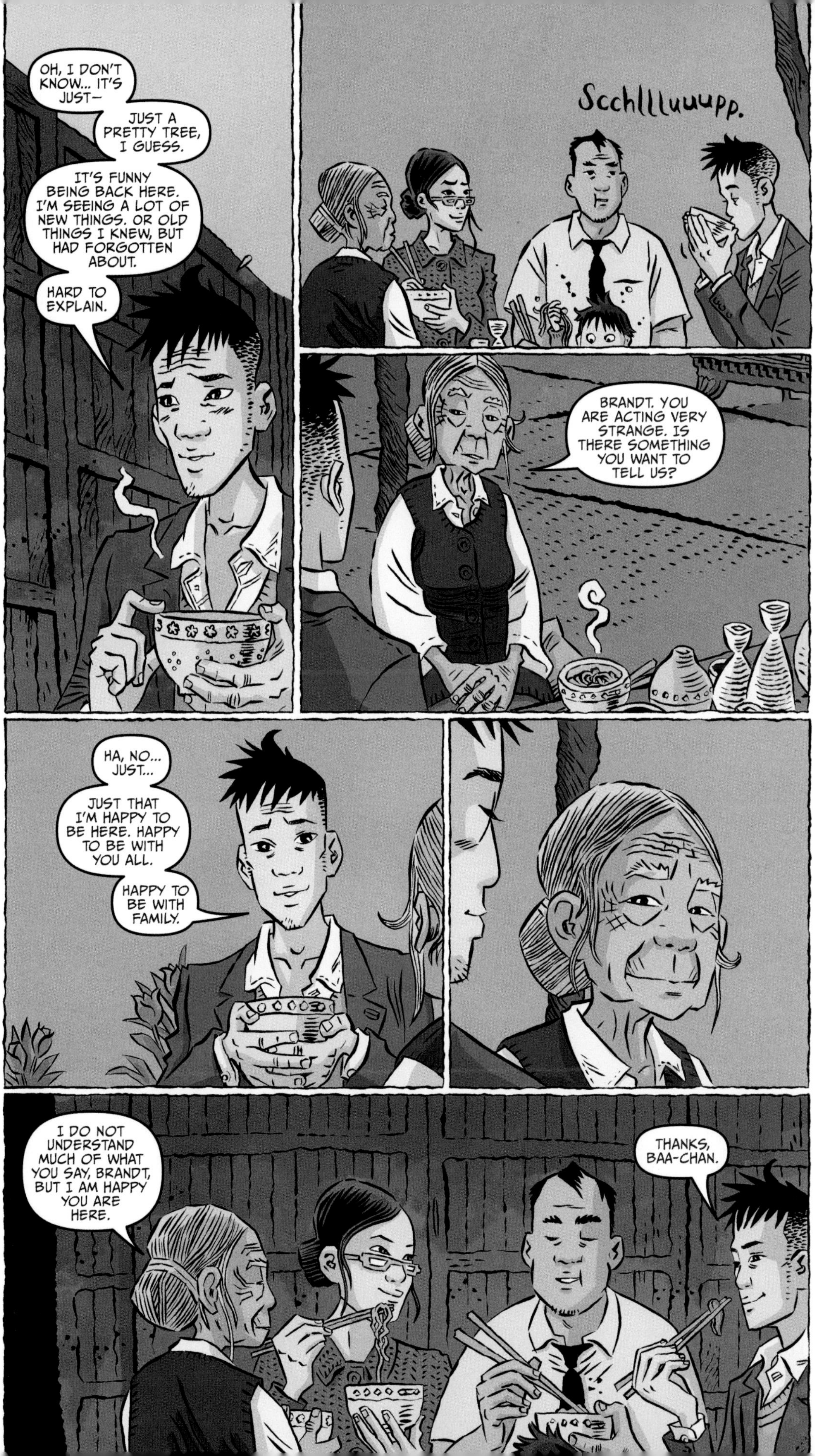
OH, I DON'T KNOW... IT'S JUST—
JUST A PRETTY TREE, I GUESS.
IT'S FUNNY BEING BACK HERE. I'M SEEING A LOT OF NEW THINGS. OR OLD THINGS I KNEW, BUT HAD FORGOTTEN ABOUT.
HARD TO EXPLAIN.
Scchllluuupp.
BRANDT. YOU ARE ACTING VERY STRANGE. IS THERE SOMETHING YOU WANT TO TELL US?
HA, NO... JUST...
JUST THAT I'M HAPPY TO BE HERE. HAPPY TO BE WITH YOU ALL.
HAPPY TO BE WITH FAMILY.
I DO NOT UNDERSTAND MUCH OF WHAT YOU SAY, BRANDT, BUT I AM HAPPY YOU ARE HERE.
THANKS, BAA-CHAN.

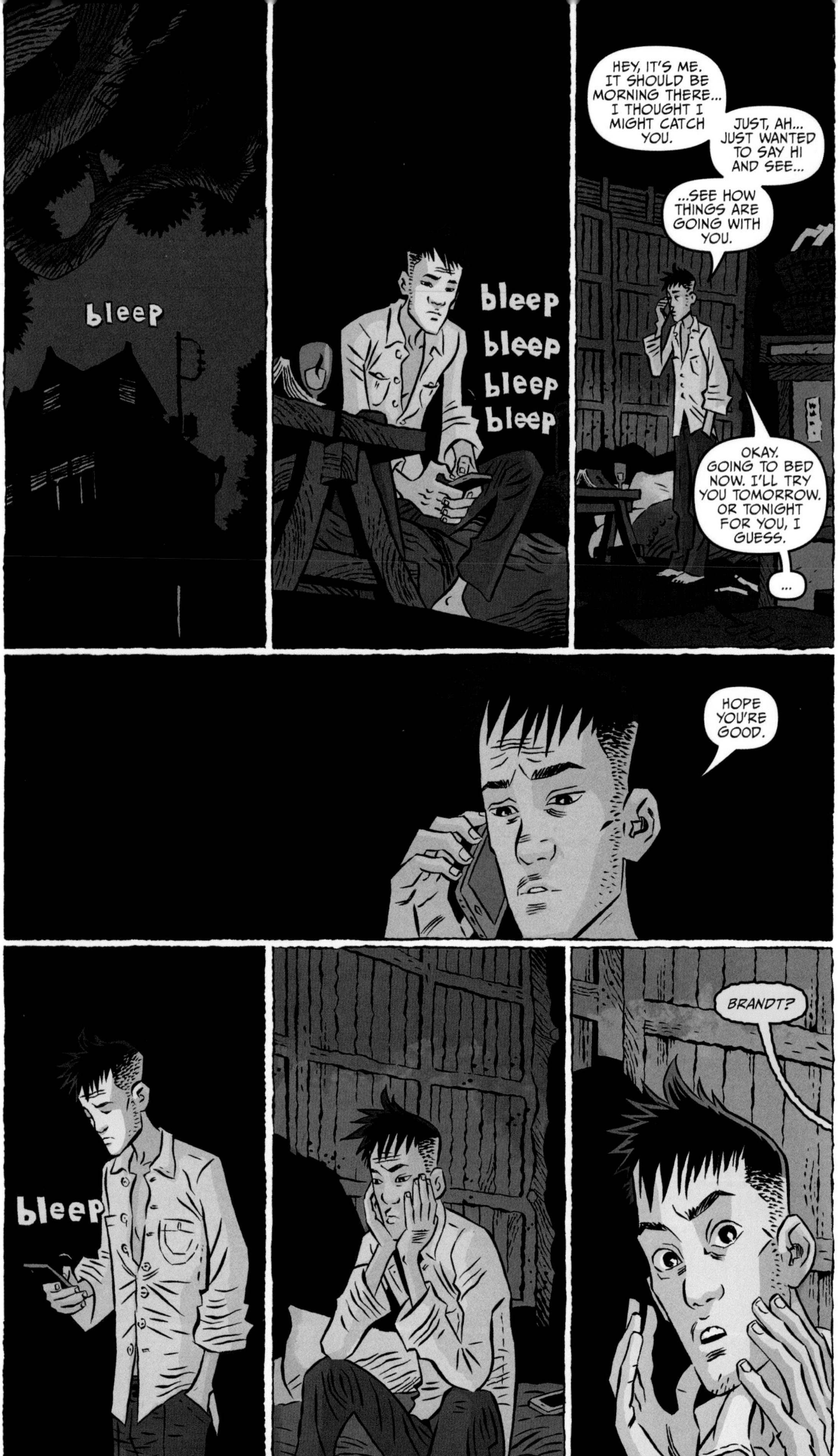
bleep
bleep
bleep
bleep
bleep
HEY, IT'S ME. IT SHOULD BE MORNING THERE... I THOUGHT I MIGHT CATCH YOU.
JUST, AH... JUST WANTED TO SAY HI AND SEE...
...SEE HOW THINGS ARE GOING WITH YOU.
OKAY. GOING TO BED NOW. I'LL TRY YOU TOMORROW. OR TONIGHT FOR YOU, I GUESS.
...
HOPE YOU'RE GOOD.
bleep
BRANDT?

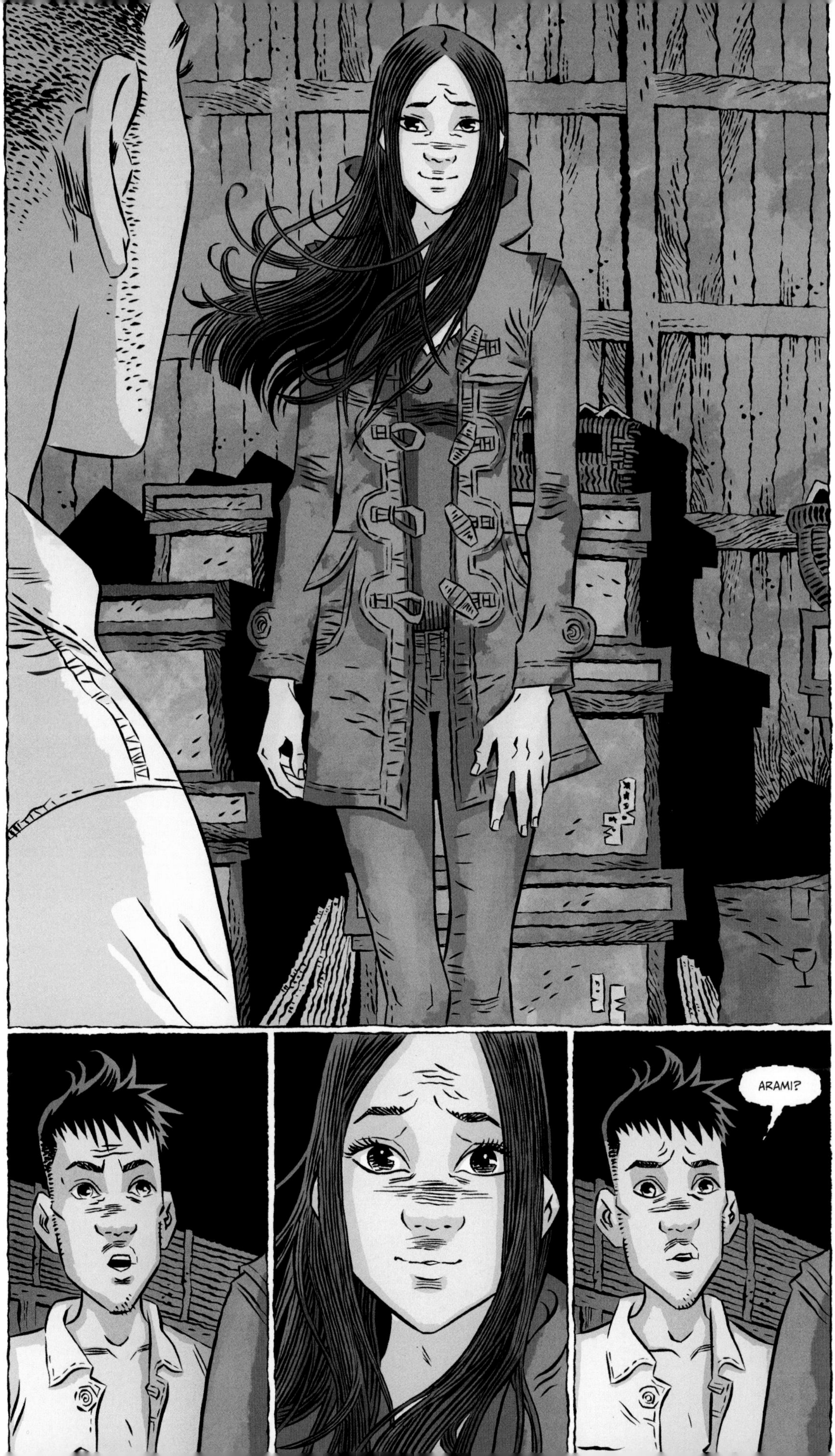
ARAMI?

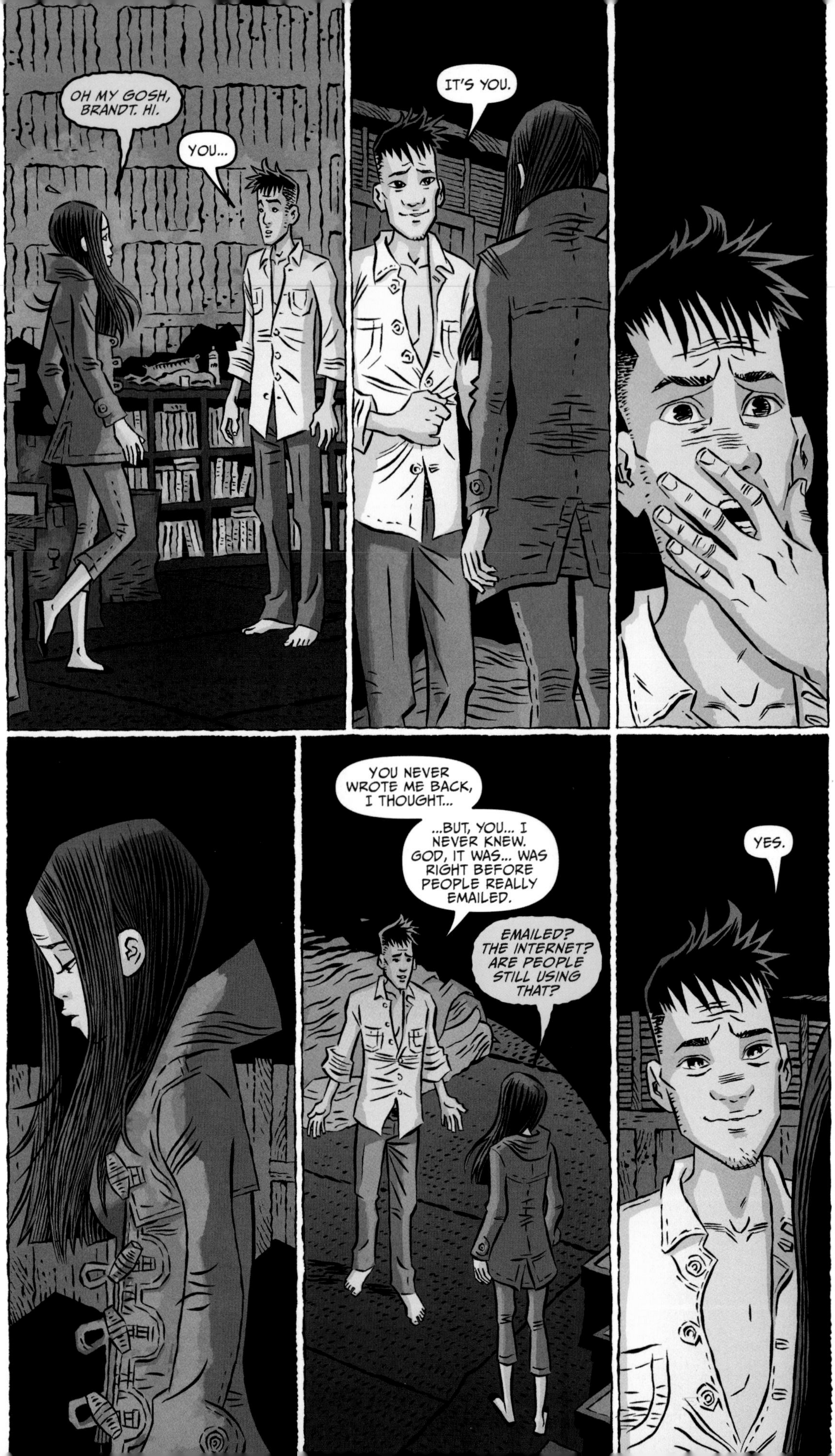
OH MY GOSH, BRANDT. HI.
YOU...
IT'S YOU.
YOU NEVER WROTE ME BACK, I THOUGHT...
...BUT, YOU... I NEVER KNEW. GOD, IT WAS... WAS RIGHT BEFORE PEOPLE REALLY EMAILED.
EMAILED? THE INTERNET? ARE PEOPLE STILL USING THAT?
YES.

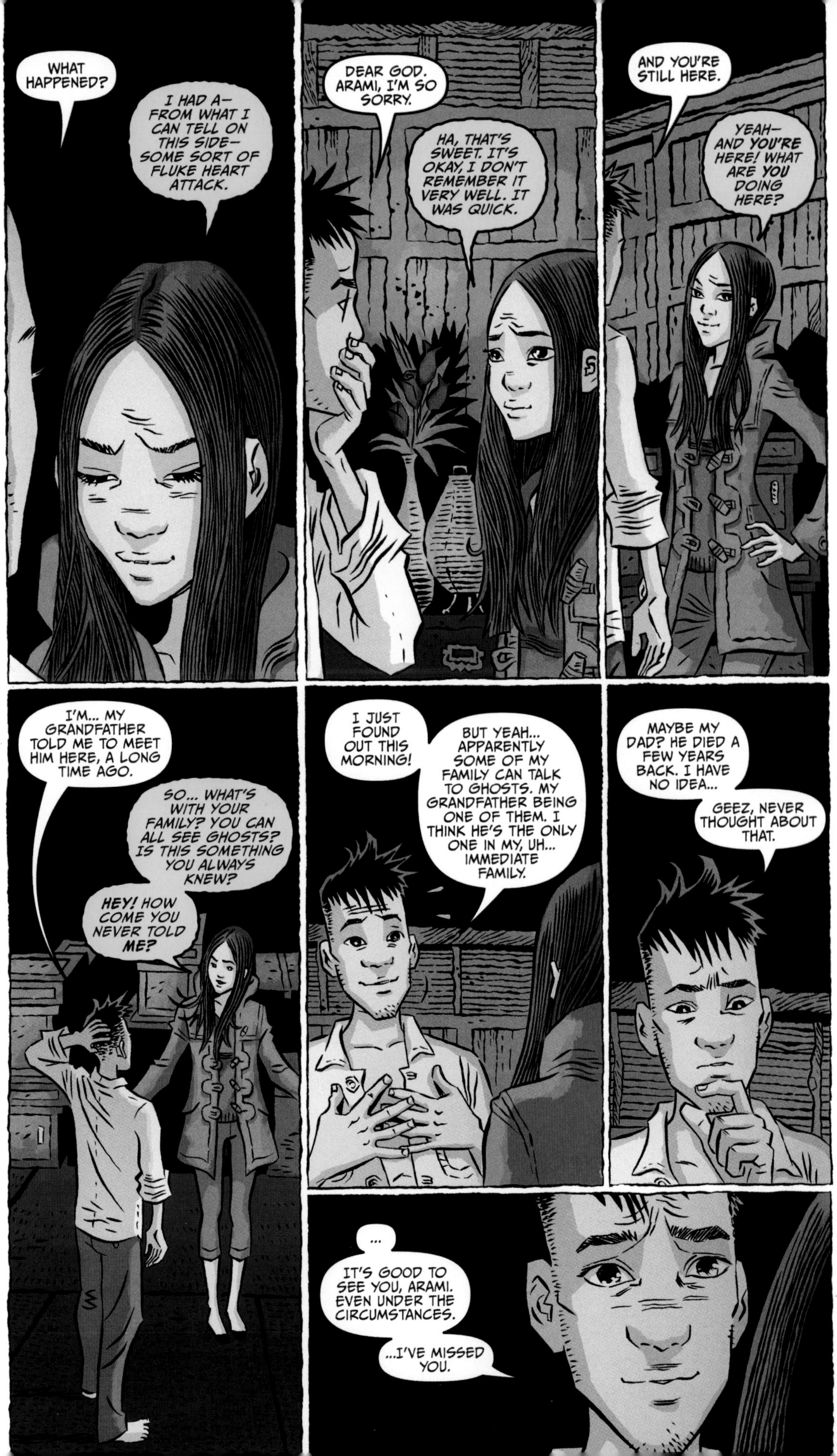
WHAT HAPPENED?
I HAD A— FROM WHAT I CAN TELL ON THIS SIDE— SOME SORT OF FLUKE HEART ATTACK.
DEAR GOD. ARAMI, I'M SO SORRY.
HA, THAT'S SWEET. IT'S OKAY, I DON'T REMEMBER IT VERY WELL. IT WAS QUICK.
AND YOU'RE STILL HERE.
YEAH— AND YOU'RE HERE! WHAT ARE YOU DOING HERE?
I'M... MY GRANDFATHER TOLD ME TO MEET HIM HERE, A LONG TIME AGO.
SO... WHAT'S WITH YOUR FAMILY? YOU CAN ALL SEE GHOSTS? IS THIS SOMETHING YOU ALWAYS KNEW?
HEY! HOW COME YOU NEVER TOLD ME?
I JUST FOUND OUT THIS MORNING!
BUT YEAH... APPARENTLY SOME OF MY FAMILY CAN TALK TO GHOSTS. MY GRANDFATHER BEING ONE OF THEM. I THINK HE'S THE ONLY ONE IN MY, UH... IMMEDIATE FAMILY.
MAYBE MY DAD? HE DIED A FEW YEARS BACK. I HAVE NO IDEA...
GEEZ, NEVER THOUGHT ABOUT THAT.
...
IT'S GOOD TO SEE YOU, ARAMI. EVEN UNDER THE CIRCUMSTANCES.
...I'VE MISSED YOU.

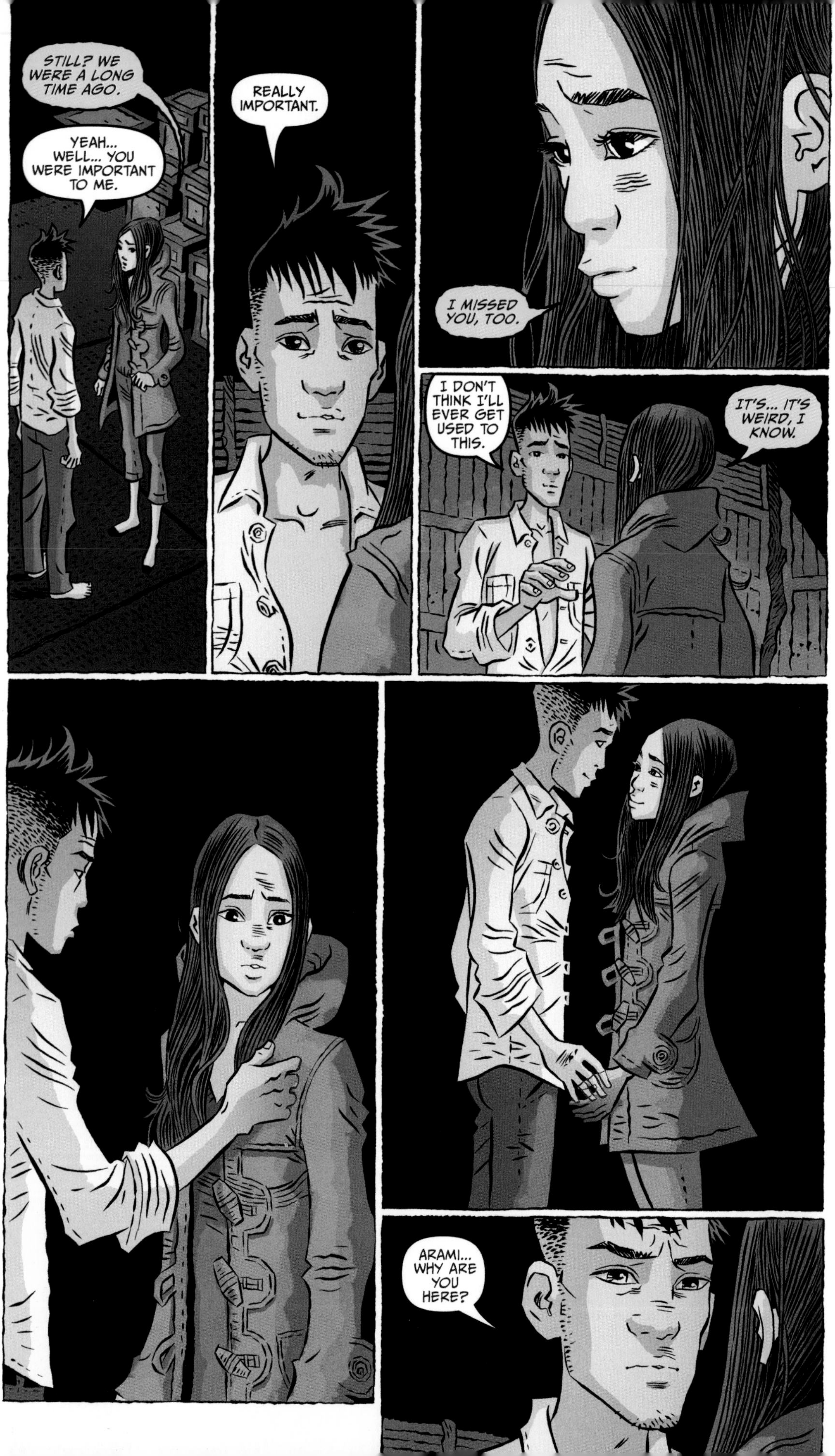
STILL? WE WERE A LONG TIME AGO.
YEAH... WELL... YOU WERE IMPORTANT TO ME.
REALLY IMPORTANT.
I MISSED YOU, TOO.
I DON'T THINK I'LL EVER GET USED TO THIS.
IT'S... IT'S WEIRD, I KNOW.
ARAMI... WHY ARE YOU HERE?

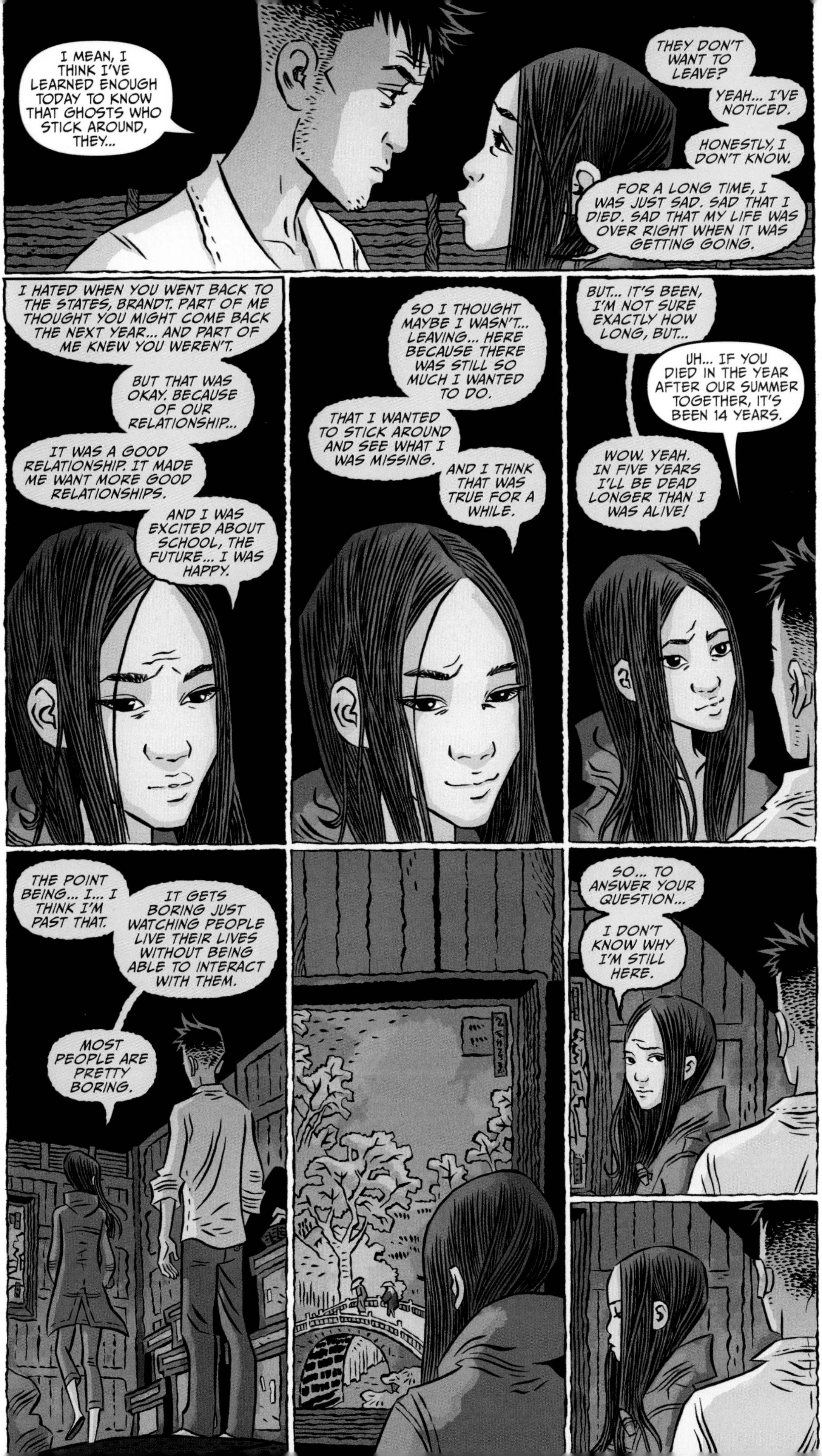

I MEAN, I THINK I'VE LEARNED ENOUGH TODAY TO KNOW THAT GHOSTS WHO STICK AROUND, THEY...
THEY DON'T WANT TO LEAVE?
YEAH... I'VE NOTICED.
HONESTLY, I DON'T KNOW.
FOR A LONG TIME, I WAS JUST SAD. SAD THAT I DIED. SAD THAT MY LIFE WAS OVER RIGHT WHEN IT WAS GETTING GOING.
I HATED WHEN YOU WENT BACK TO THE STATES, BRANDT. PART OF ME THOUGHT YOU MIGHT COME BACK THE NEXT YEAR... AND PART OF ME KNEW YOU WEREN'T.
BUT THAT WAS OKAY. BECAUSE OF OUR RELATIONSHIP...
IT WAS A GOOD RELATIONSHIP. IT MADE ME WANT MORE GOOD RELATIONSHIPS.
AND I WAS EXCITED ABOUT SCHOOL, THE FUTURE... I WAS HAPPY.
SO I THOUGHT MAYBE I WASN'T... LEAVING... HERE BECAUSE THERE WAS STILL SO MUCH I WANTED TO DO.
THAT I WANTED TO STICK AROUND AND SEE WHAT I WAS MISSING.
AND I THINK THAT WAS TRUE FOR A WHILE.
BUT... IT'S BEEN, I'M NOT SURE EXACTLY HOW LONG, BUT...
UH... IF YOU DIED IN THE YEAR AFTER OUR SUMMER TOGETHER, IT'S BEEN 14 YEARS.
WOW. YEAH. IN FIVE YEARS I'LL BE DEAD LONGER THAN I WAS ALIVE!
THE POINT BEING... I... I THINK I'M PAST THAT.
IT GETS BORING JUST WATCHING PEOPLE LIVE THEIR LIVES WITHOUT BEING ABLE TO INTERACT WITH THEM.
MOST PEOPLE ARE PRETTY BORING.
SO... TO ANSWER YOUR QUESTION...
I DON'T KNOW WHY I'M STILL HERE.

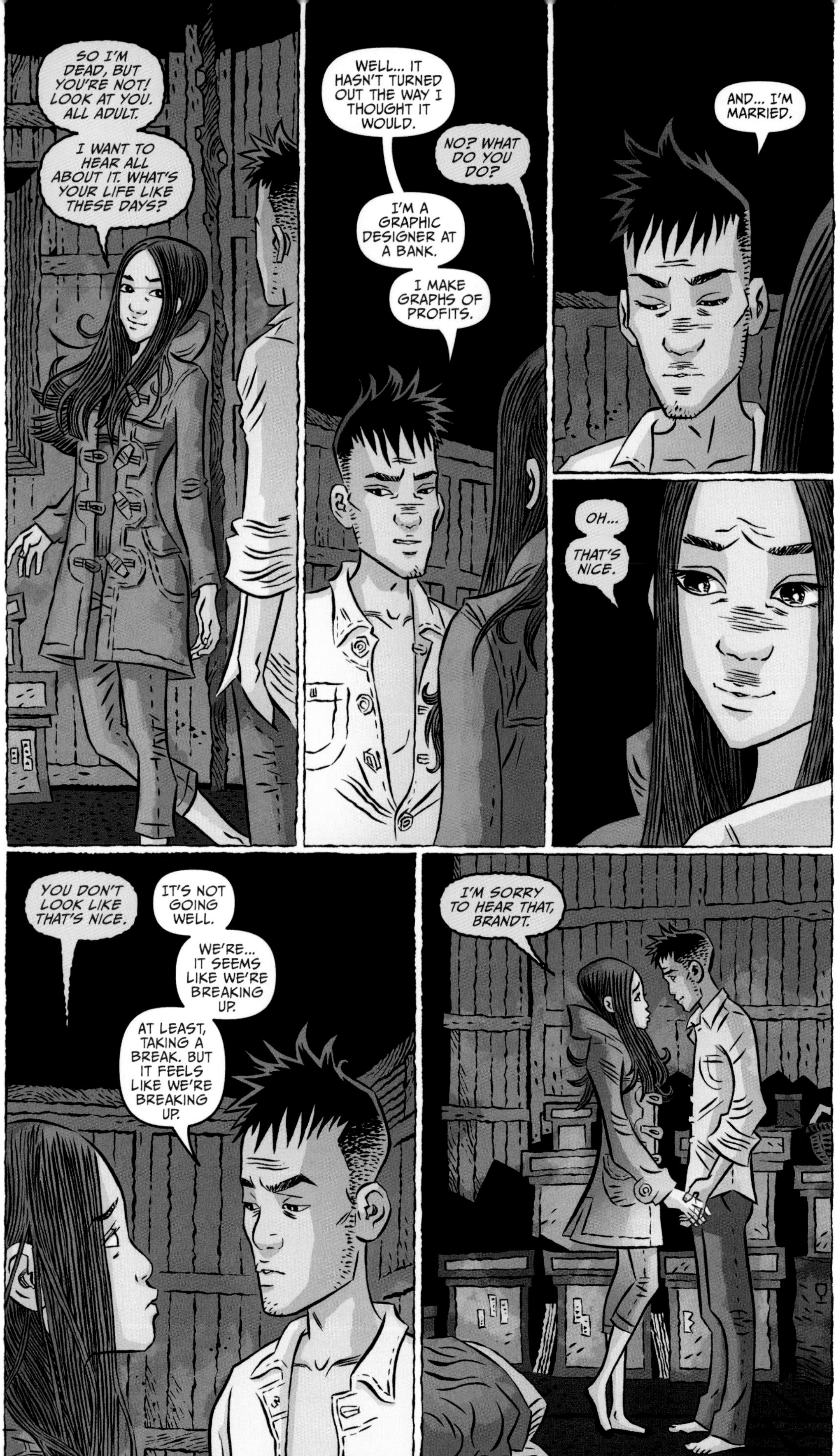
SO I'M DEAD, BUT YOU'RE NOT! LOOK AT YOU. ALL ADULT.
I WANT TO HEAR ALL ABOUT IT. WHAT'S YOUR LIFE LIKE THESE DAYS?
WELL... IT HASN'T TURNED OUT THE WAY I THOUGHT IT WOULD.
NO? WHAT DO YOU DO?
I'M A GRAPHIC DESIGNER AT A BANK.
I MAKE GRAPHS OF PROFITS.
AND... I'M MARRIED.
OH...
THAT'S NICE.
YOU DON'T LOOK LIKE THAT'S NICE.
IT'S NOT GOING WELL.
WE'RE... IT SEEMS LIKE WE'RE BREAKING UP.
AT LEAST, TAKING A BREAK. BUT IT FEELS LIKE WE'RE BREAKING UP.
I'M SORRY TO HEAR THAT, BRANDT.

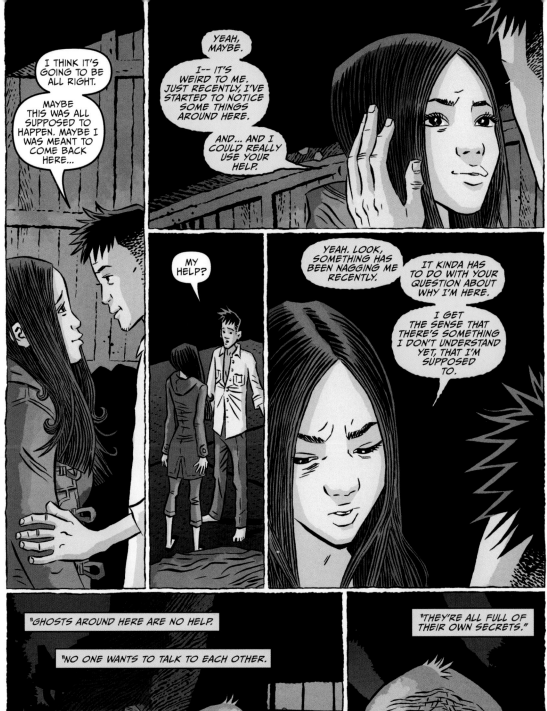

I THINK IT'S GOING TO BE ALL RIGHT.

MAYBE THIS WAS ALL SUPPOSED TO HAPPEN. MAYBE I WAS MEANT TO COME BACK HERE...

YEAH, MAYBE.

I-- IT'S WEIRD TO ME. JUST RECENTLY, I'VE STARTED TO NOTICE SOME THINGS AROUND HERE.

AND... AND I COULD REALLY USE YOUR HELP.

MY HELP?

YEAH. LOOK, SOMETHING HAS BEEN NAGGING ME RECENTLY.

IT KINDA HAS TO DO WITH YOUR QUESTION ABOUT WHY I'M HERE.

I GET THE SENSE THAT THERE'S SOMETHING I DON'T UNDERSTAND YET, THAT I'M SUPPOSED TO.

"GHOSTS AROUND HERE ARE NO HELP."

"NO ONE WANTS TO TALK TO EACH OTHER.

"THEY'RE ALL FULL OF THEIR OWN SECRETS."

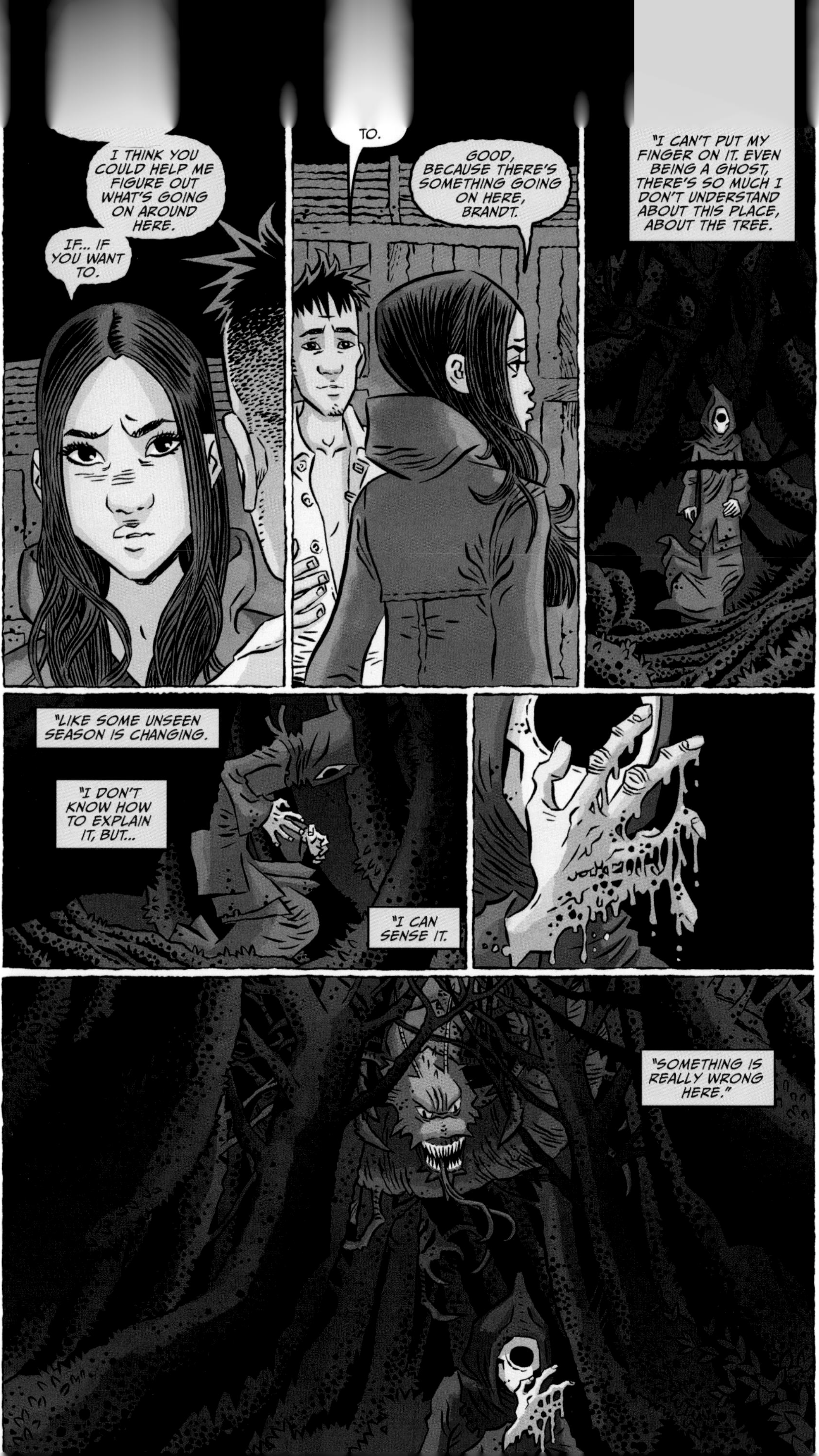

I THINK YOU COULD HELP ME FIGURE OUT WHAT'S GOING ON AROUND HERE.
IF... IF YOU WANT TO.
TO.
GOOD, BECAUSE THERE'S SOMETHING GOING ON HERE, BRANDT.
"I CAN'T PUT MY FINGER ON IT. EVEN BEING A GHOST, THERE'S SO MUCH I DON'T UNDERSTAND ABOUT THIS PLACE, ABOUT THE TREE.
"LIKE SOME UNSEEN SEASON IS CHANGING.
"I DON'T KNOW HOW TO EXPLAIN IT, BUT...
"I CAN SENSE IT.
"SOMETHING IS REALLY WRONG HERE."

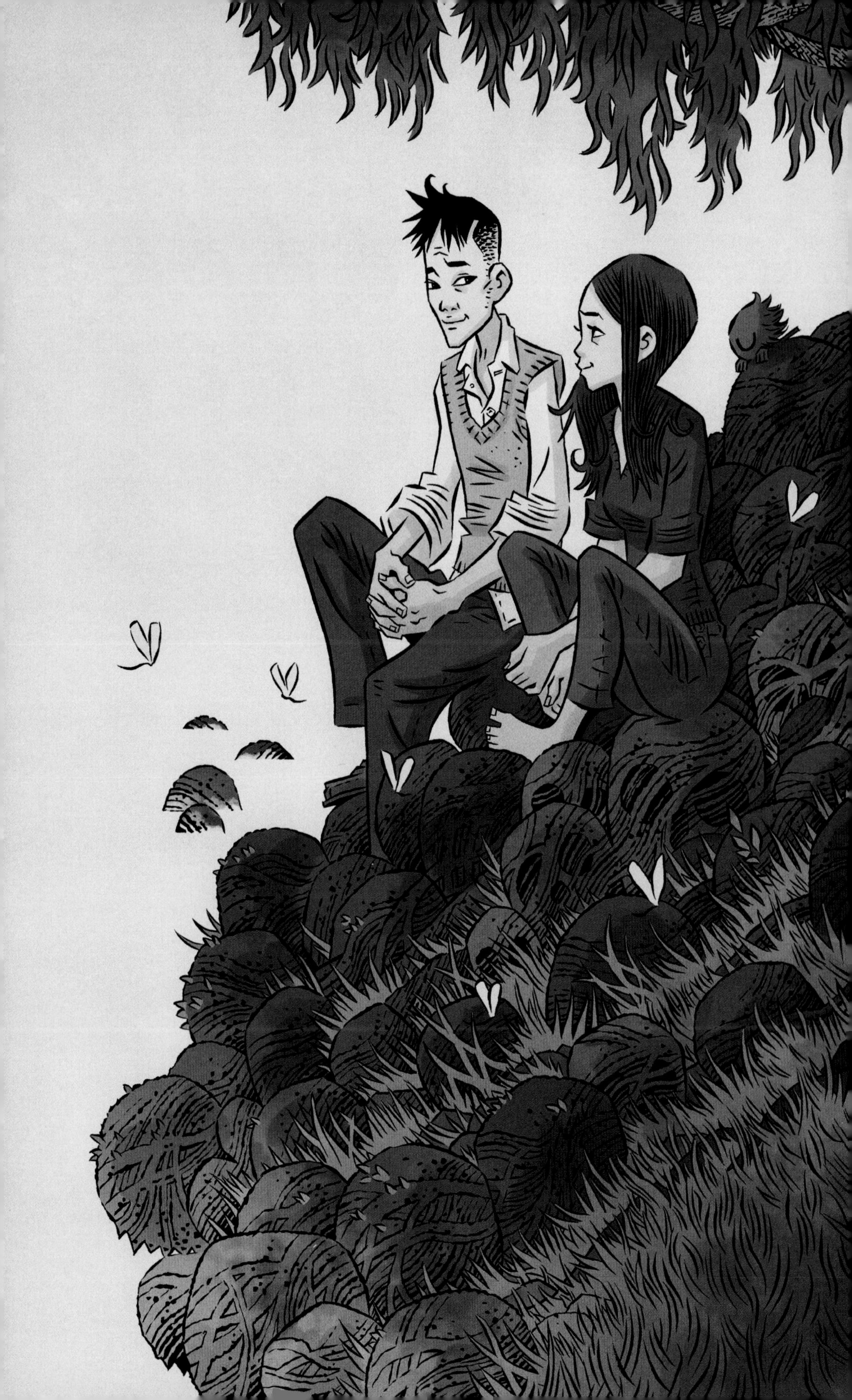

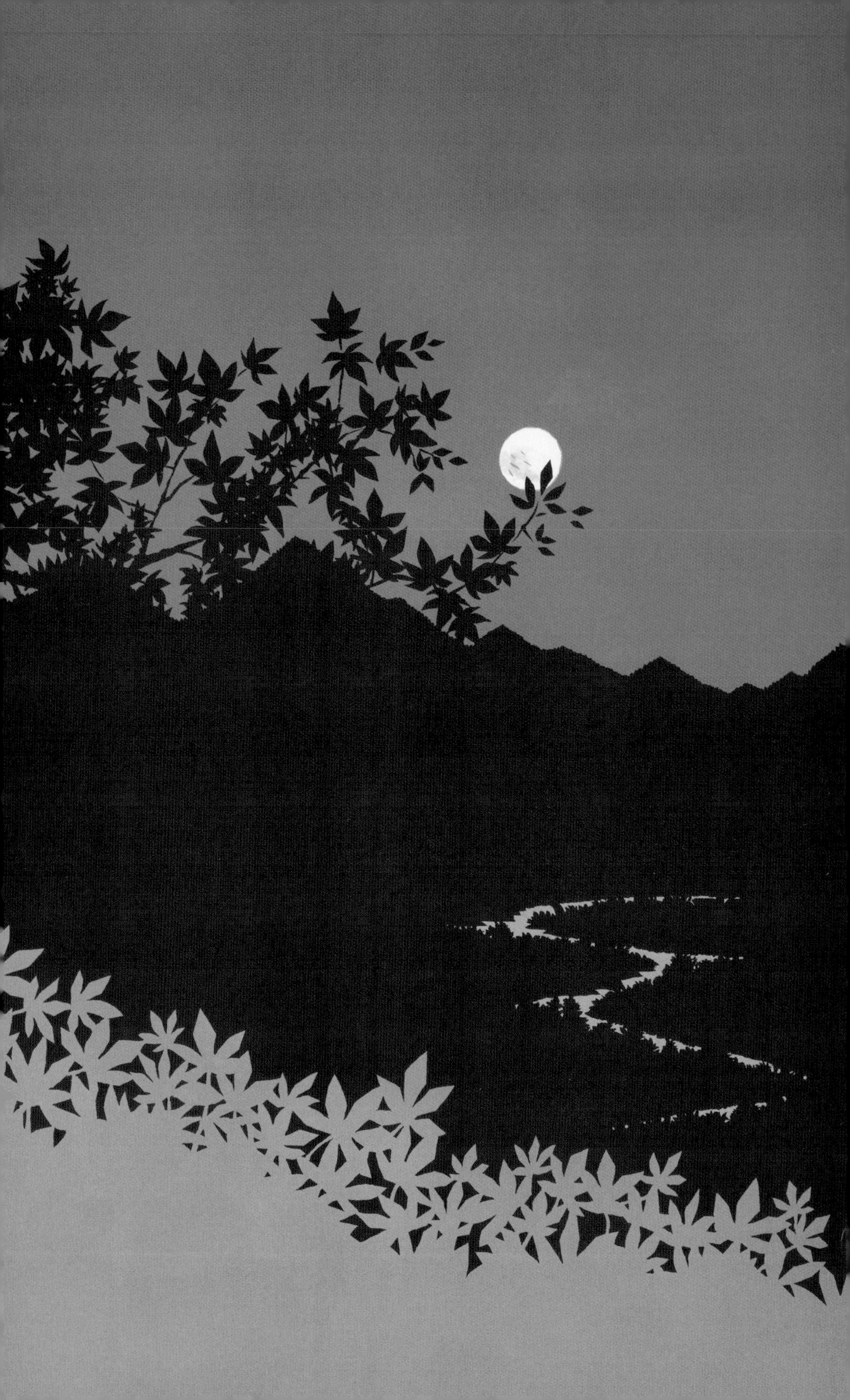

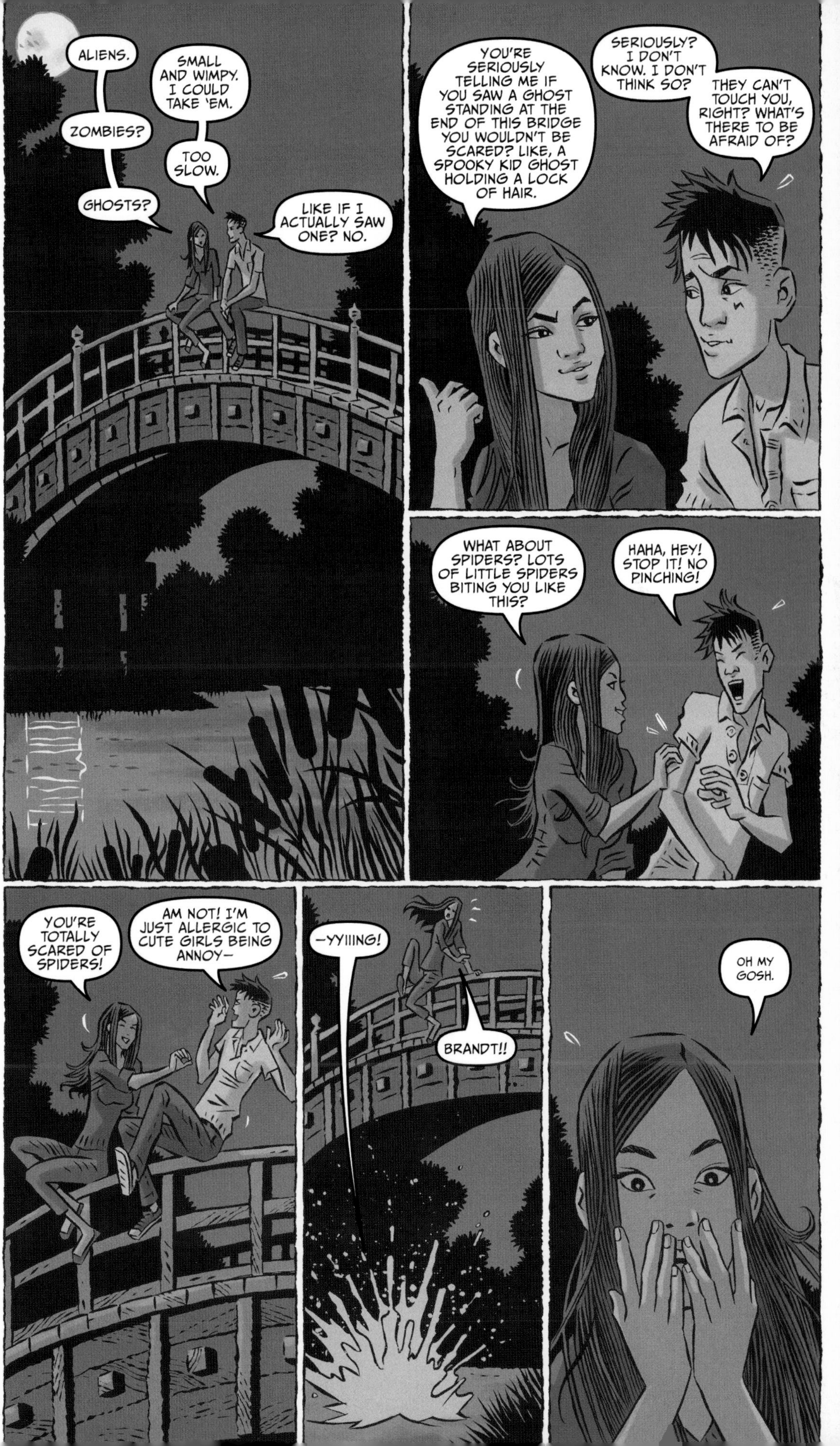
ALIENS.
SMALL AND WIMPY. I COULD TAKE 'EM.
ZOMBIES?
TOO SLOW.
GHOSTS?
LIKE IF I ACTUALLY SAW ONE? NO.
YOU'RE SERIOUSLY TELLING ME IF YOU SAW A GHOST STANDING AT THE END OF THIS BRIDGE YOU WOULDN'T BE SCARED? LIKE, A SPOOKY KID GHOST HOLDING A LOCK OF HAIR.
SERIOUSLY? I DON'T KNOW. I DON'T THINK SO?
THEY CAN'T TOUCH YOU, RIGHT? WHAT'S THERE TO BE AFRAID OF?
WHAT ABOUT SPIDERS? LOTS OF LITTLE SPIDERS BITING YOU LIKE THIS?
HAHA, HEY! STOP IT! NO PINCHING!
YOU'RE TOTALLY SCARED OF SPIDERS!
AM NOT! I'M JUST ALLERGIC TO CUTE GIRLS BEING ANNOY—
—YYIIING!
BRANDT!!
OH MY GOSH.

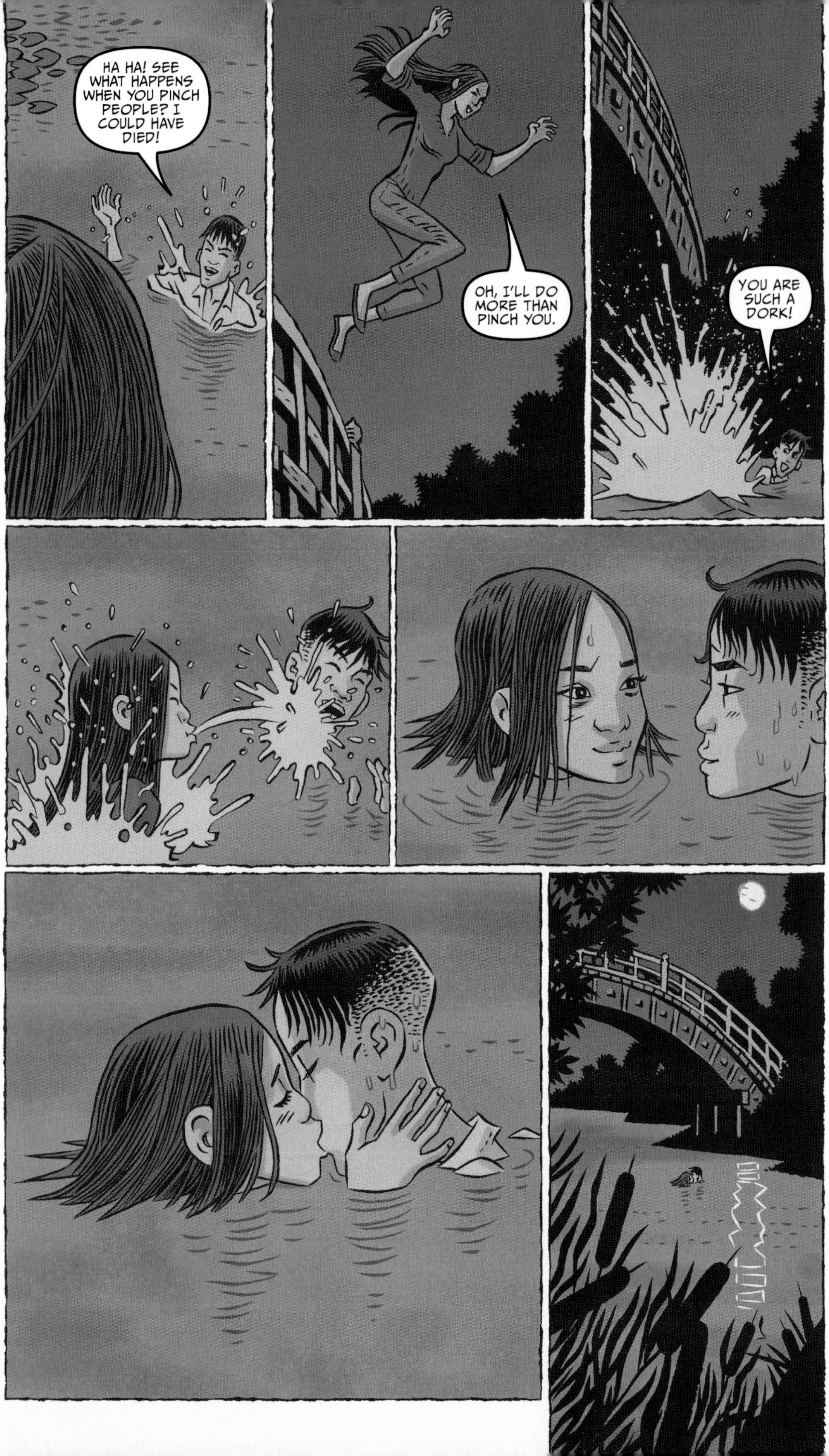
HA HA! SEE WHAT HAPPENS WHEN YOU PINCH PEOPLE? I COULD HAVE DIED!
OH, I'LL DO MORE THAN PINCH YOU.
YOU ARE SUCH A DORK!

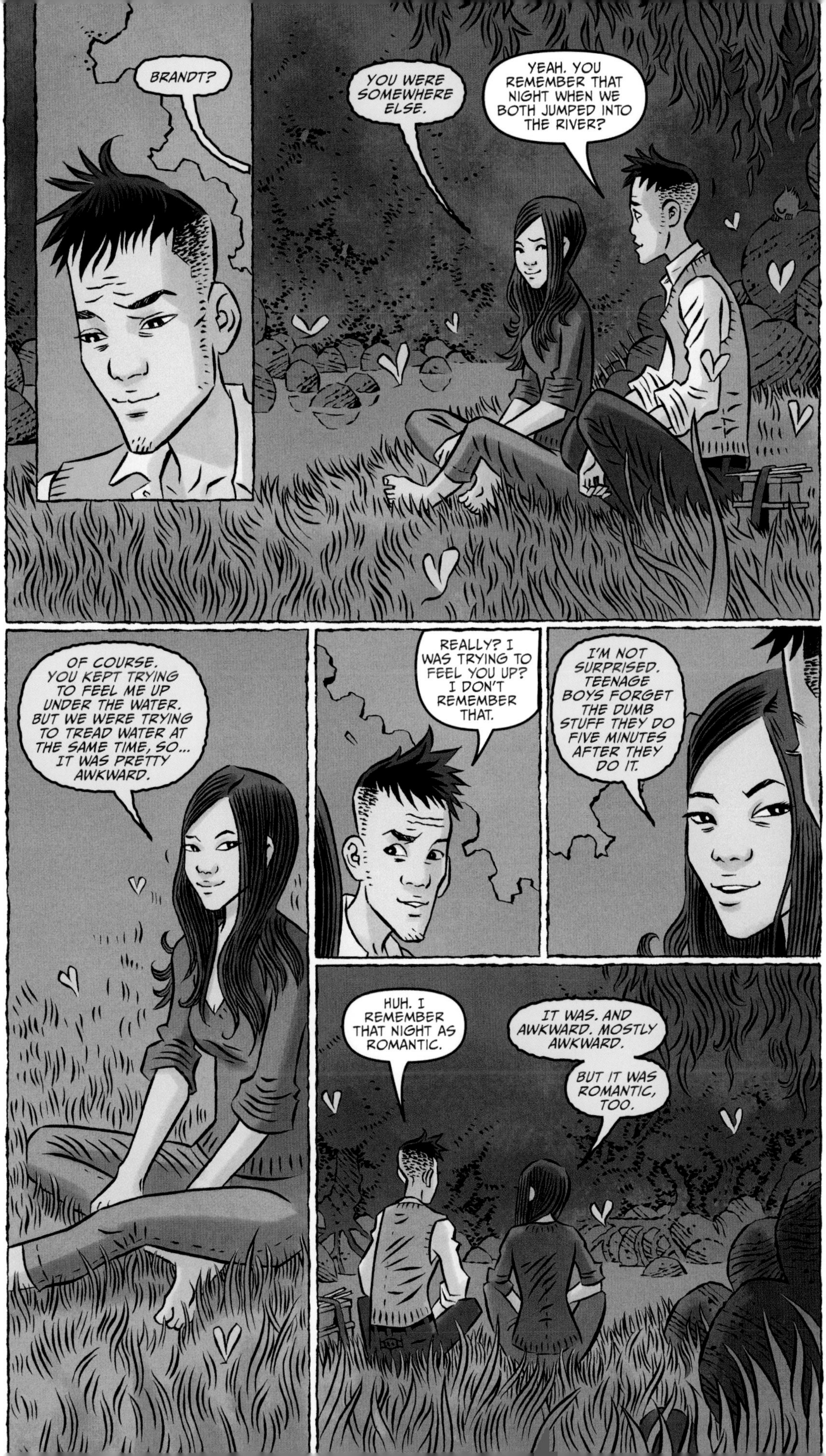
BRANDT?
YOU WERE SOMEWHERE ELSE.
YEAH. YOU REMEMBER THAT NIGHT WHEN WE BOTH JUMPED INTO THE RIVER?
OF COURSE. YOU KEPT TRYING TO FEEL ME UP UNDER THE WATER. BUT WE WERE TRYING TO TREAD WATER AT THE SAME TIME, SO... IT WAS PRETTY AWKWARD.
REALLY? I WAS TRYING TO FEEL YOU UP? I DON'T REMEMBER THAT.
I'M NOT SURPRISED. TEENAGE BOYS FORGET THE DUMB STUFF THEY DO FIVE MINUTES AFTER THEY DO IT.
HUH. I REMEMBER THAT NIGHT AS ROMANTIC.
IT WAS. AND AWKWARD. MOSTLY AWKWARD.
BUT IT WAS ROMANTIC, TOO.

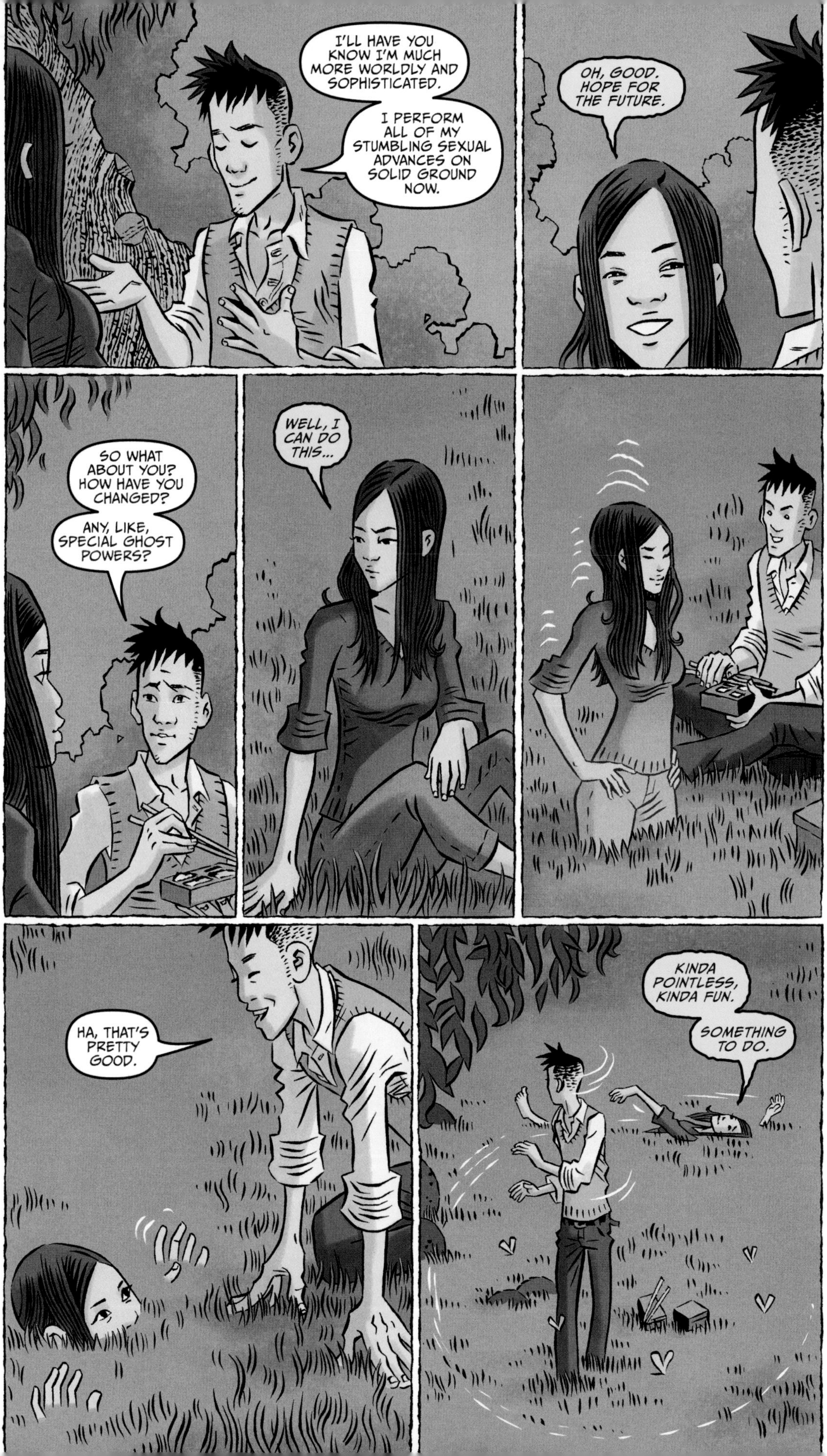
I'LL HAVE YOU KNOW I'M MUCH MORE WORLDLY AND SOPHISTICATED.
I PERFORM ALL OF MY STUMBLING SEXUAL ADVANCES ON SOLID GROUND NOW.
OH, GOOD. HOPE FOR THE FUTURE.
SO WHAT ABOUT YOU? HOW HAVE YOU CHANGED?
ANY, LIKE, SPECIAL GHOST POWERS?
WELL, I CAN DO THIS...
HA, THAT'S PRETTY GOOD.
KINDA POINTLESS, KINDA FUN.
SOMETHING TO DO.

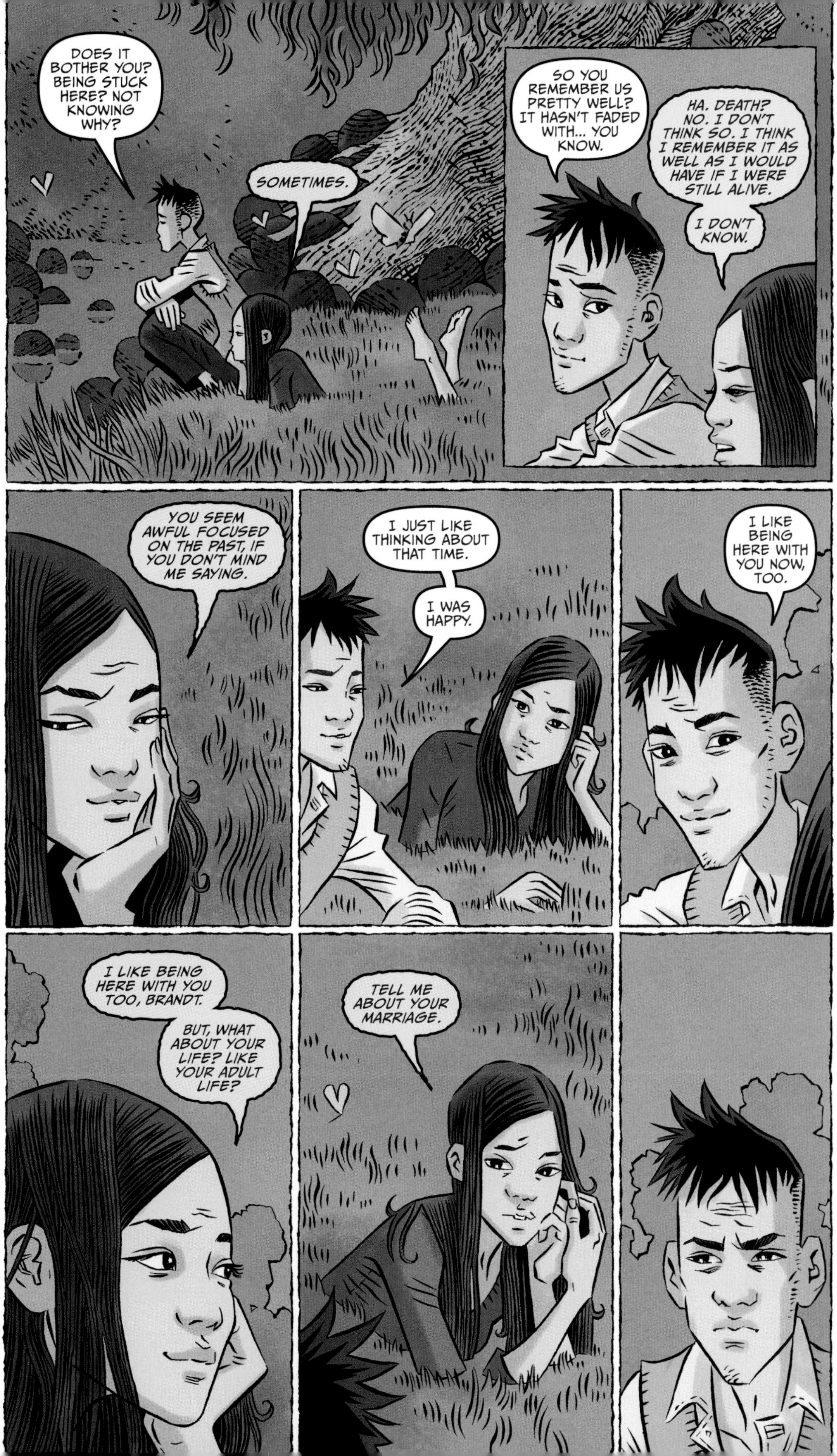
DOES IT BOTHER YOU? BEING STUCK HERE? NOT KNOWING WHY?
SOMETIMES.
SO YOU REMEMBER US PRETTY WELL? IT HASN'T FADED WITH... YOU KNOW.
HA. DEATH? NO. I DON'T THINK SO. I THINK I REMEMBER IT AS WELL AS I WOULD HAVE IF I WERE STILL ALIVE.
I DON'T KNOW.
YOU SEEM AWFUL FOCUSED ON THE PAST, IF YOU DON'T MIND ME SAYING.
I JUST LIKE THINKING ABOUT THAT TIME.
I WAS HAPPY.
I LIKE BEING HERE WITH YOU NOW, TOO.
I LIKE BEING HERE WITH YOU TOO, BRANDT.
BUT, WHAT ABOUT YOUR LIFE? LIKE YOUR ADULT LIFE?
TELL ME ABOUT YOUR MARRIAGE.

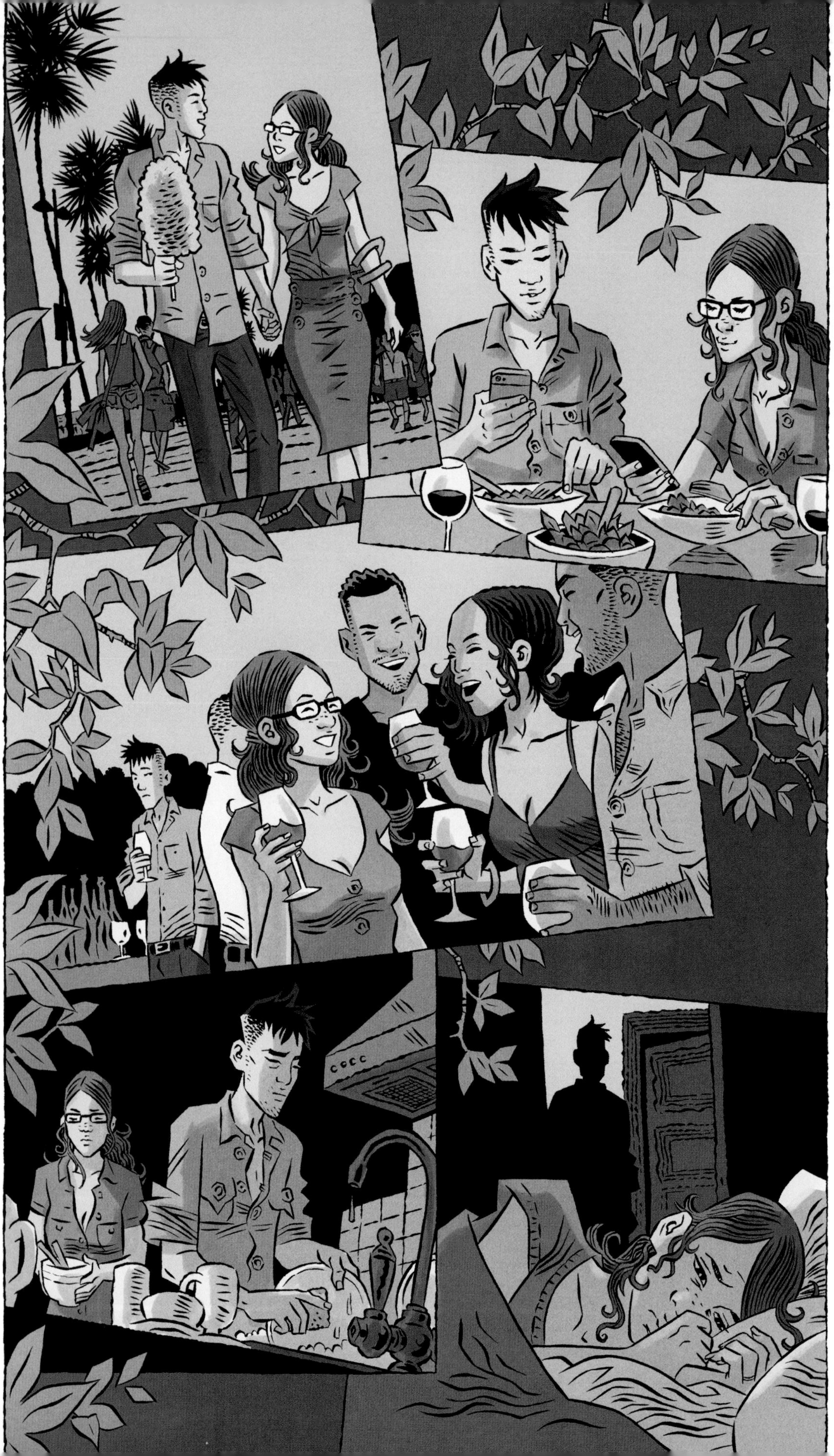

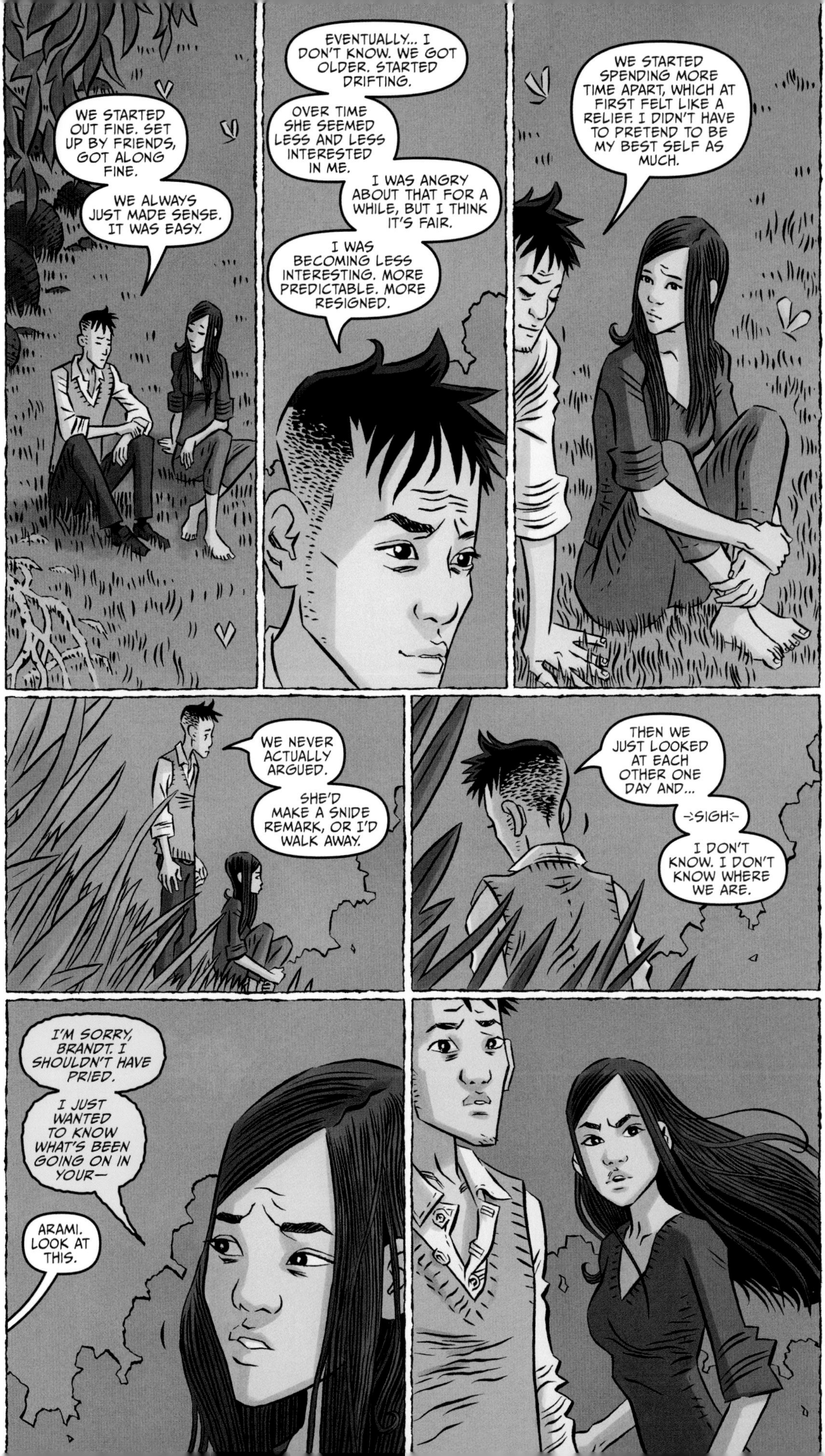
WE STARTED OUT FINE. SET UP BY FRIENDS, GOT ALONG FINE.
WE ALWAYS JUST MADE SENSE. IT WAS EASY.
EVENTUALLY... I DON'T KNOW. WE GOT OLDER. STARTED DRIFTING.
OVER TIME SHE SEEMED LESS AND LESS INTERESTED IN ME.
I WAS ANGRY ABOUT THAT FOR A WHILE, BUT I THINK IT'S FAIR.
I WAS BECOMING LESS INTERESTING. MORE PREDICTABLE. MORE RESIGNED.
WE STARTED SPENDING MORE TIME APART, WHICH AT FIRST FELT LIKE A RELIEF. I DIDN'T HAVE TO PRETEND TO BE MY BEST SELF AS MUCH.
WE NEVER ACTUALLY ARGUED.
SHE'D MAKE A SNIDE REMARK, OR I'D WALK AWAY.
THEN WE JUST LOOKED AT EACH OTHER ONE DAY AND...
SIGH
I DON'T KNOW. I DON'T KNOW WHERE WE ARE.
I'M SORRY, BRANDT. I SHOULDN'T HAVE PRIED.
I JUST WANTED TO KNOW WHAT'S BEEN GOING ON IN YOUR—
ARAMI. LOOK AT THIS.

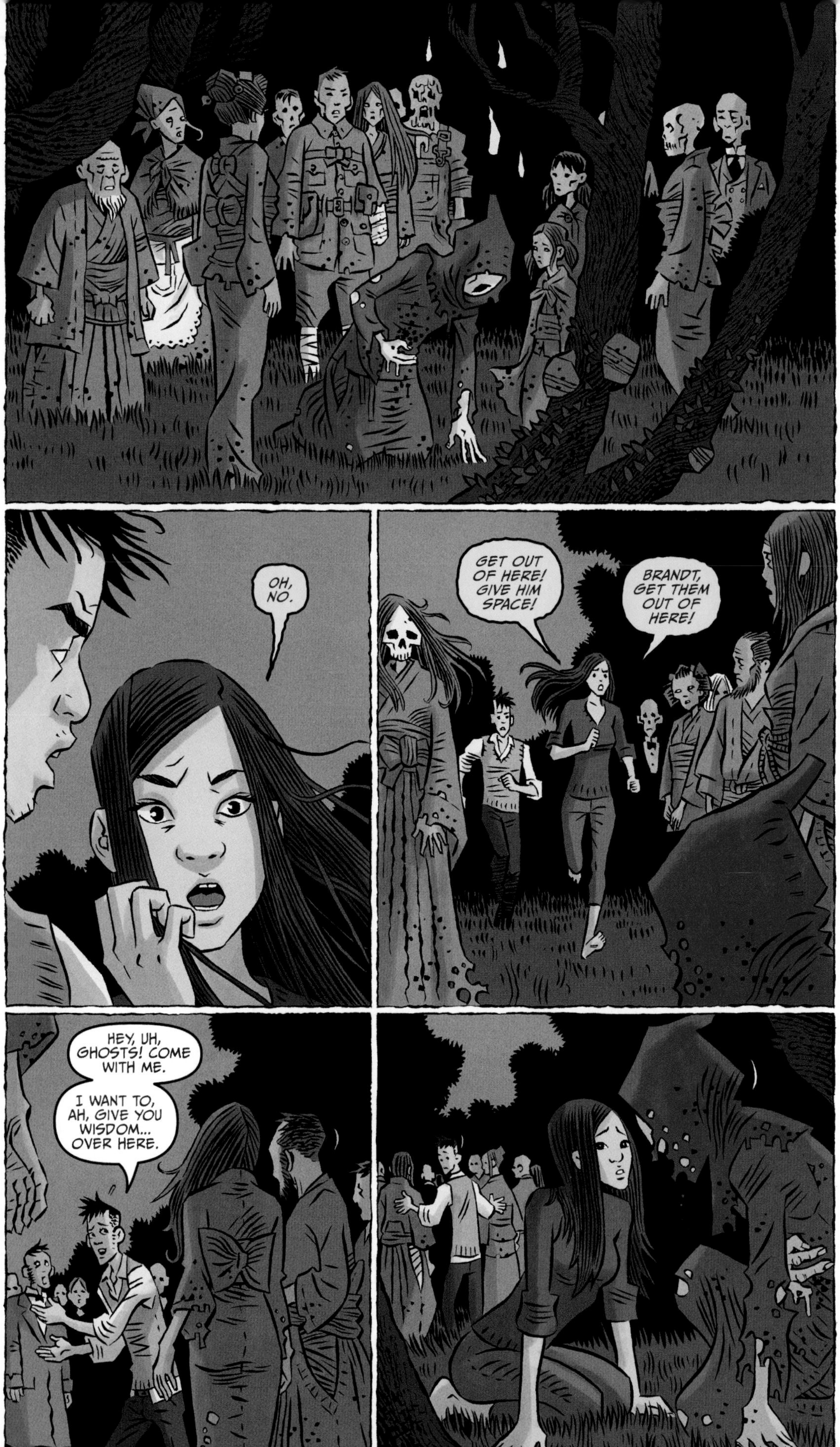
OH, NO.
GET OUT OF HERE! GIVE HIM SPACE!
BRANDT, GET THEM OUT OF HERE!
HEY, UH, GHOSTS! COME WITH ME.
I WANT TO, AH, GIVE YOU WISDOM... OVER HERE.

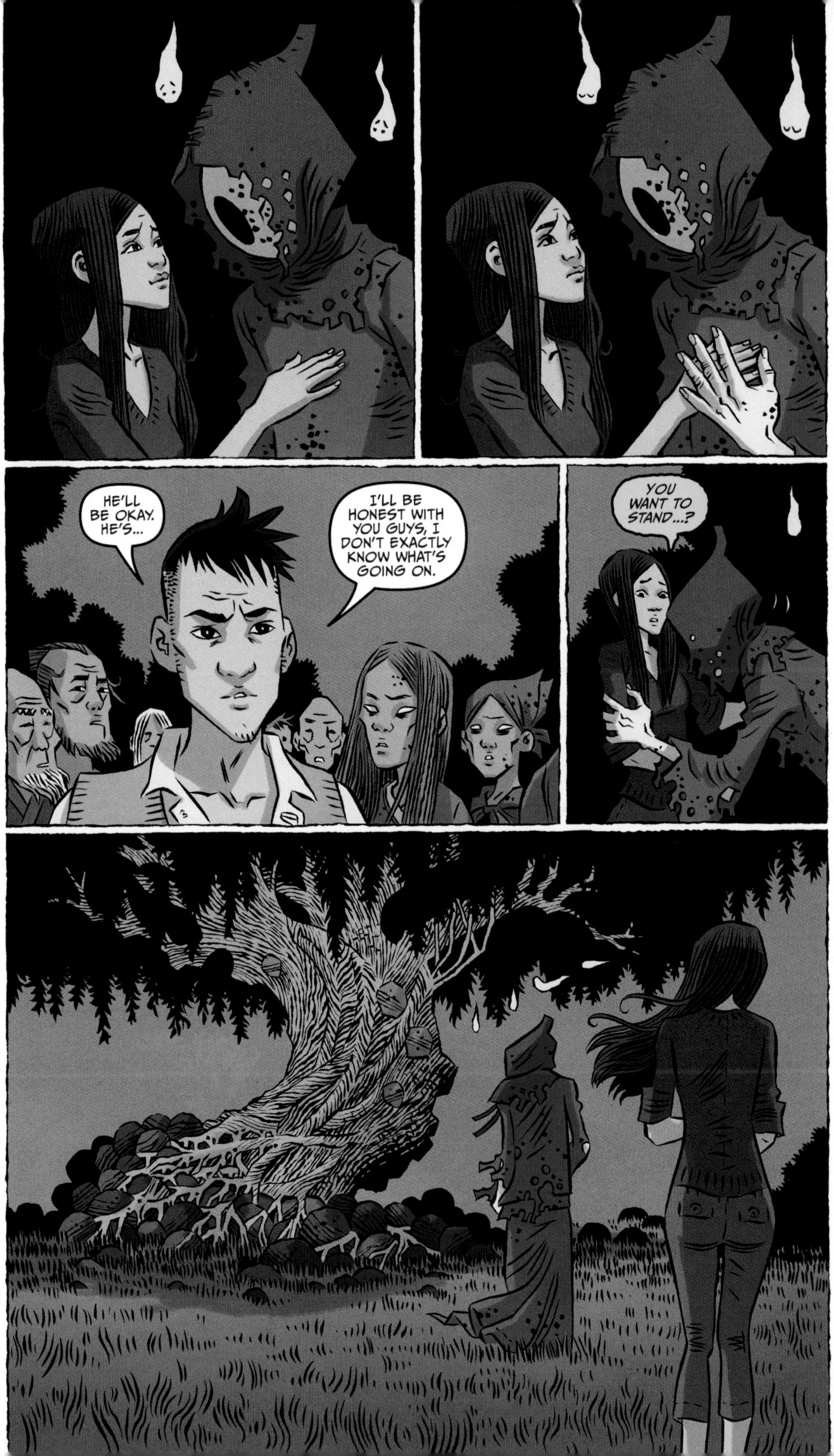
HE'LL BE OKAY. HE'S...
I'LL BE HONEST WITH YOU GUYS, I DON'T EXACTLY KNOW WHAT'S GOING ON.
YOU WANT TO STAND...?

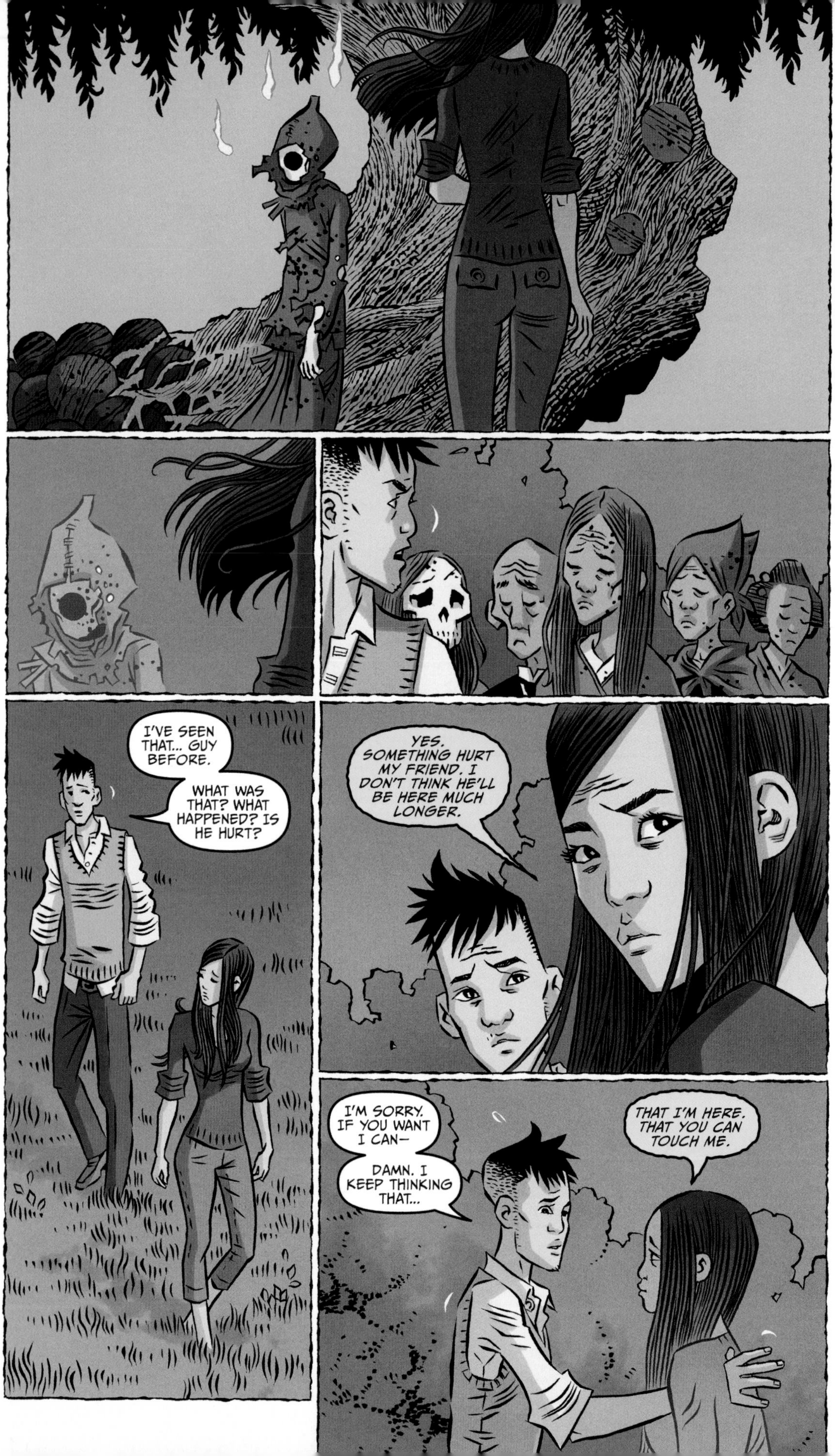
I'VE SEEN THAT... GUY BEFORE.
WHAT WAS THAT? WHAT HAPPENED? IS HE HURT?
YES. SOMETHING HURT MY FRIEND. I DON'T THINK HE'LL BE HERE MUCH LONGER.
I'M SORRY. IF YOU WANT I CAN—
DAMN. I KEEP THINKING THAT...
THAT I'M HERE. THAT YOU CAN TOUCH ME.

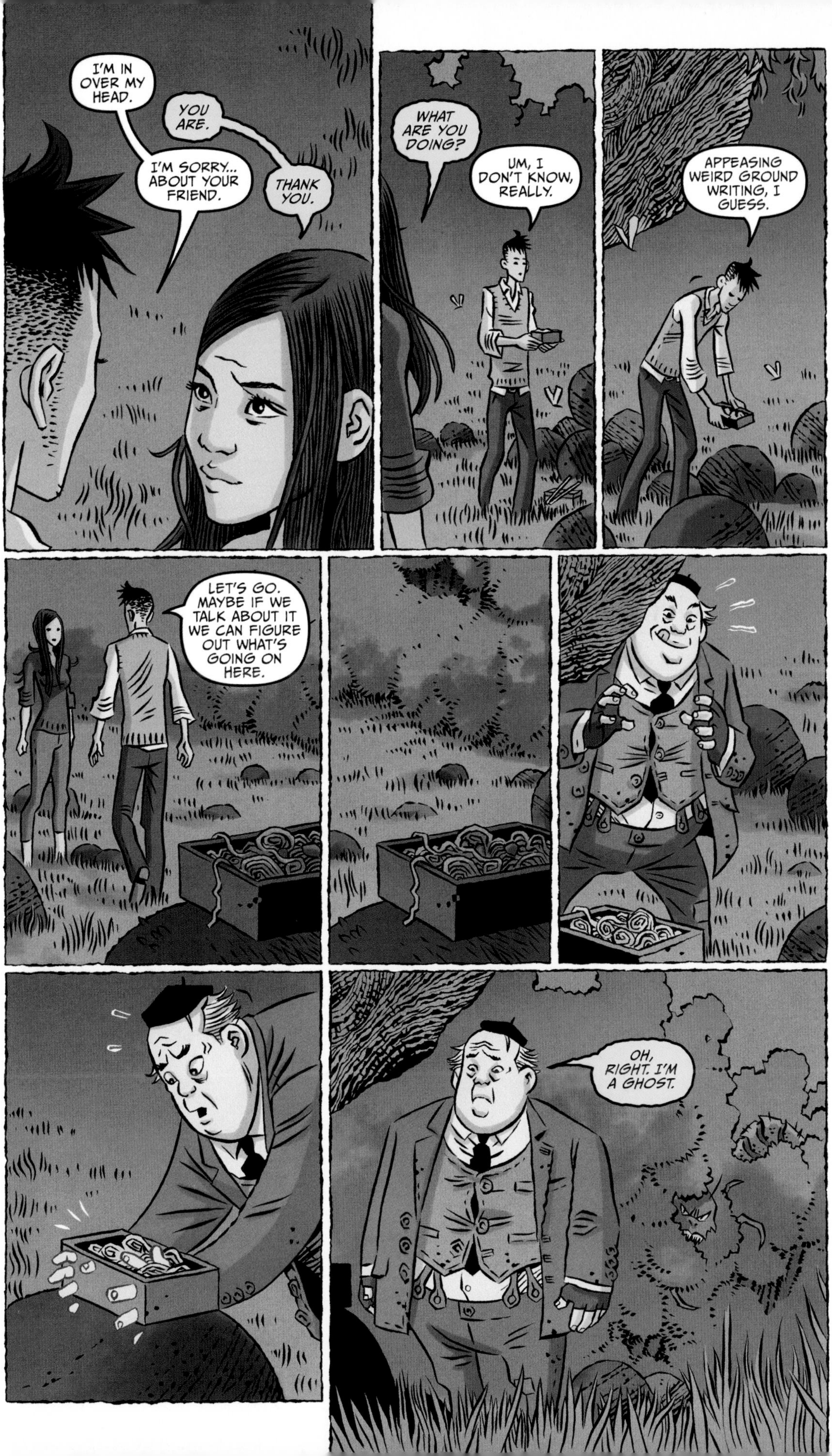
I'M IN OVER MY HEAD.
YOU ARE.
I'M SORRY... ABOUT YOUR FRIEND.
THANK YOU.
WHAT ARE YOU DOING?
UM, I DON'T KNOW, REALLY.
APPEASING WEIRD GROUND WRITING, I GUESS.
LET'S GO. MAYBE IF WE TALK ABOUT IT WE CAN FIGURE OUT WHAT'S GOING ON HERE.
OH, RIGHT. I'M A GHOST.

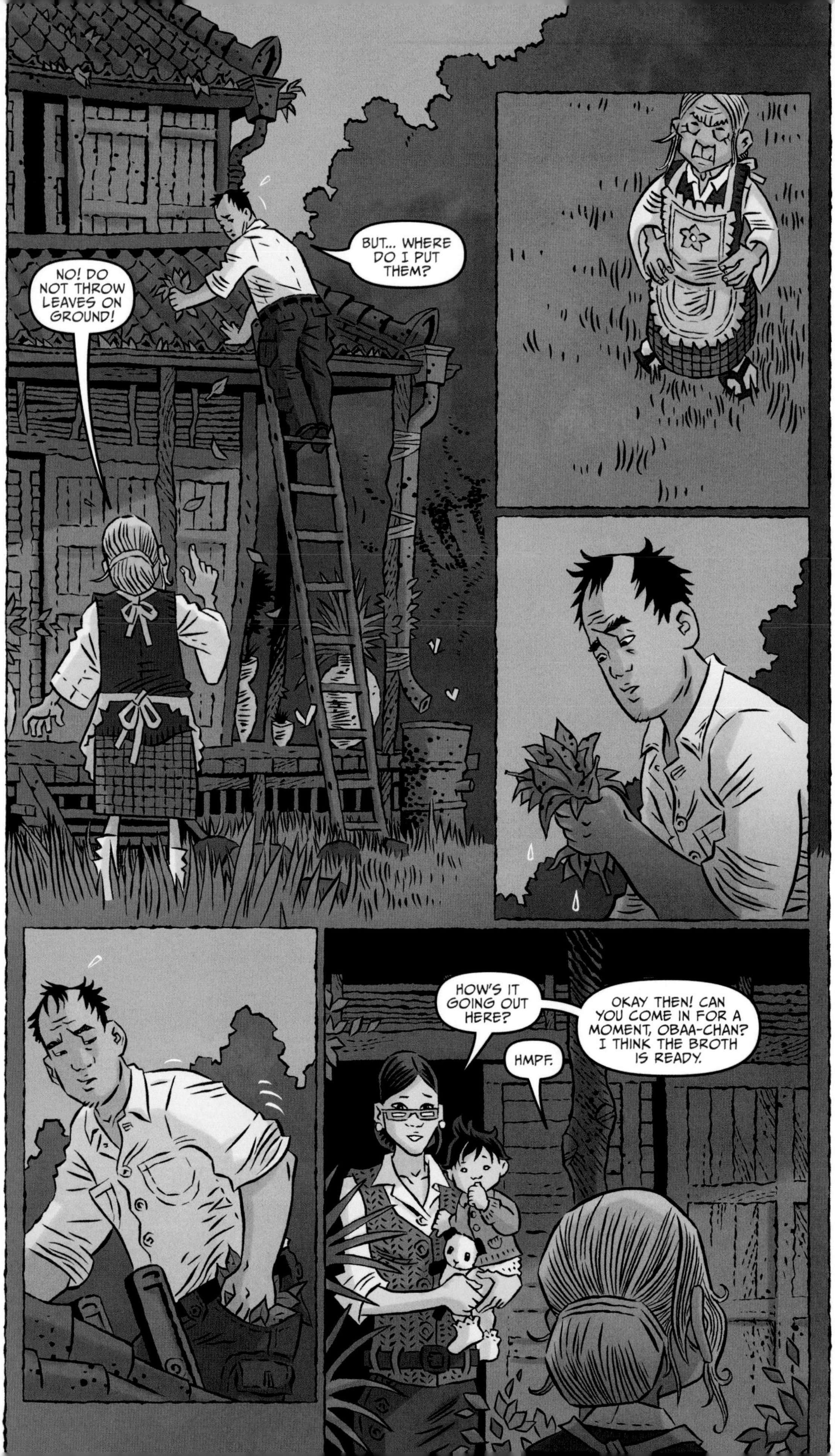
NO! DO NOT THROW LEAVES ON GROUND!
BUT... WHERE DO I PUT THEM?
HOW'S IT GOING OUT HERE?
HMPF.
OKAY THEN! CAN YOU COME IN FOR A MOMENT, OBAA-CHAN? I THINK THE BROTH IS READY.

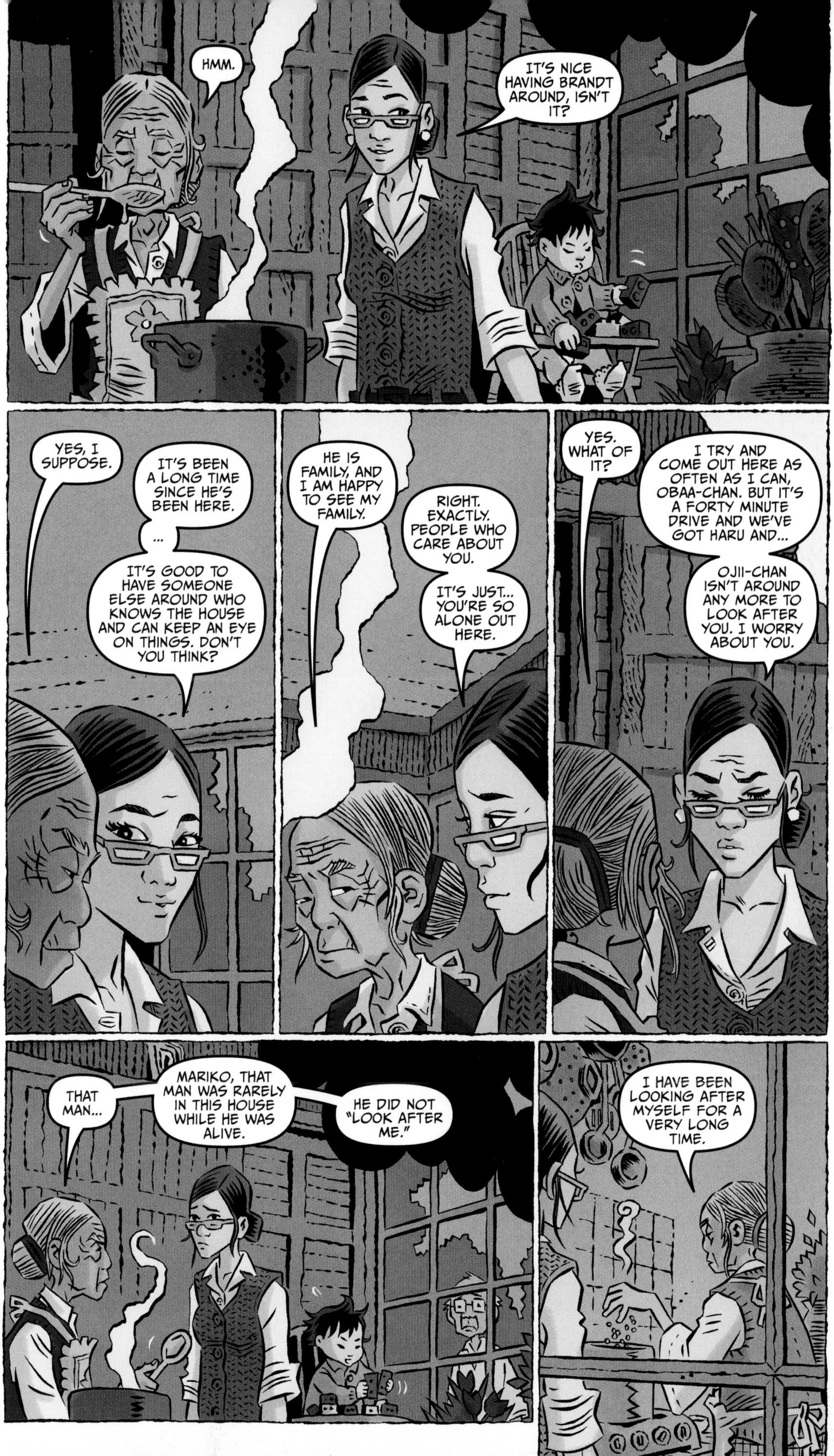
HMM.
IT'S NICE HAVING BRANDT AROUND, ISN'T IT?
YES, I SUPPOSE.
IT'S BEEN A LONG TIME SINCE HE'S BEEN HERE.
...
IT'S GOOD TO HAVE SOMEONE ELSE AROUND WHO KNOWS THE HOUSE AND CAN KEEP AN EYE ON THINGS. DON'T YOU THINK?
HE IS FAMILY, AND I AM HAPPY TO SEE MY FAMILY.
RIGHT. EXACTLY. PEOPLE WHO CARE ABOUT YOU.
IT'S JUST... YOU'RE SO ALONE OUT HERE.
YES. WHAT OF IT?
I TRY AND COME OUT HERE AS OFTEN AS I CAN, OBAA-CHAN. BUT IT'S A FORTY MINUTE DRIVE AND WE'VE GOT HARU AND...
OJII-CHAN ISN'T AROUND ANY MORE TO LOOK AFTER YOU. I WORRY ABOUT YOU.
THAT MAN...
MARIKO, THAT MAN WAS RARELY IN THIS HOUSE WHILE HE WAS ALIVE.
HE DID NOT "LOOK AFTER ME."
I HAVE BEEN LOOKING AFTER MYSELF FOR A VERY LONG TIME.

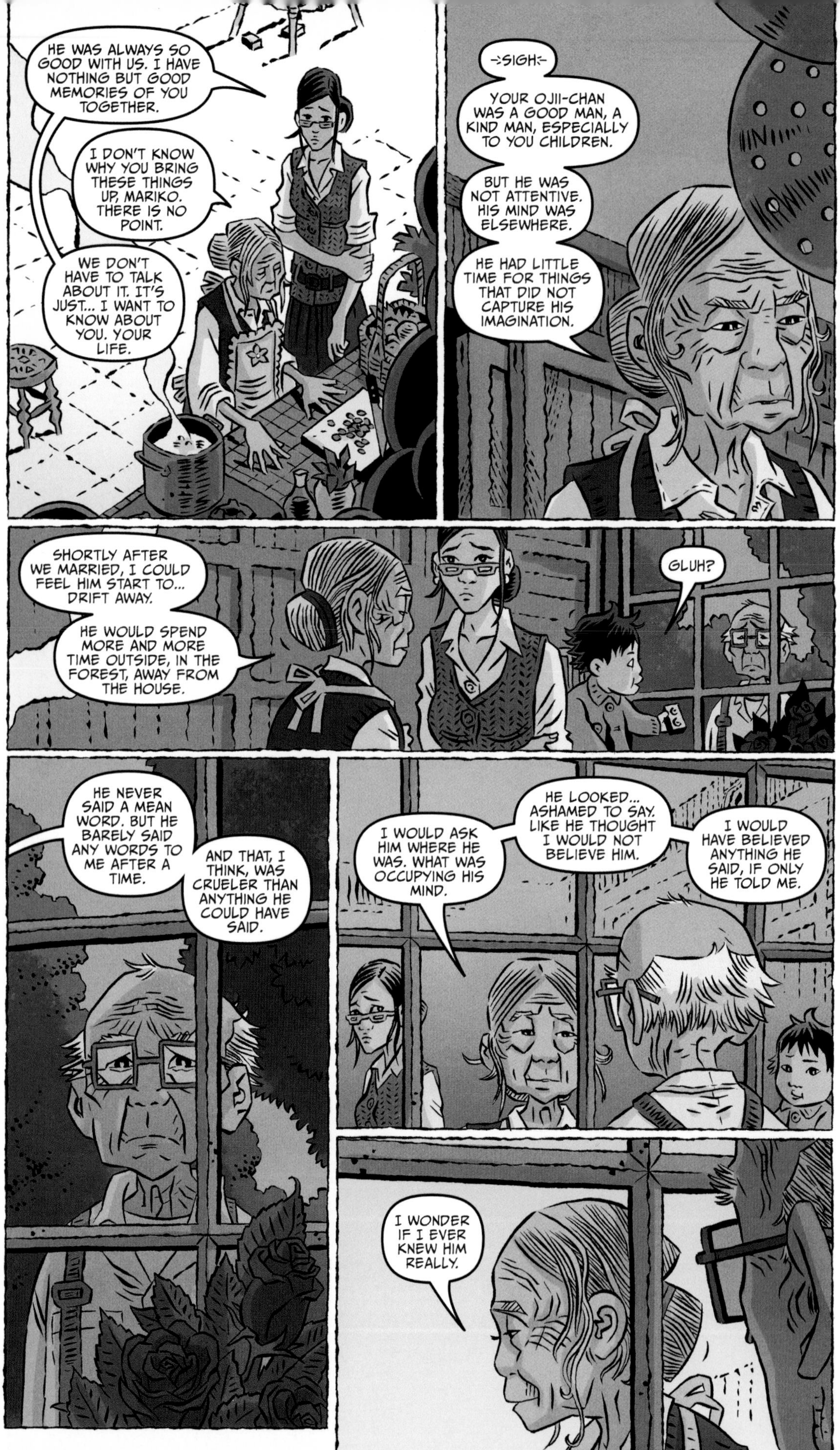
HE WAS ALWAYS SO GOOD WITH US. I HAVE NOTHING BUT GOOD MEMORIES OF YOU TOGETHER.
I DON'T KNOW WHY YOU BRING THESE THINGS UP, MARIKO. THERE IS NO POINT.
WE DON'T HAVE TO TALK ABOUT IT. IT'S JUST... I WANT TO KNOW ABOUT YOU. YOUR LIFE.
-SIGH-
YOUR OJII-CHAN WAS A GOOD MAN, A KIND MAN, ESPECIALLY TO YOU CHILDREN.
BUT HE WAS NOT ATTENTIVE. HIS MIND WAS ELSEWHERE.
HE HAD LITTLE TIME FOR THINGS THAT DID NOT CAPTURE HIS IMAGINATION.
SHORTLY AFTER WE MARRIED, I COULD FEEL HIM START TO... DRIFT AWAY.
HE WOULD SPEND MORE AND MORE TIME OUTSIDE, IN THE FOREST, AWAY FROM THE HOUSE.
GLUH?
HE NEVER SAID A MEAN WORD. BUT HE BARELY SAID ANY WORDS TO ME AFTER A TIME.
AND THAT, I THINK, WAS CRUELER THAN ANYTHING HE COULD HAVE SAID.
I WOULD ASK HIM WHERE HE WAS. WHAT WAS OCCUPYING HIS MIND.
HE LOOKED... ASHAMED TO SAY. LIKE HE THOUGHT I WOULD NOT BELIEVE HIM.
I WOULD HAVE BELIEVED ANYTHING HE SAID, IF ONLY HE TOLD ME.
I WONDER IF I EVER KNEW HIM REALLY.

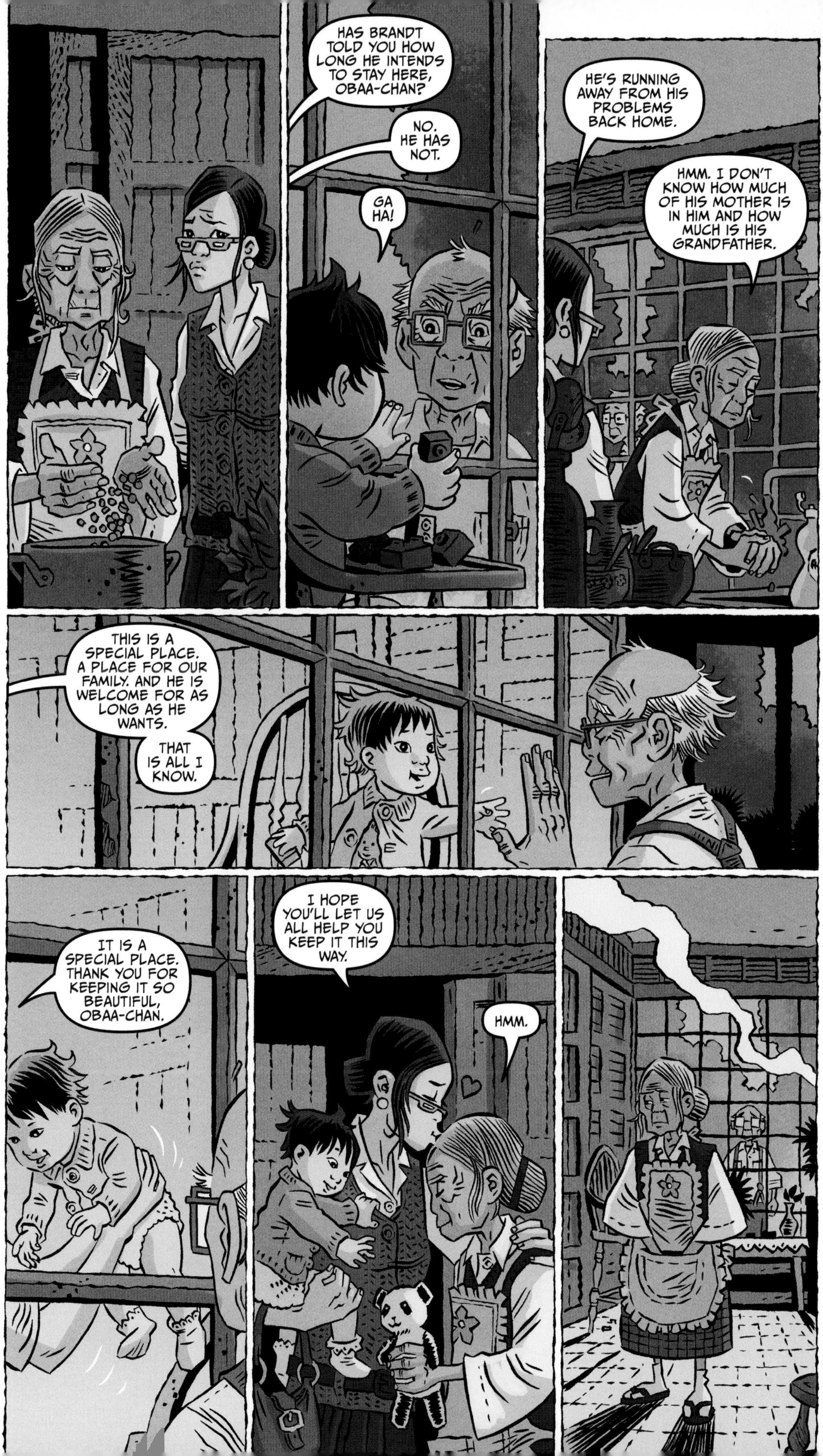
HAS BRANDT TOLD YOU HOW LONG HE INTENDS TO STAY HERE, OBAA-CHAN?
NO. HE HAS NOT.
GA HA!
HE'S RUNNING AWAY FROM HIS PROBLEMS BACK HOME.
HMM. I DON'T KNOW HOW MUCH OF HIS MOTHER IS IN HIM AND HOW MUCH IS HIS GRANDFATHER.
THIS IS A SPECIAL PLACE. A PLACE FOR OUR FAMILY. AND HE IS WELCOME FOR AS LONG AS HE WANTS.
THAT IS ALL I KNOW.
IT IS A SPECIAL PLACE. THANK YOU FOR KEEPING IT SO BEAUTIFUL, OBAA-CHAN.
I HOPE YOU'LL LET US ALL HELP YOU KEEP IT THIS WAY.
HMM.

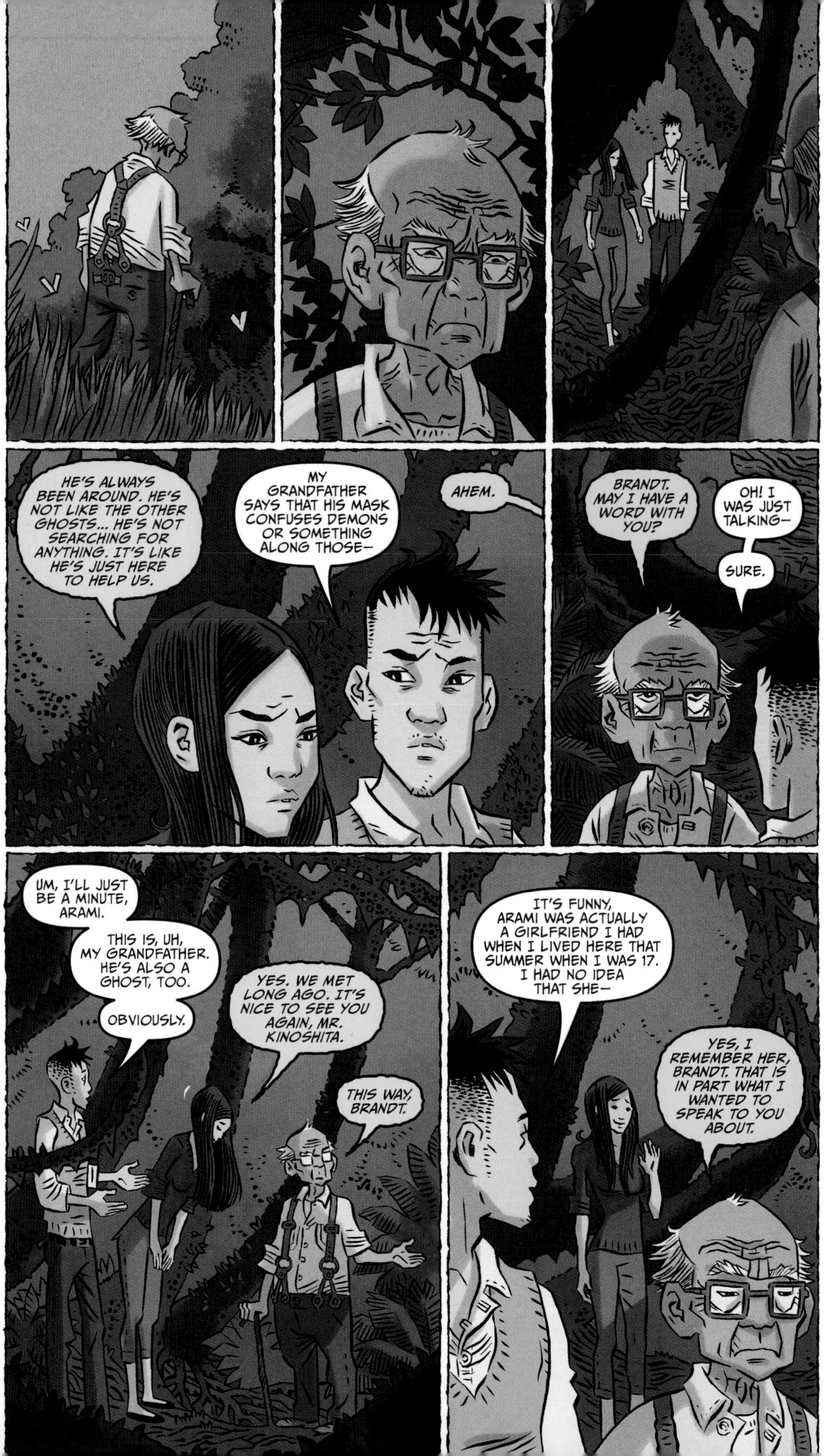
HE'S ALWAYS BEEN AROUND. HE'S NOT LIKE THE OTHER GHOSTS... HE'S NOT SEARCHING FOR ANYTHING. IT'S LIKE HE'S JUST HERE TO HELP US.
MY GRANDFATHER SAYS THAT HIS MASK CONFUSES DEMONS OR SOMETHING ALONG THOSE—
AHEM.
BRANDT. MAY I HAVE A WORD WITH YOU?
OH! I WAS JUST TALKING—
SURE.
UM, I'LL JUST BE A MINUTE, ARAMI.
THIS IS, UH, MY GRANDFATHER. HE'S ALSO A GHOST, TOO.
OBVIOUSLY.
YES. WE MET LONG AGO. IT'S NICE TO SEE YOU AGAIN, MR. KINOSHITA.
THIS WAY, BRANDT.
IT'S FUNNY, ARAMI WAS ACTUALLY A GIRLFRIEND I HAD WHEN I LIVED HERE THAT SUMMER WHEN I WAS 17. I HAD NO IDEA THAT SHE—
YES, I REMEMBER HER, BRANDT. THAT IS IN PART WHAT I WANTED TO SPEAK TO YOU ABOUT.

YOU ARE SPENDING TOO MUCH TIME HERE.
WHAT DO YOU MEAN? I JUST GOT HERE TWO DAYS AGO...
YOU ARE SPENDING TOO MUCH TIME AT THE TREE. WITH THE GHOSTS.
WITH... ARAMI.
WITH ALL DUE RESPECT, JII-CHAN, I DON'T THINK YOU HAVE ANY RIGHT TO JUDGE ME OR WHAT I'M DOING.
YOU ARE WRONG. I HAVE EVERY RIGHT. I AM YOUR ELDER AND I KNOW THIS PLACE.
I KNOW WHAT IT DOES.
THIS PLACE... IT IS AN ESCAPE FROM THE REAL WORLD. IT CAN BE INTOXICATING. A PORTAL TO A DIFFERENT TIME.
IT IS EASY TO BECOME A DIFFERENT PERSON HERE, AMONG THE GHOSTS. SOMEONE WHO HELPS.
A PERSON, PERHAPS, WHO YOU ARE MORE COMFORTABLE BEING.
THE FACT THAT THE GHOST OF SOMEONE YOU CARED ABOUT IS ALSO HERE...
IT IS DANGEROUS, AND IT IS NOT BEST FOR YOU.
WHEN I TOLD YOU TO RETURN HERE ALL THOSE YEARS AGO... IT WAS WRONG. I WAS IN LOVE WITH THE IDEA OF BEING A MAN AMONG GHOSTS. I WANTED TO PASS IT ALONG AND I THOUGHT YOU MIGHT ONE DAY BE LIKE I WAS.
BUT I WAS WRONG. NO GOOD CAN COME OF THIS PLACE FOR YOU, BRANDT. YOU SHOULD LEAVE.
YOU THINK I DON'T KNOW THAT? YOU THINK I DON'T KNOW WHAT'S GOING ON? YOU THINK I'M AN IDIOT?
I KNOW I'M SPENDING TOO MUCH TIME HERE.
AND... AND... I DON'T CARE.

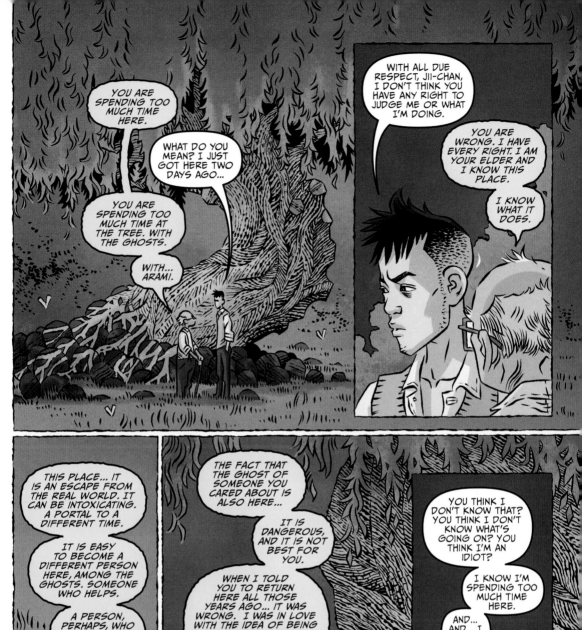

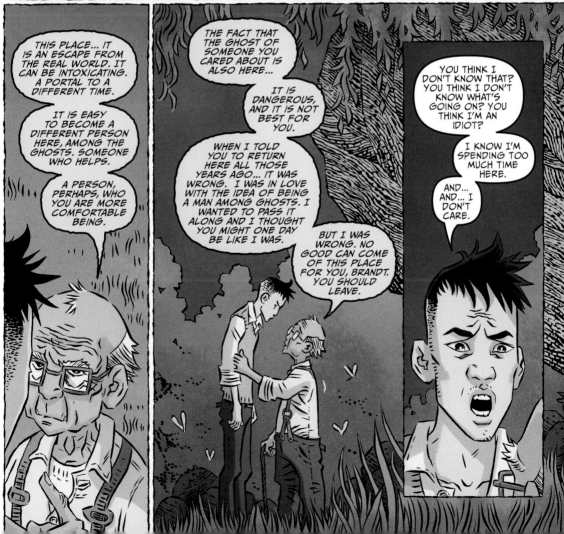

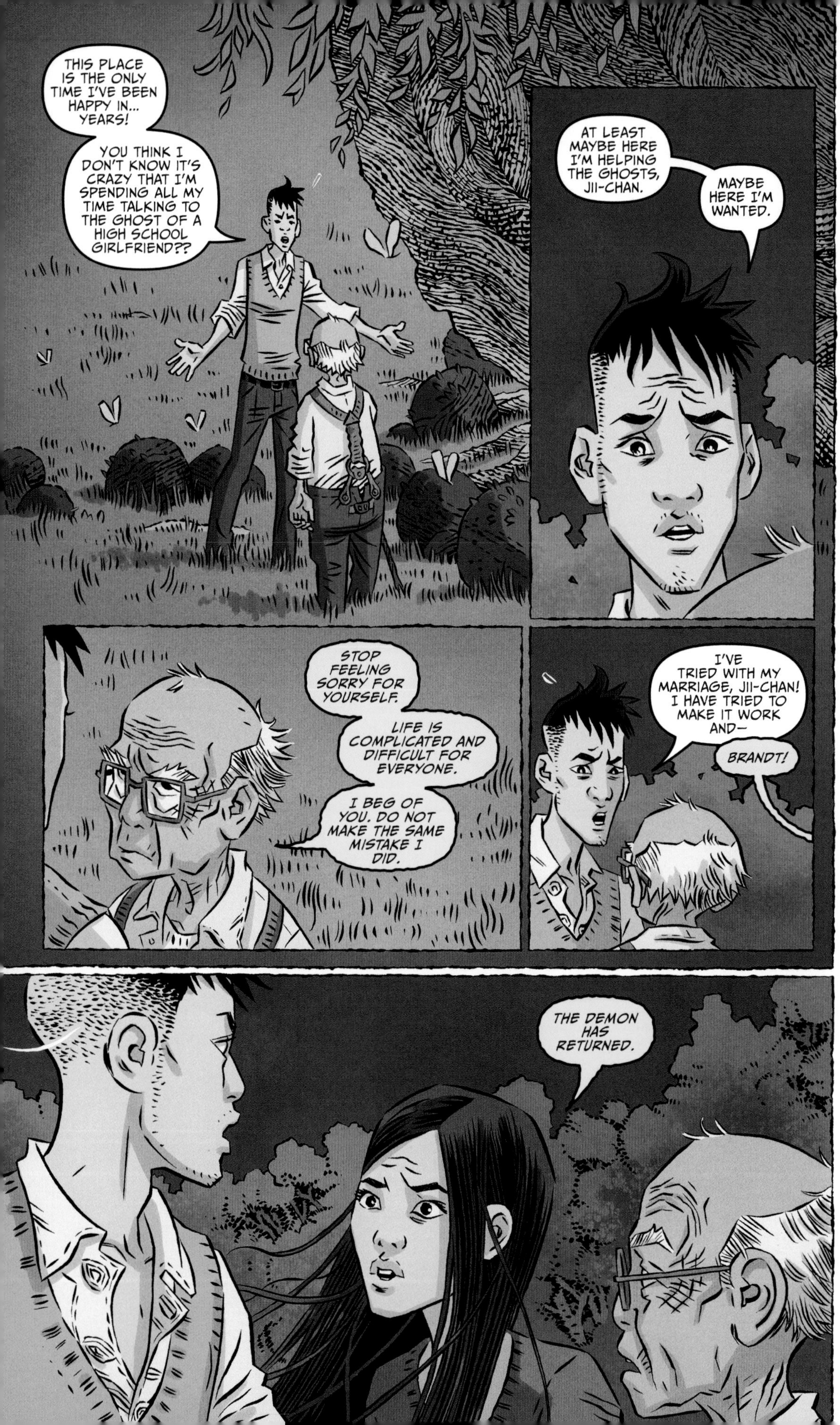

THIS PLACE IS THE ONLY TIME I'VE BEEN HAPPY IN... YEARS!
YOU THINK I DON'T KNOW IT'S CRAZY THAT I'M SPENDING ALL MY TIME TALKING TO THE GHOST OF A HIGH SCHOOL GIRLFRIEND??
AT LEAST MAYBE HERE I'M HELPING THE GHOSTS, JII-CHAN.
MAYBE HERE I'M WANTED.
STOP FEELING SORRY FOR YOURSELF.
LIFE IS COMPLICATED AND DIFFICULT FOR EVERYONE.
I BEG OF YOU. DO NOT MAKE THE SAME MISTAKE I DID.
I'VE TRIED WITH MY MARRIAGE, JII-CHAN! I HAVE TRIED TO MAKE IT WORK AND—
BRANDT!
THE DEMON HAS RETURNED.

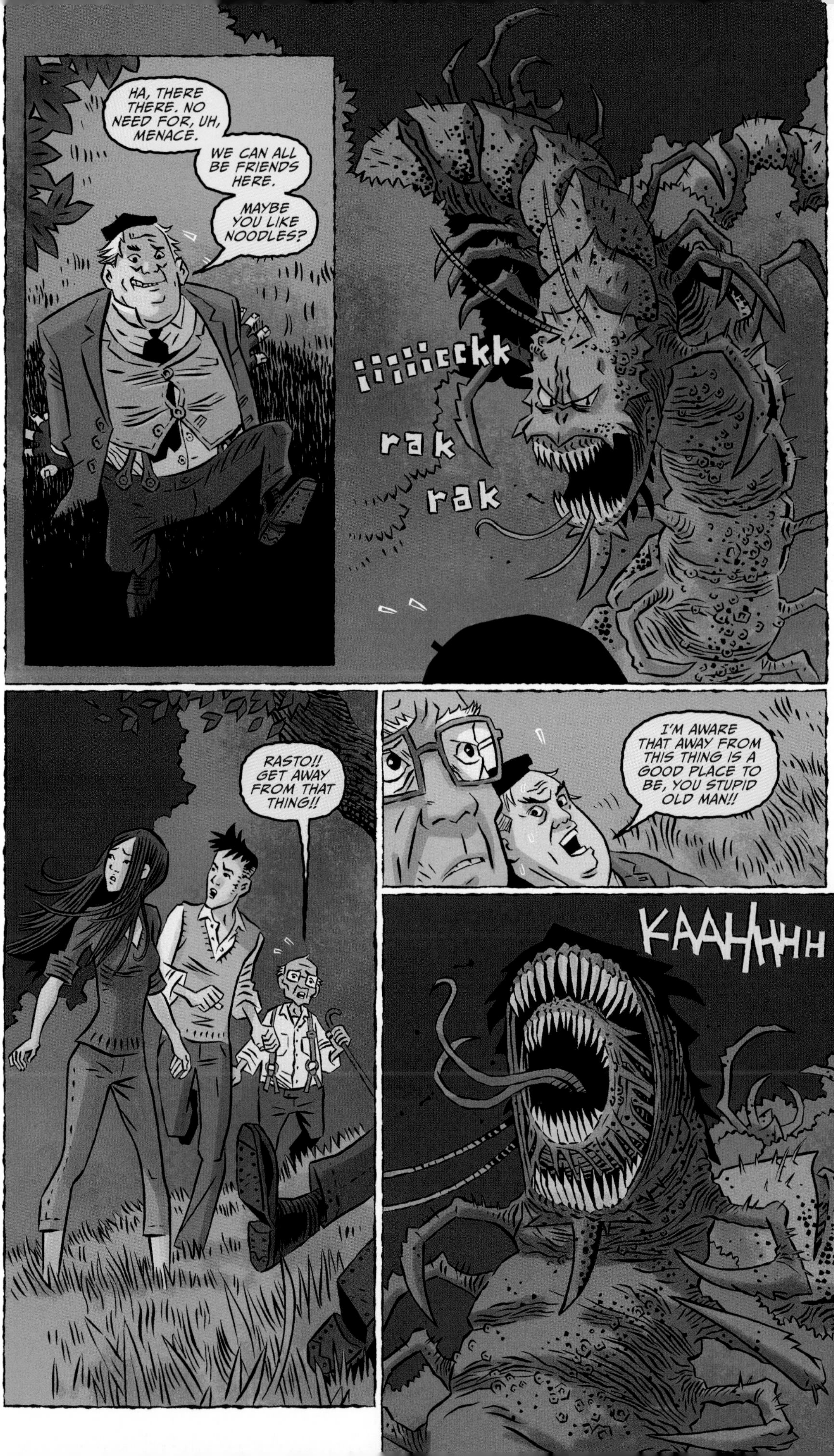

HA, THERE THERE. NO NEED FOR, UH, MENACE.
WE CAN ALL BE FRIENDS HERE.
MAYBE YOU LIKE NOODLES?
iiiiiickk
rak
rak
RASTO!! GET AWAY FROM THAT THING!!
I'M AWARE THAT AWAY FROM THIS THING IS A GOOD PLACE TO BE, YOU STUPID OLD MAN!!
KAAHHHHH

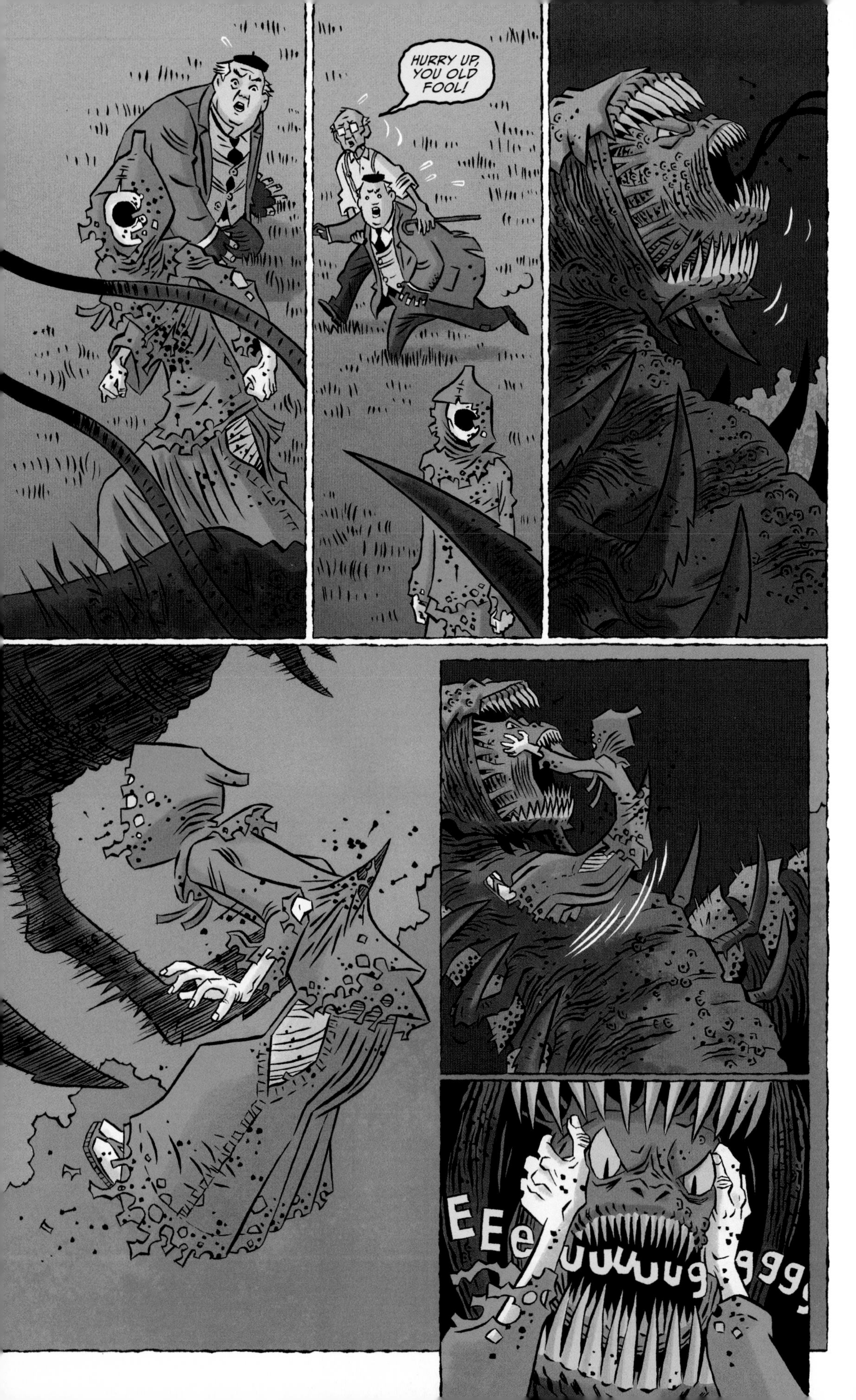
HURRY UP, YOU OLD FOOL!
EEeuuuuug9999

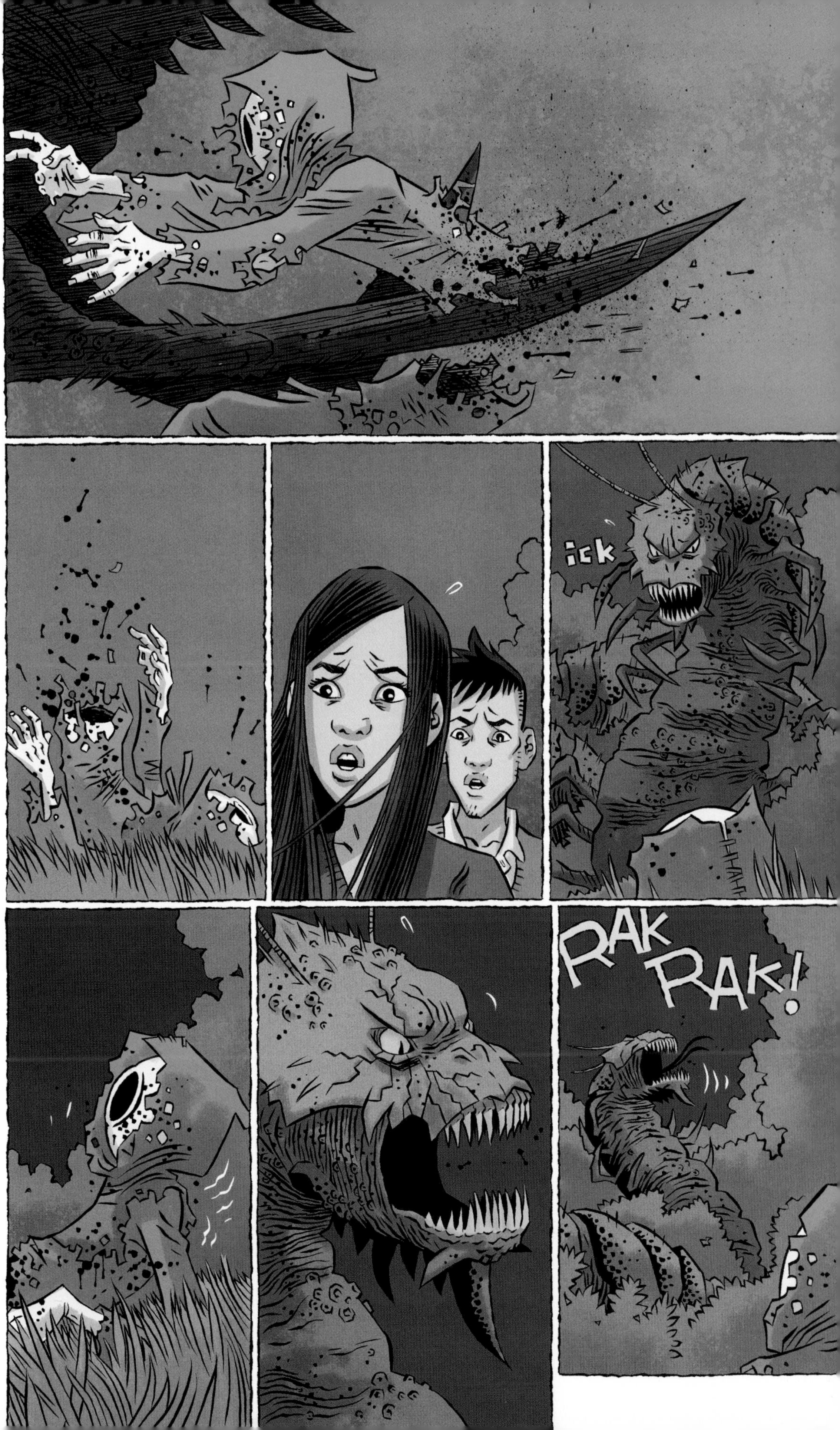
ick
RAK
RAK!

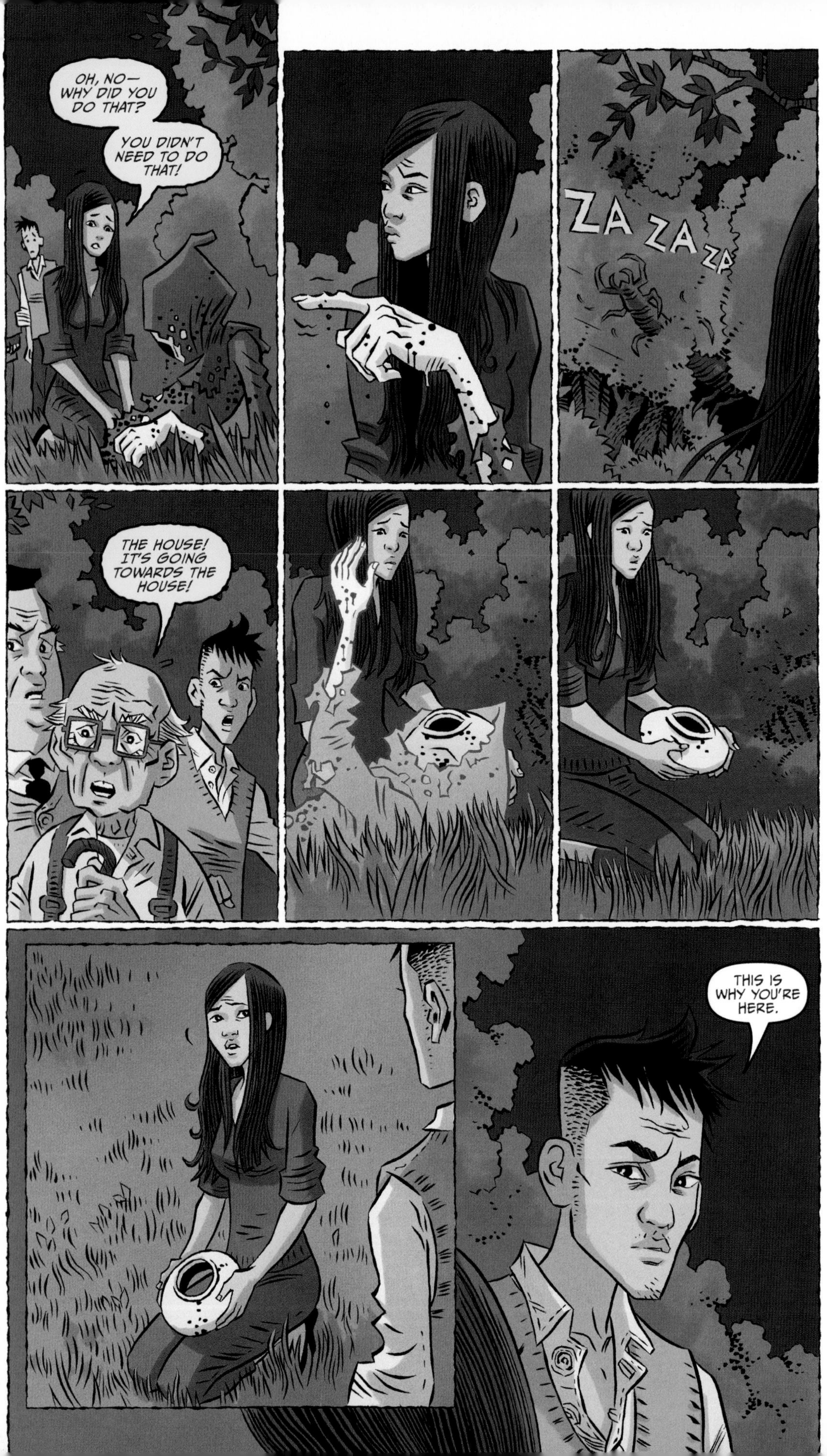
OH, NO—
WHY DID YOU DO THAT?
YOU DIDN'T NEED TO DO THAT!
ZA ZA ZAP
THE HOUSE! IT'S GOING TOWARDS THE HOUSE!
THIS IS WHY YOU'RE HERE.

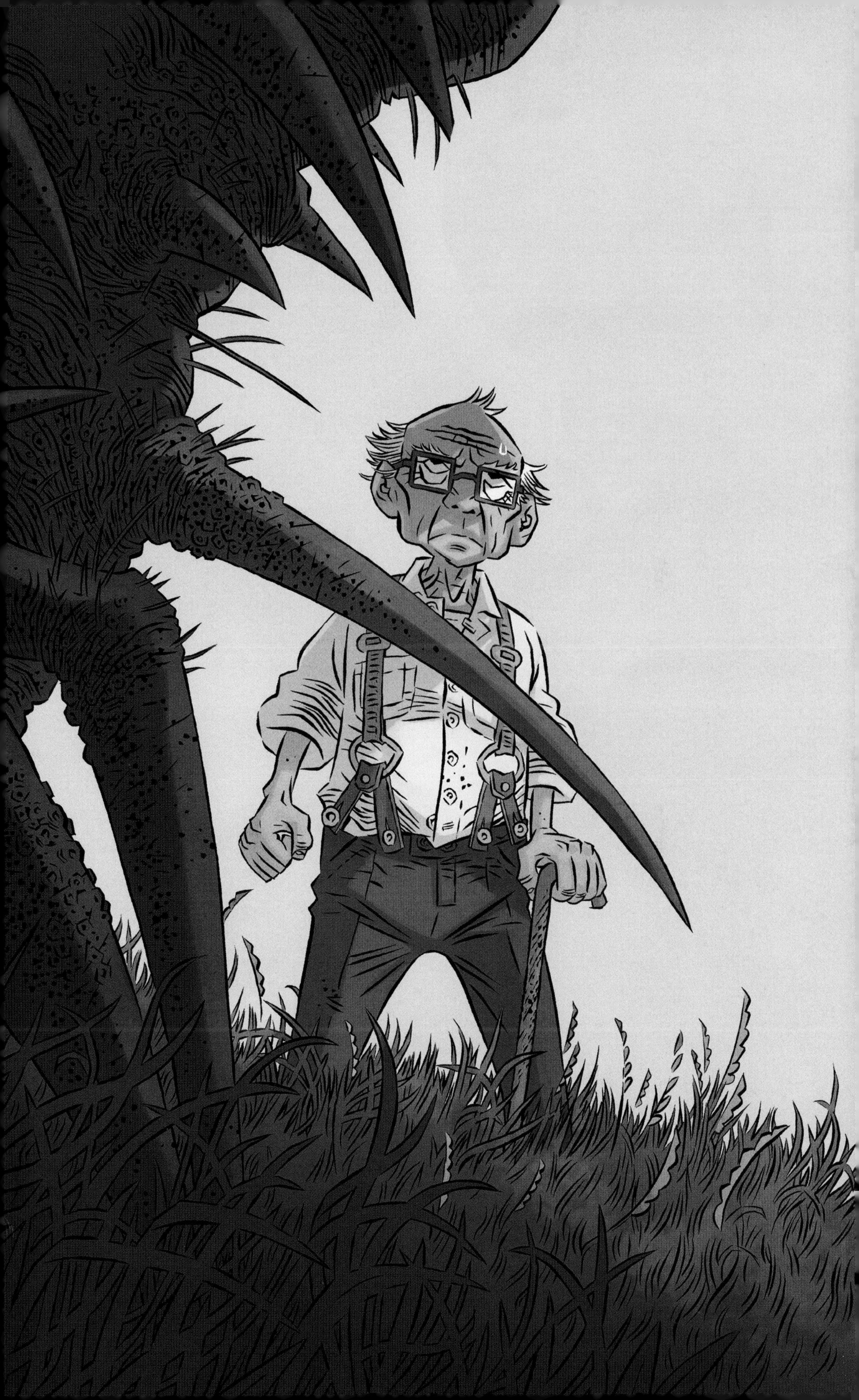

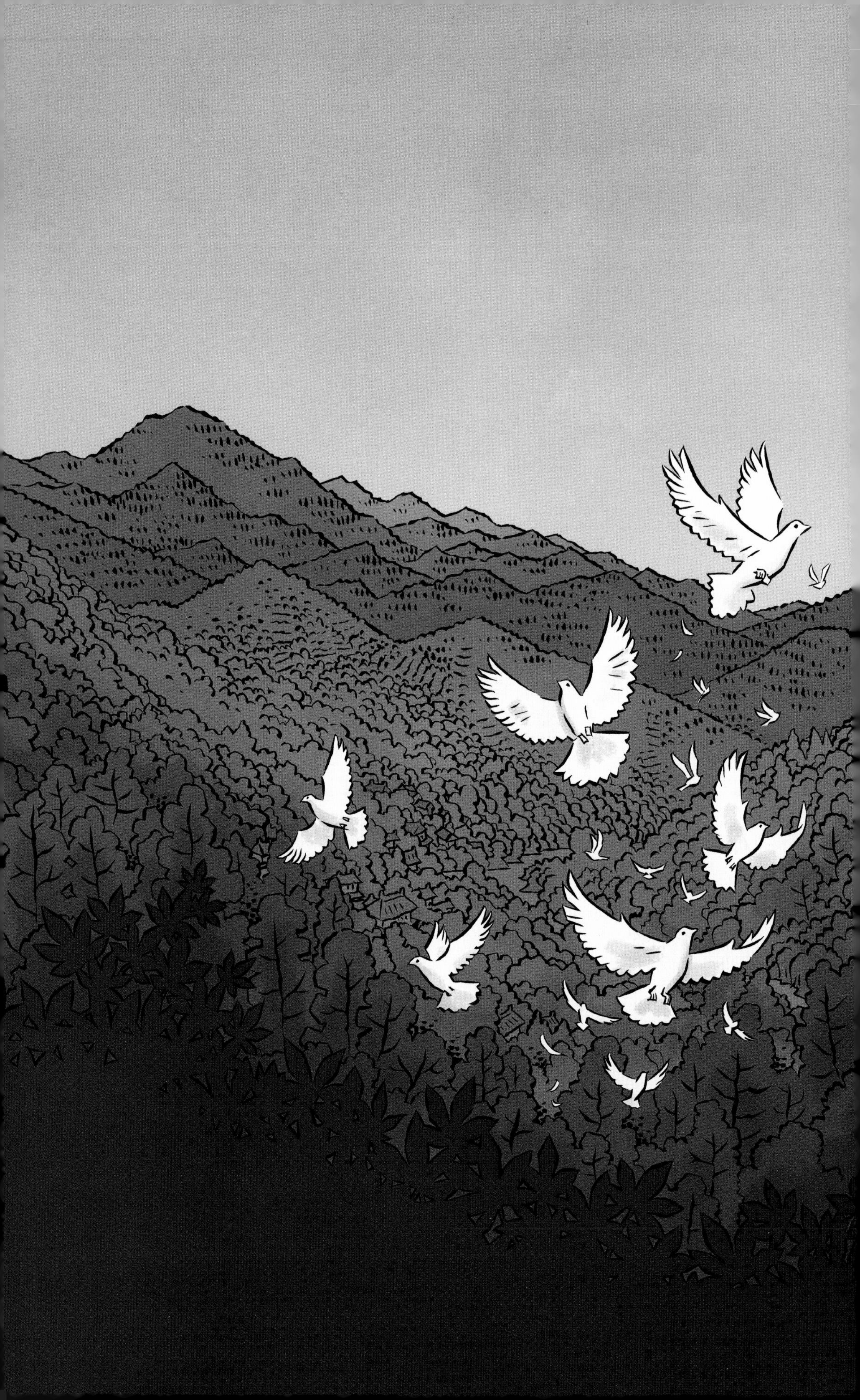

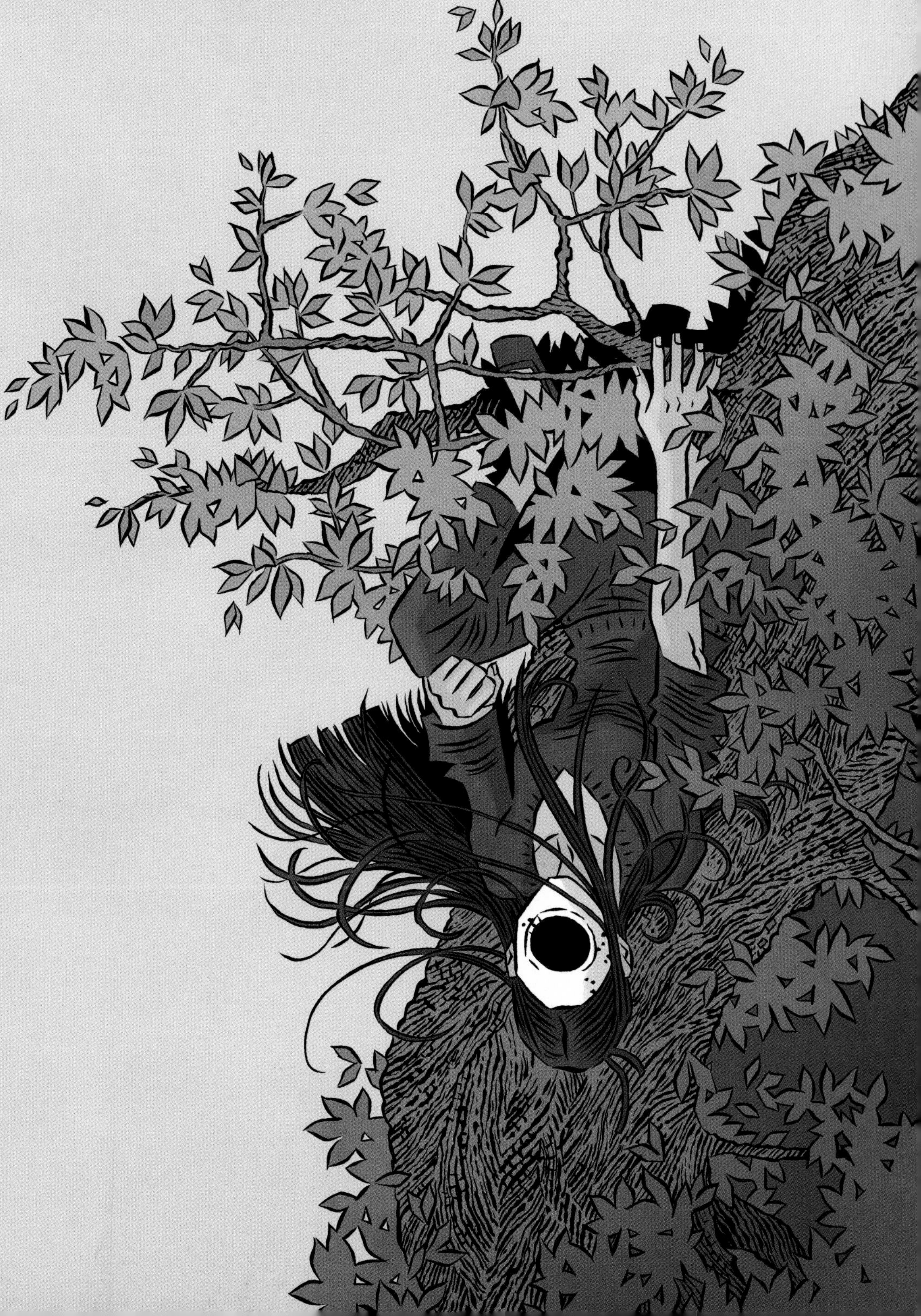

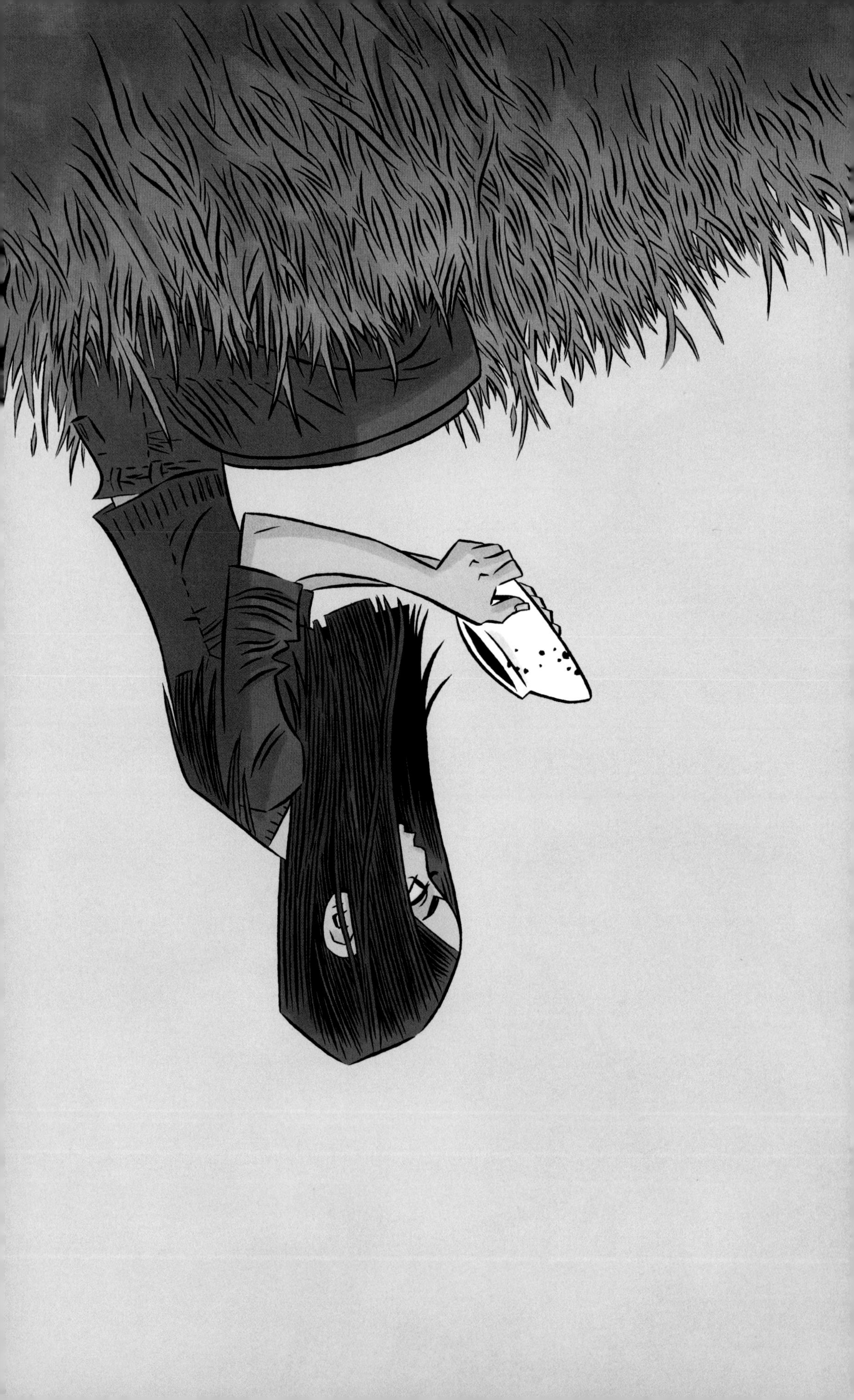

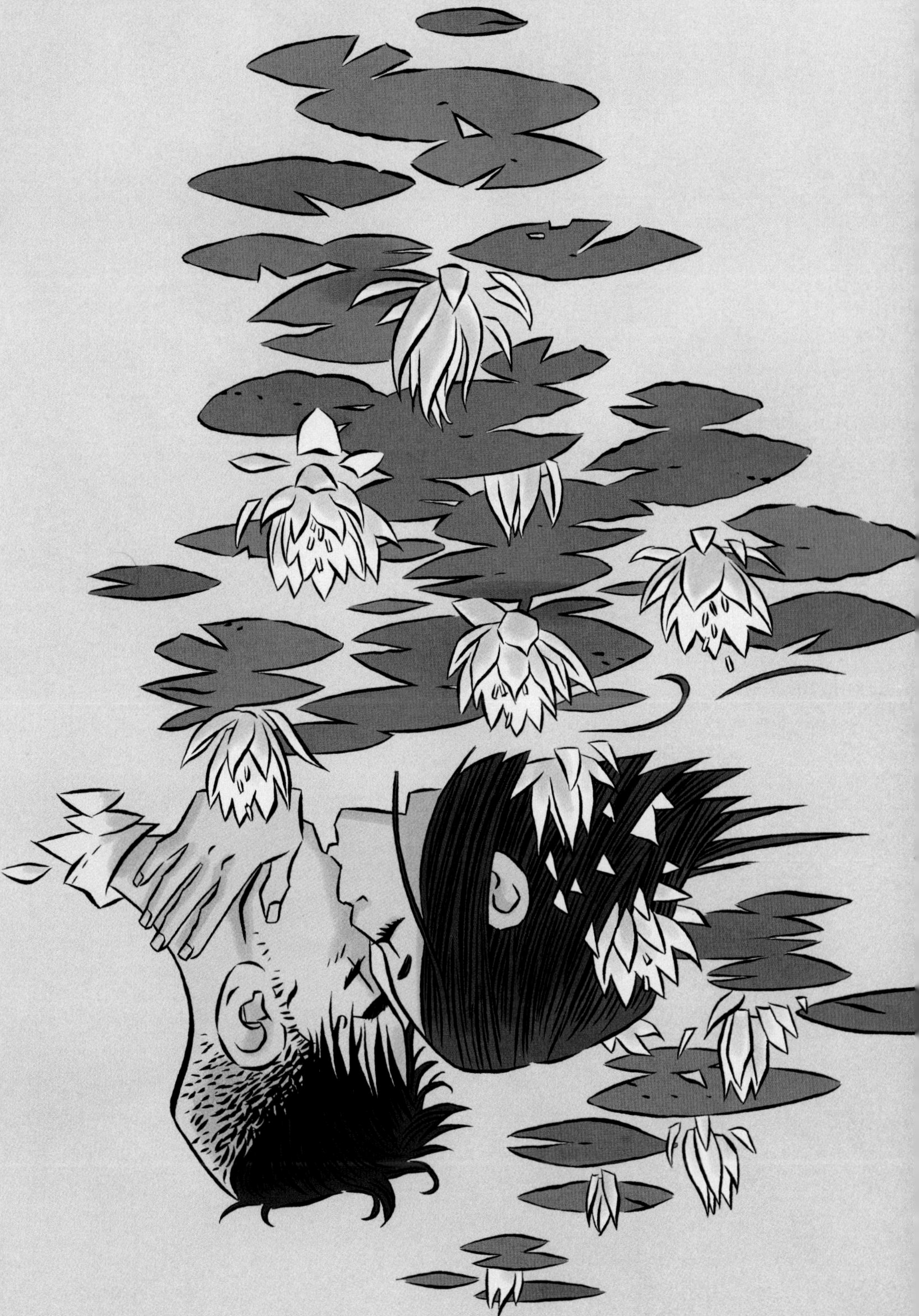

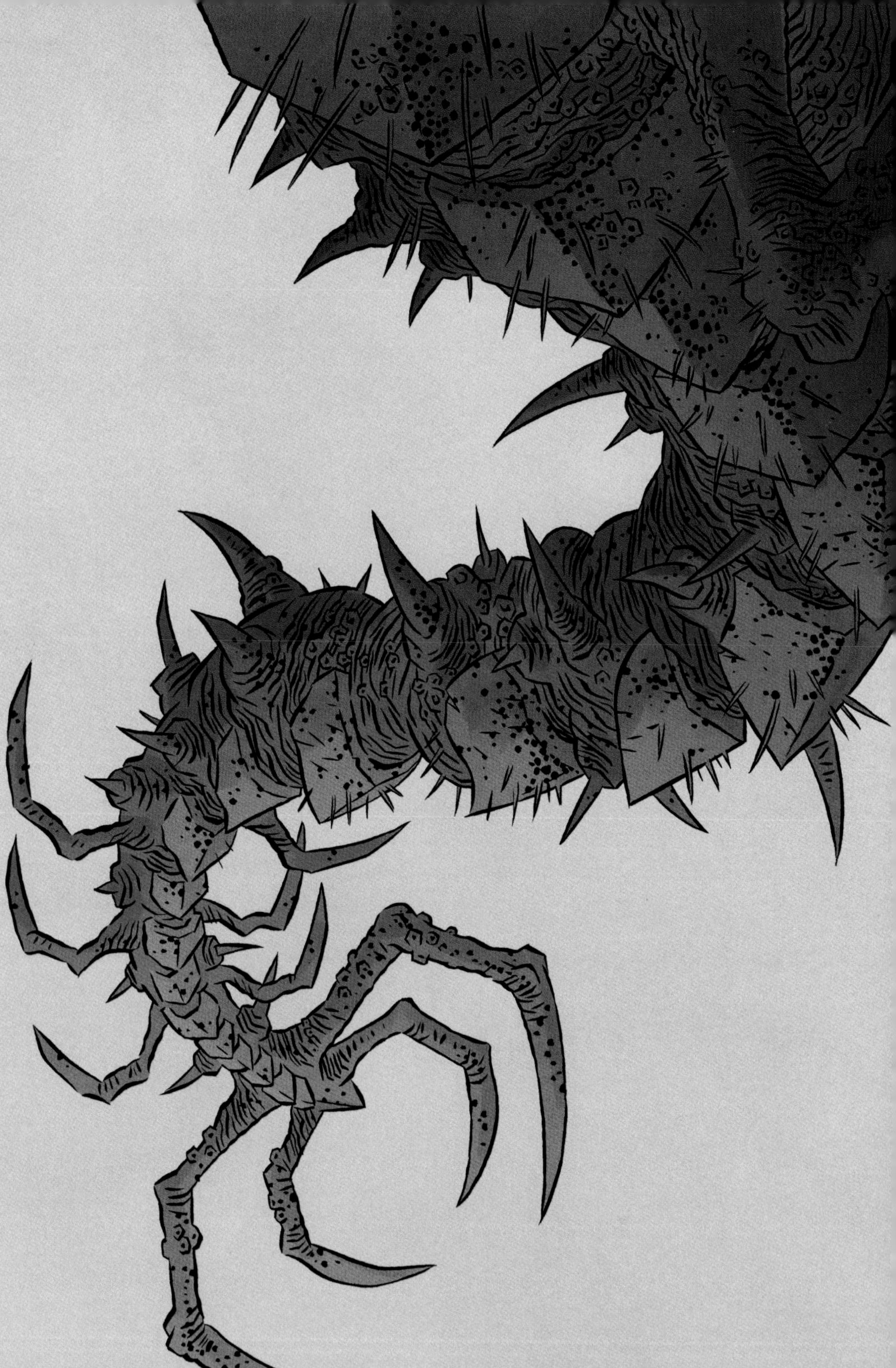

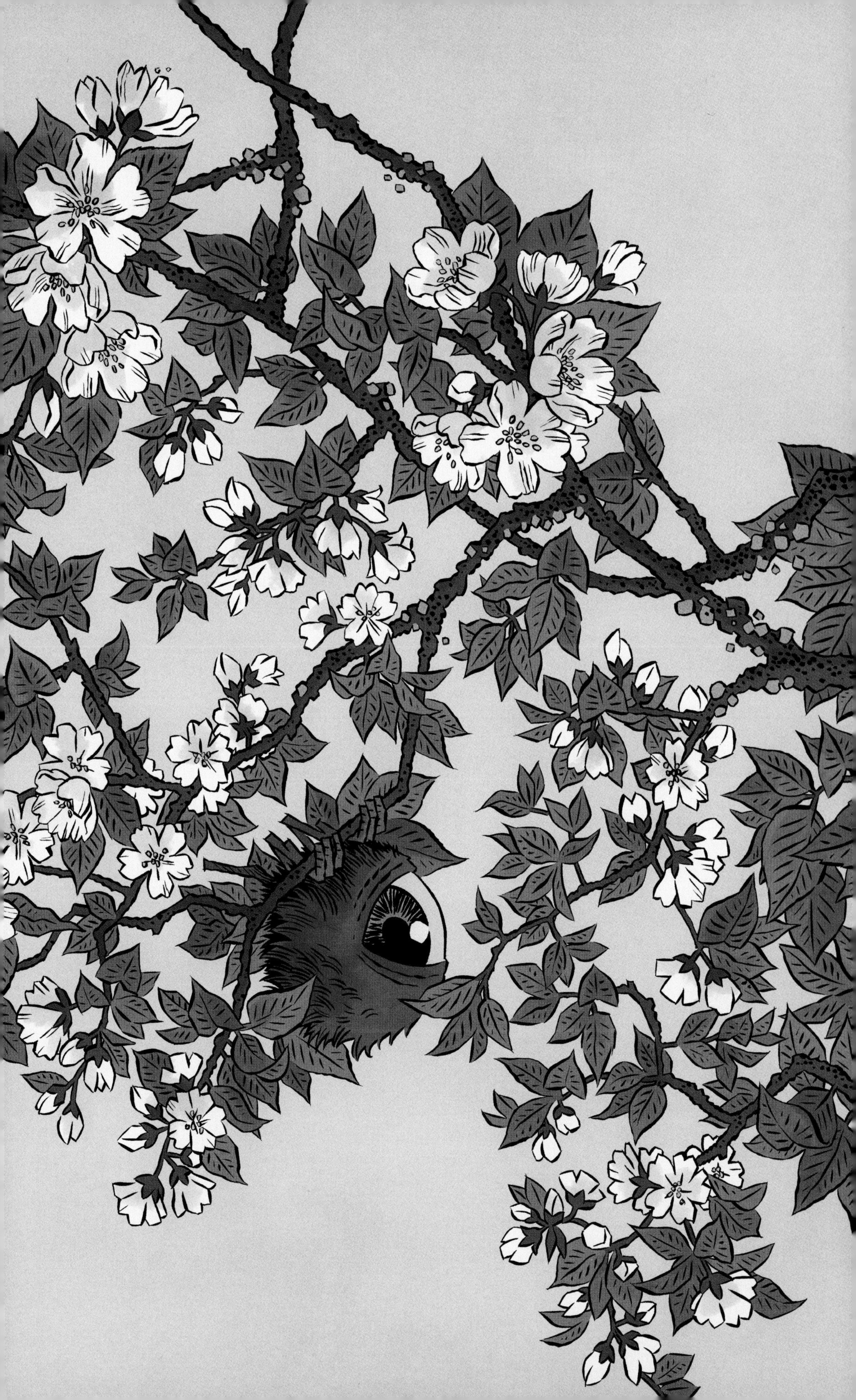

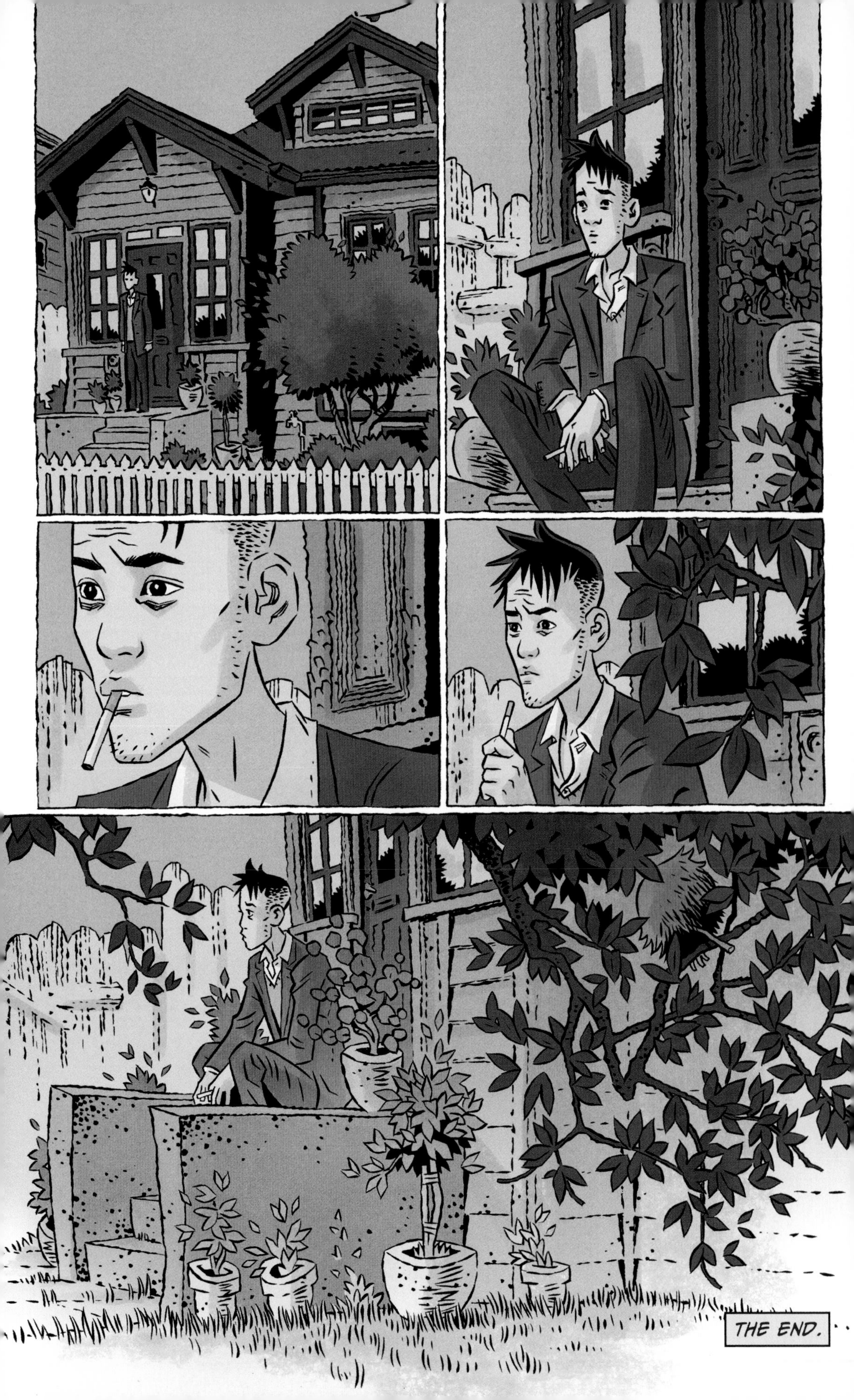
THE END.

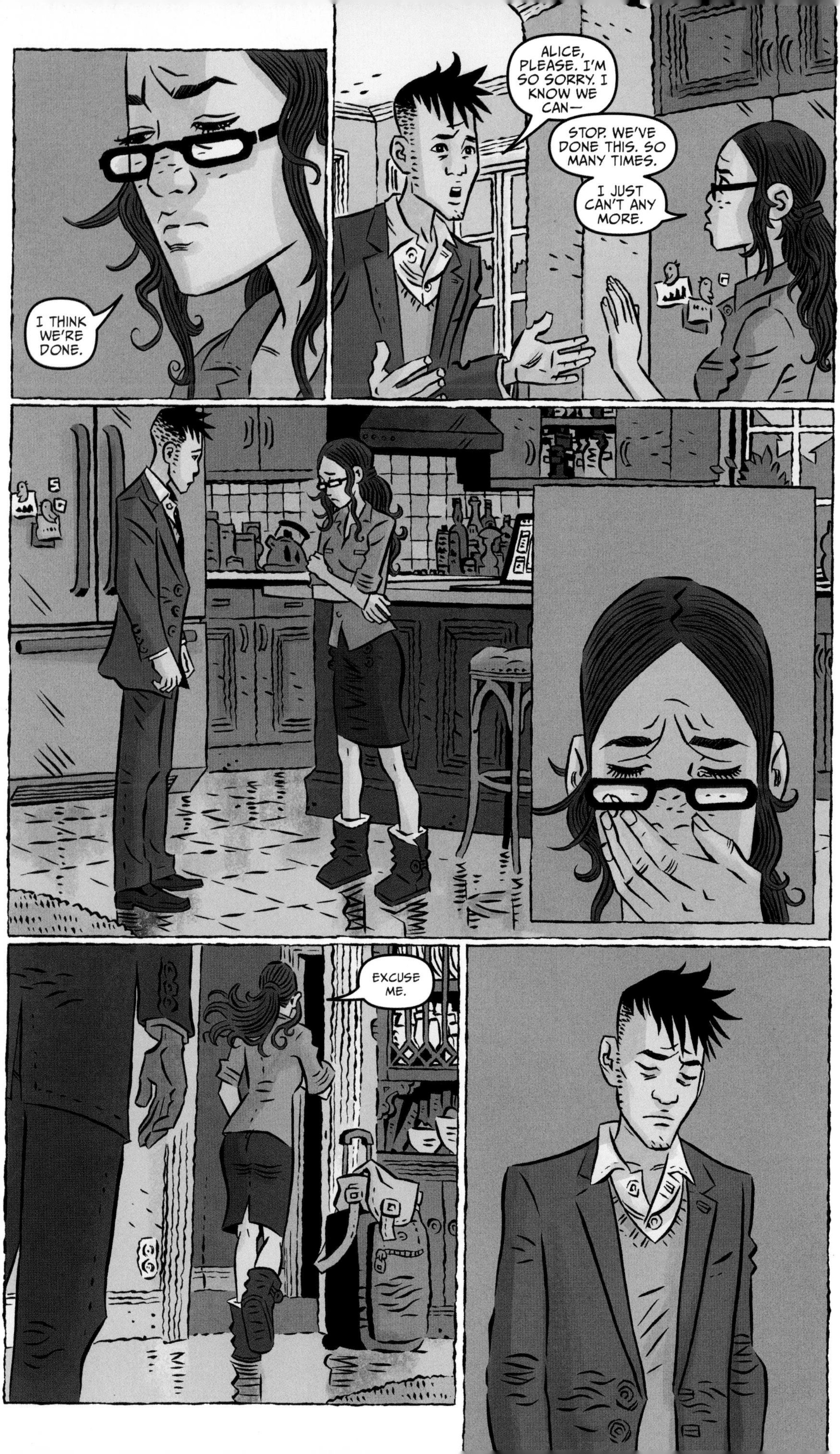
I THINK WE'RE DONE.
ALICE, PLEASE. I'M SO SORRY. I KNOW WE CAN—
STOP. WE'VE DONE THIS. SO MANY TIMES.
I JUST CAN'T ANY MORE.
EXCUSE ME.

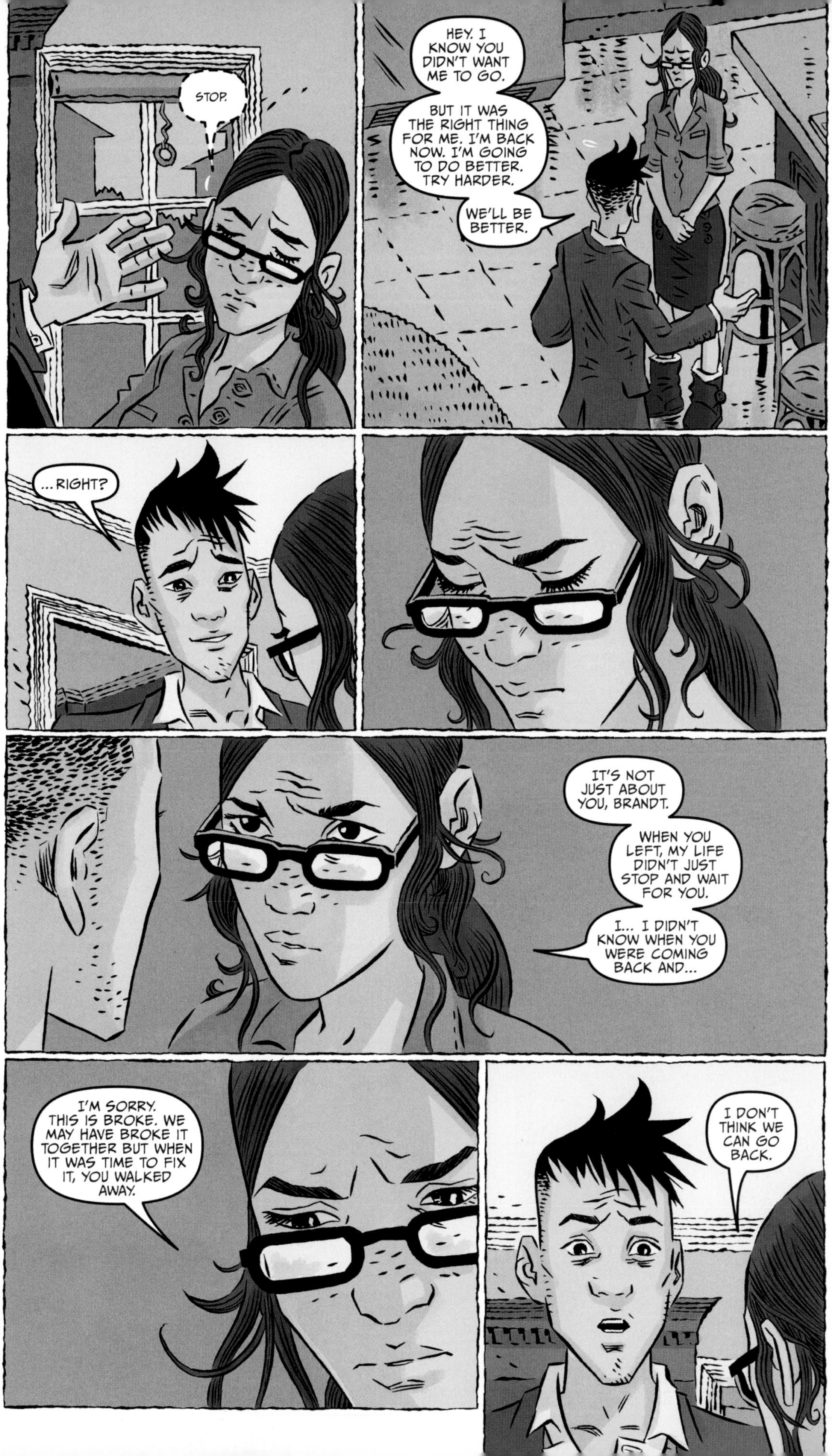
STOP.
HEY. I KNOW YOU DIDN'T WANT ME TO GO.
BUT IT WAS THE RIGHT THING FOR ME. I'M BACK NOW. I'M GOING TO DO BETTER. TRY HARDER.
WE'LL BE BETTER.
...RIGHT?
IT'S NOT JUST ABOUT YOU, BRANDT.
WHEN YOU LEFT, MY LIFE DIDN'T JUST STOP AND WAIT FOR YOU.
I... I DIDN'T KNOW WHEN YOU WERE COMING BACK AND...
I'M SORRY. THIS IS BROKE. WE MAY HAVE BROKE IT TOGETHER BUT WHEN IT WAS TIME TO FIX IT, YOU WALKED AWAY.
I DON'T THINK WE CAN GO BACK.

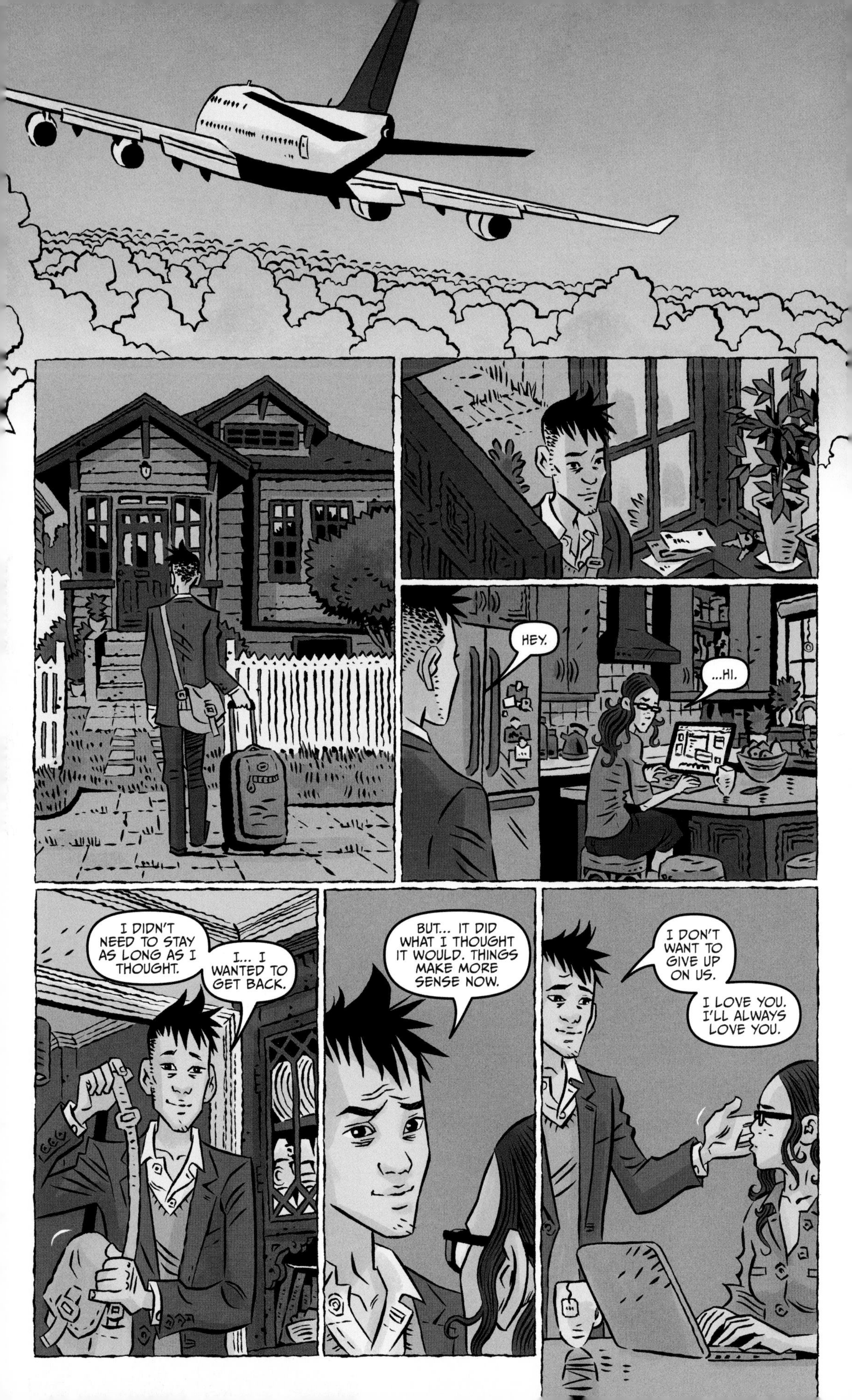
HEY.
...HI.
I DIDN'T NEED TO STAY AS LONG AS I THOUGHT.
I... I WANTED TO GET BACK.
BUT... IT DID WHAT I THOUGHT IT WOULD. THINGS MAKE MORE SENSE NOW.
I DON'T WANT TO GIVE UP ON US.
I LOVE YOU. I'LL ALWAYS LOVE YOU.

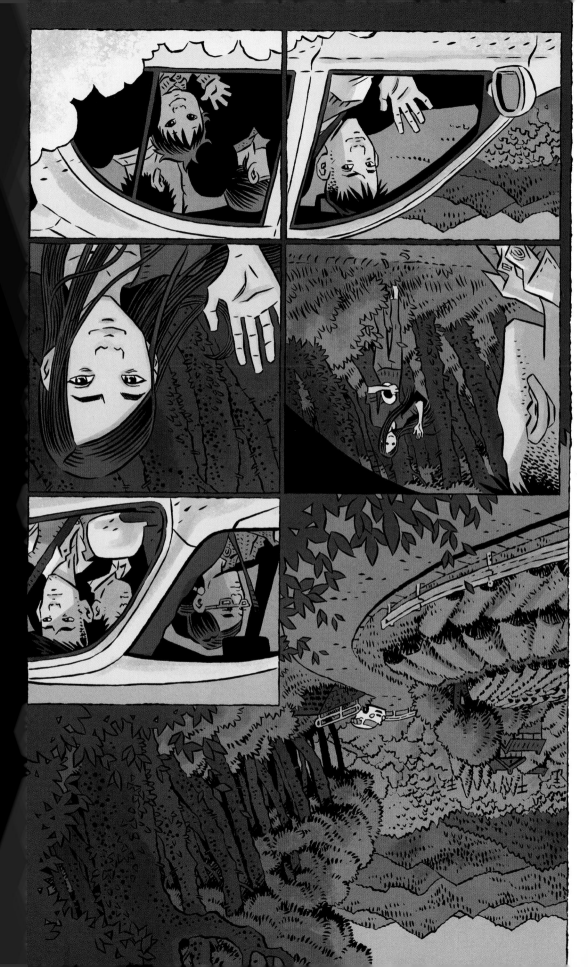

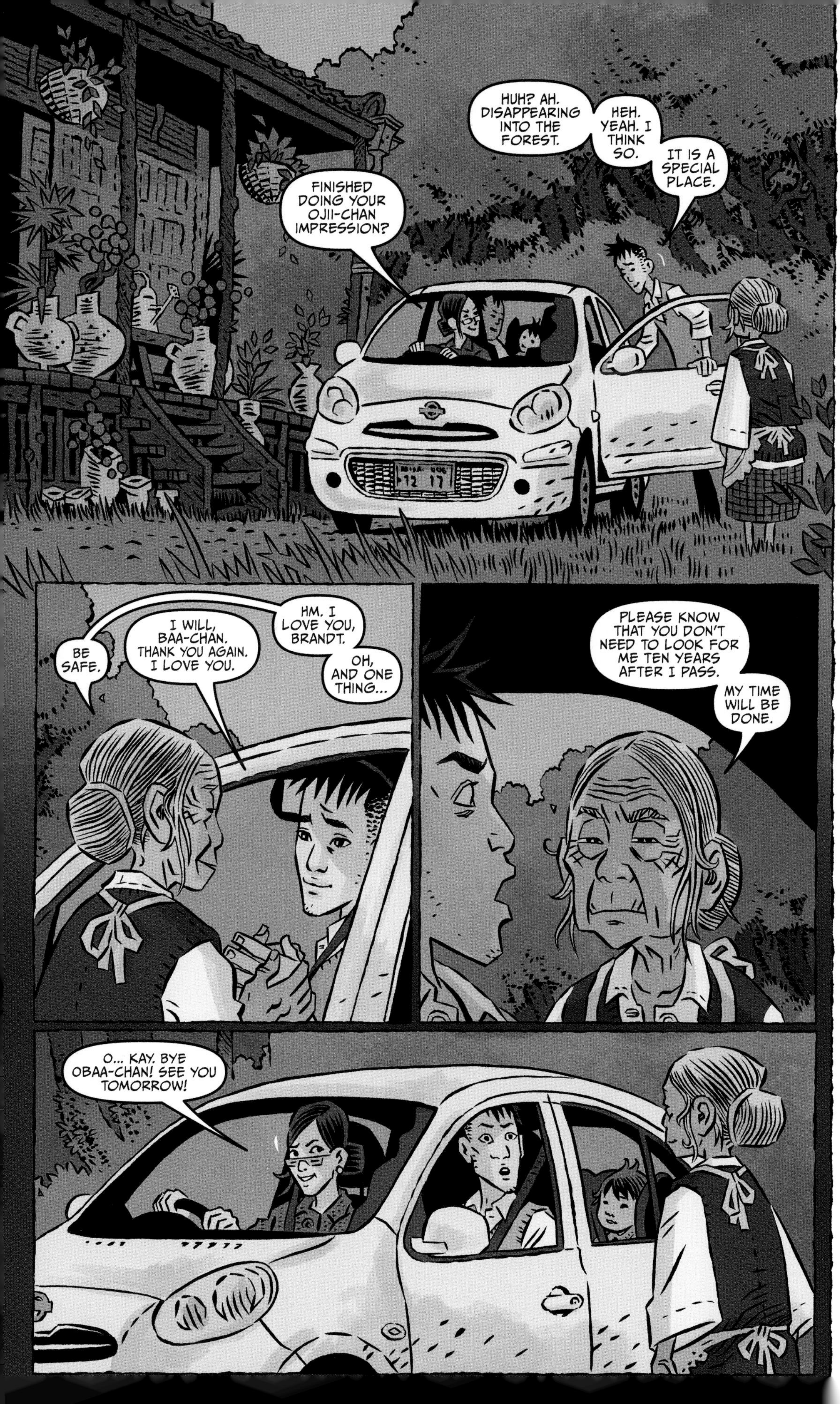
FINISHED DOING YOUR OJII-CHAN IMPRESSION?
HUH? AH. DISAPPEARING INTO THE FOREST.
HEH. YEAH. I THINK SO.
IT IS A SPECIAL PLACE.
BE SAFE.
I WILL, BAA-CHAN. THANK YOU AGAIN. I LOVE YOU.
HM. I LOVE YOU, BRANDT.
OH, AND ONE THING...
PLEASE KNOW THAT YOU DON'T NEED TO LOOK FOR ME TEN YEARS AFTER I PASS.
MY TIME WILL BE DONE.
O... KAY. BYE OBAA-CHAN! SEE YOU TOMORROW!

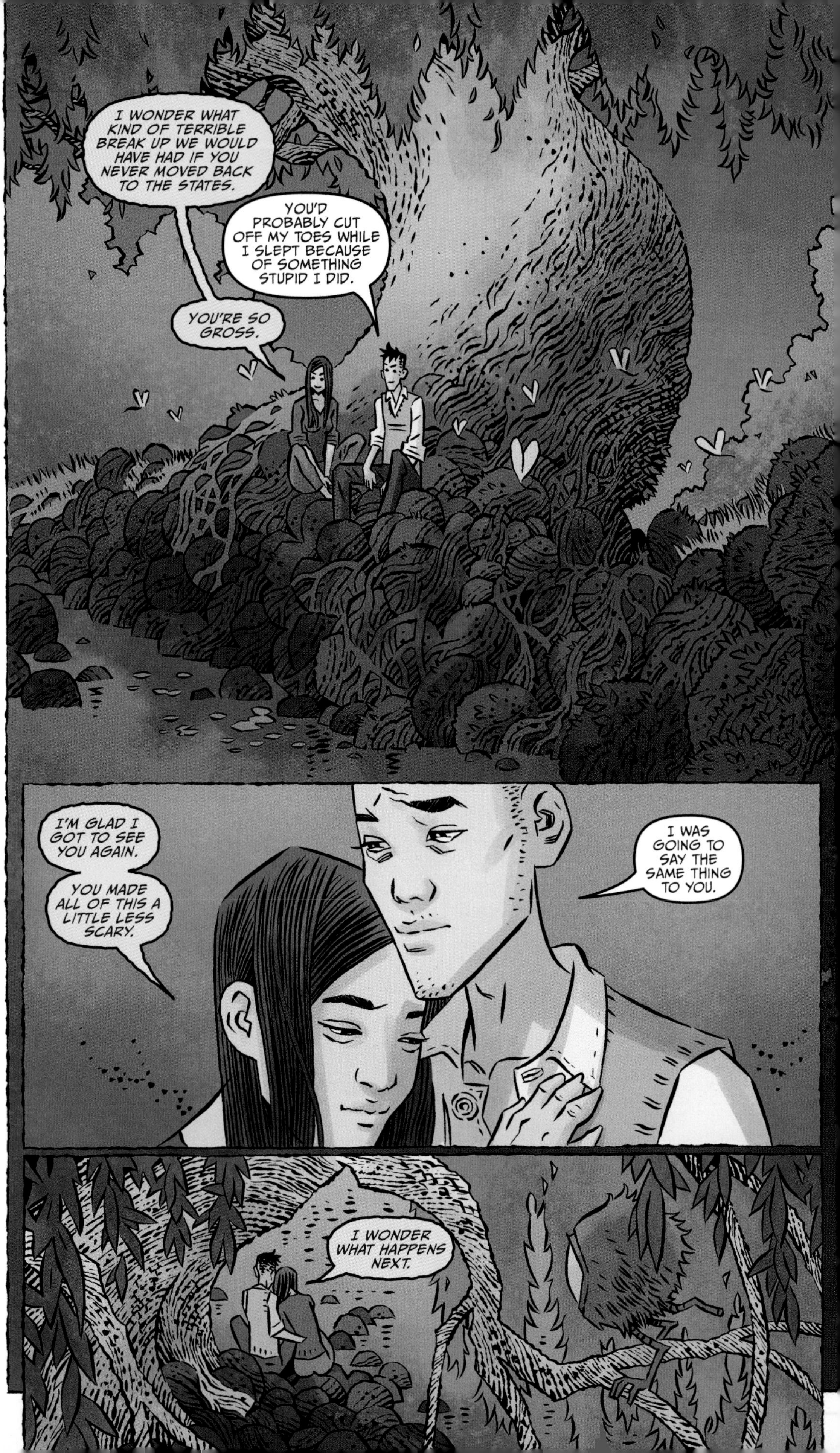
I WONDER WHAT KIND OF TERRIBLE BREAK UP WE WOULD HAVE HAD IF YOU NEVER MOVED BACK TO THE STATES.
YOU'D PROBABLY CUT OFF MY TOES WHILE I SLEPT BECAUSE OF SOMETHING STUPID I DID.
YOU'RE SO GROSS.
I'M GLAD I GOT TO SEE YOU AGAIN.
YOU MADE ALL OF THIS A LITTLE LESS SCARY.
I WAS GOING TO SAY THE SAME THING TO YOU.
I WONDER WHAT HAPPENS NEXT.

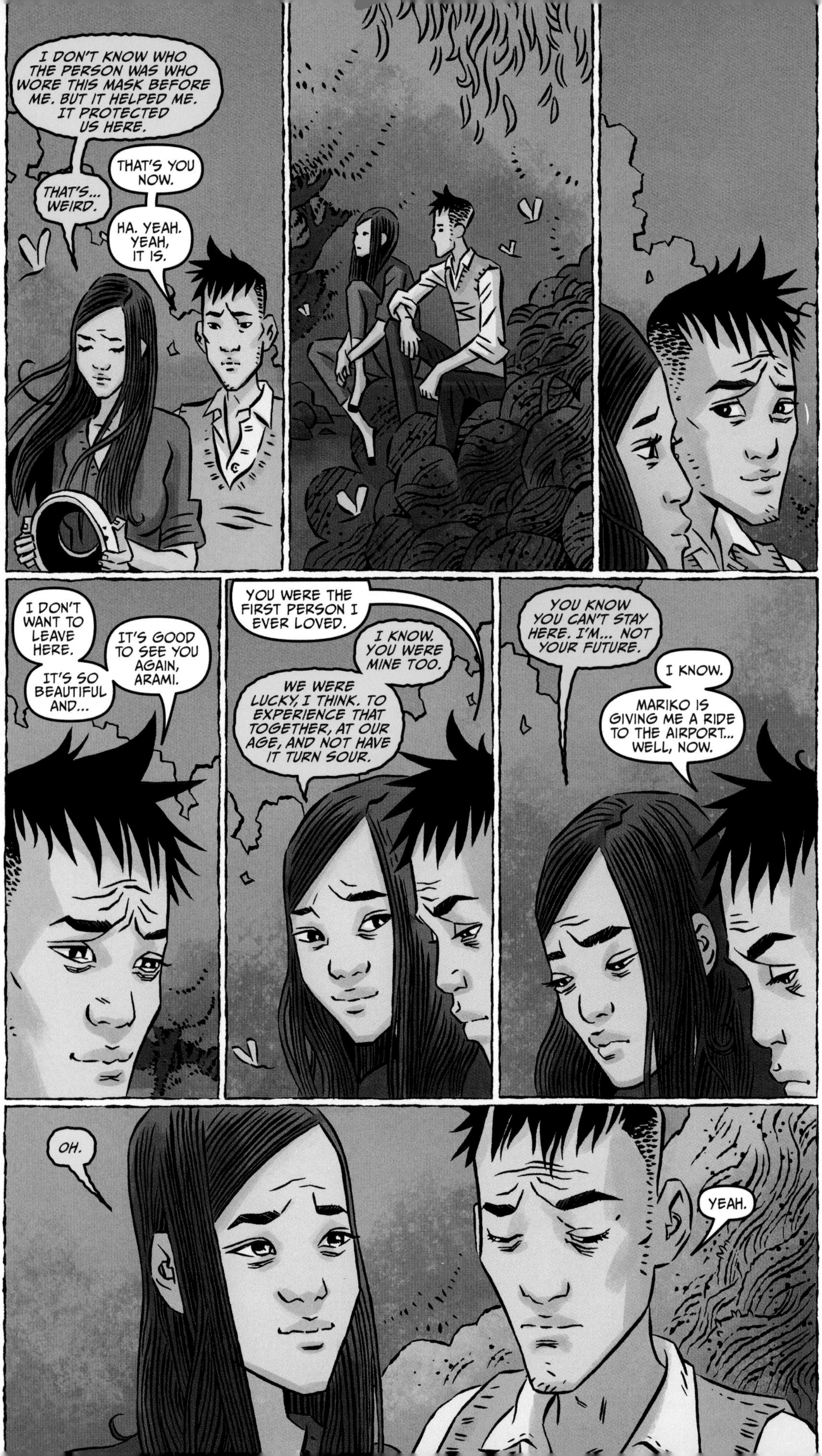
I DON'T KNOW WHO THE PERSON WAS WHO WORE THIS MASK BEFORE ME. BUT IT HELPED ME. IT PROTECTED US HERE.
THAT'S... WEIRD.
THAT'S YOU NOW.
HA. YEAH. YEAH, IT IS.
I DON'T WANT TO LEAVE HERE.
IT'S SO BEAUTIFUL AND...
IT'S GOOD TO SEE YOU AGAIN, ARAMI.
YOU WERE THE FIRST PERSON I EVER LOVED.
I KNOW. YOU WERE MINE TOO.
WE WERE LUCKY, I THINK. TO EXPERIENCE THAT TOGETHER, AT OUR AGE, AND NOT HAVE IT TURN SOUR.
YOU KNOW YOU CAN'T STAY HERE. I'M... NOT YOUR FUTURE.
I KNOW.
MARIKO IS GIVING ME A RIDE TO THE AIRPORT... WELL, NOW.
OH.
YEAH.

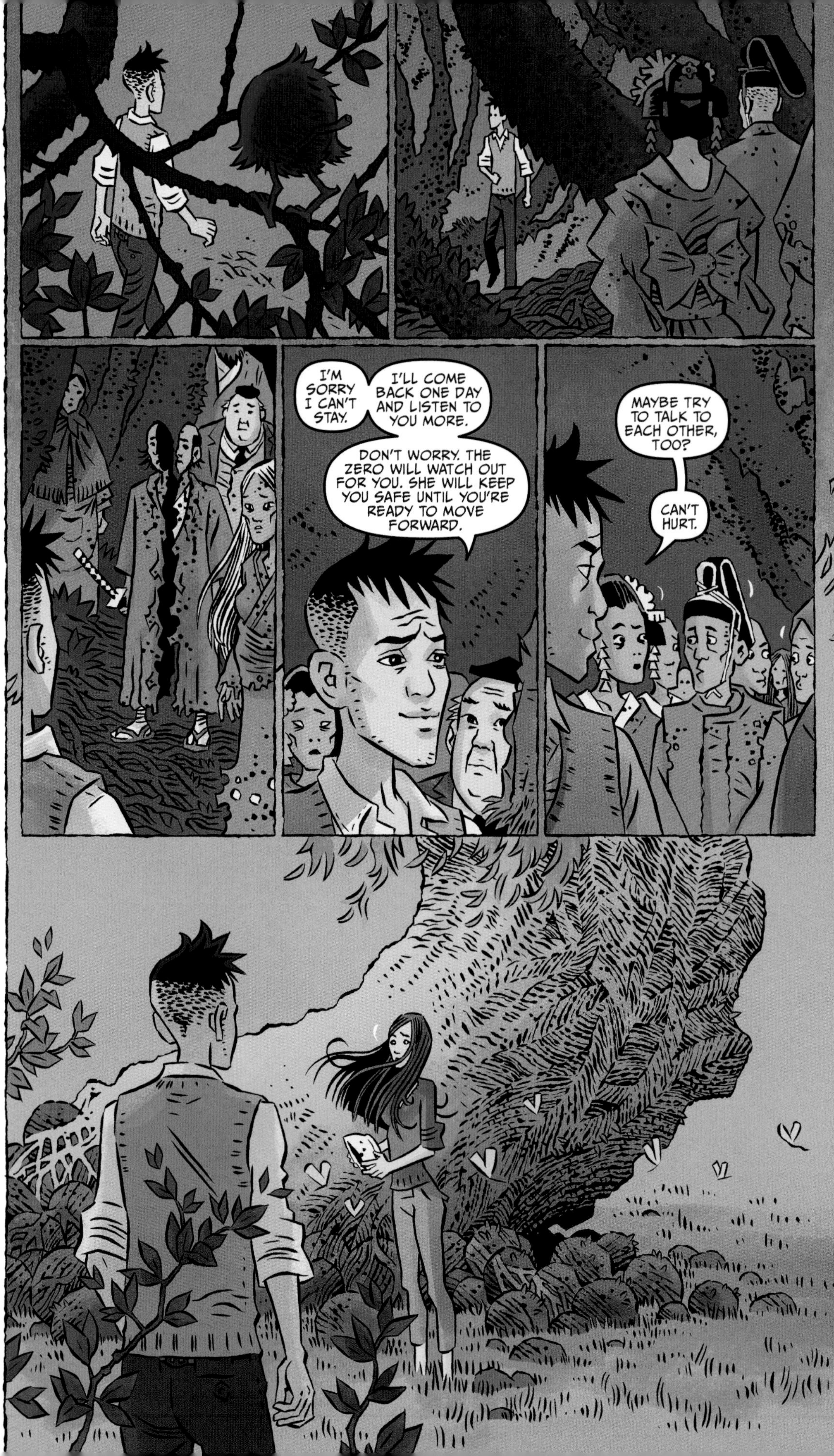
I'M SORRY I CAN'T STAY.
I'LL COME BACK ONE DAY AND LISTEN TO YOU MORE.
DON'T WORRY. THE ZERO WILL WATCH OUT FOR YOU. SHE WILL KEEP YOU SAFE UNTIL YOU'RE READY TO MOVE FORWARD.
MAYBE TRY TO TALK TO EACH OTHER, TOO?
CAN'T HURT.

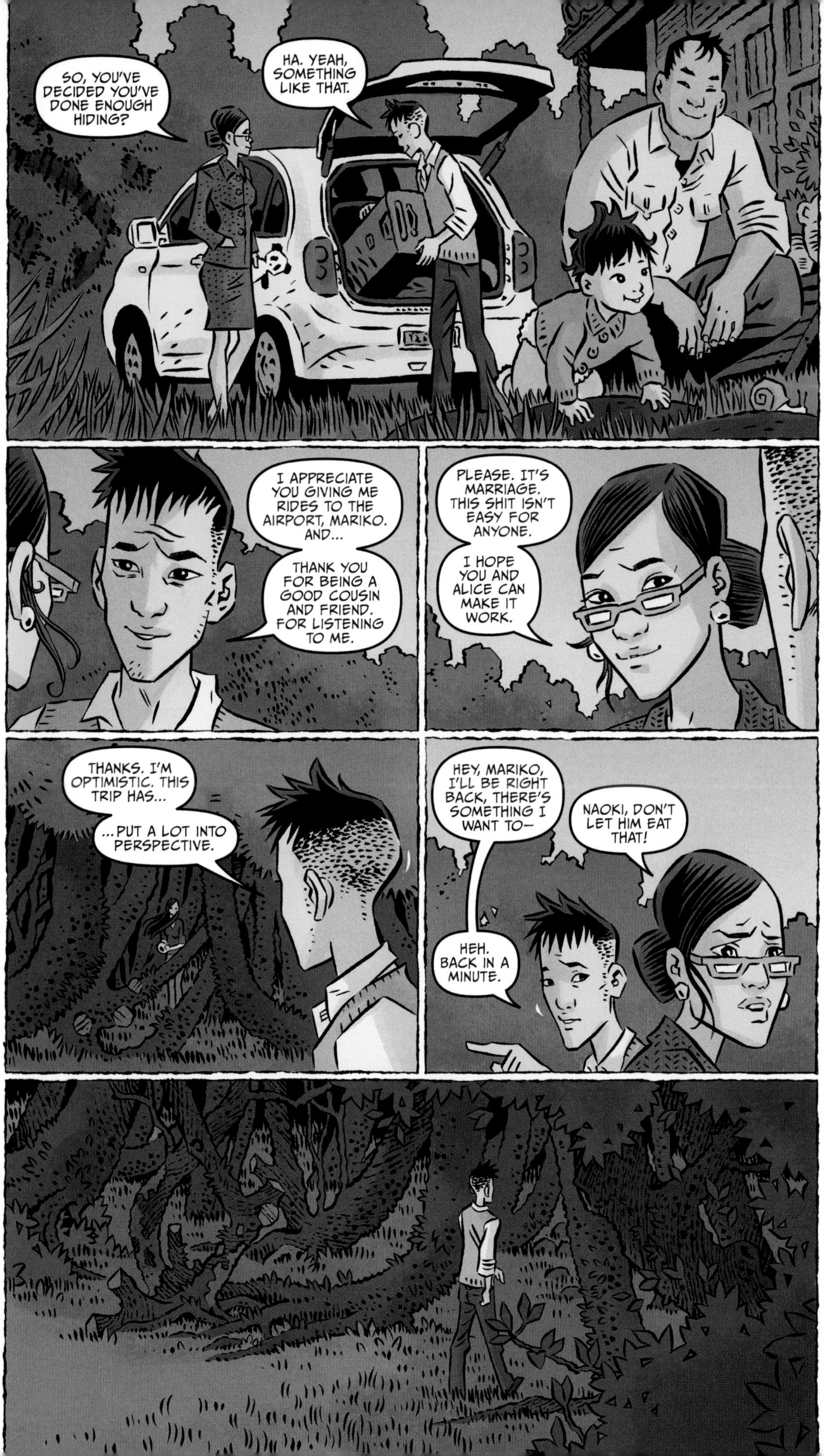
SO, YOU'VE DECIDED YOU'VE DONE ENOUGH HIDING?
HA. YEAH, SOMETHING LIKE THAT.
I APPRECIATE YOU GIVING ME RIDES TO THE AIRPORT, MARIKO. AND...
THANK YOU FOR BEING A GOOD COUSIN AND FRIEND. FOR LISTENING TO ME.
PLEASE. IT'S MARRIAGE. THIS SHIT ISN'T EASY FOR ANYONE.
I HOPE YOU AND ALICE CAN MAKE IT WORK.
THANKS. I'M OPTIMISTIC. THIS TRIP HAS...
...PUT A LOT INTO PERSPECTIVE.
HEY, MARIKO, I'LL BE RIGHT BACK, THERE'S SOMETHING I WANT TO—
NAOKI, DON'T LET HIM EAT THAT!
HEH. BACK IN A MINUTE.

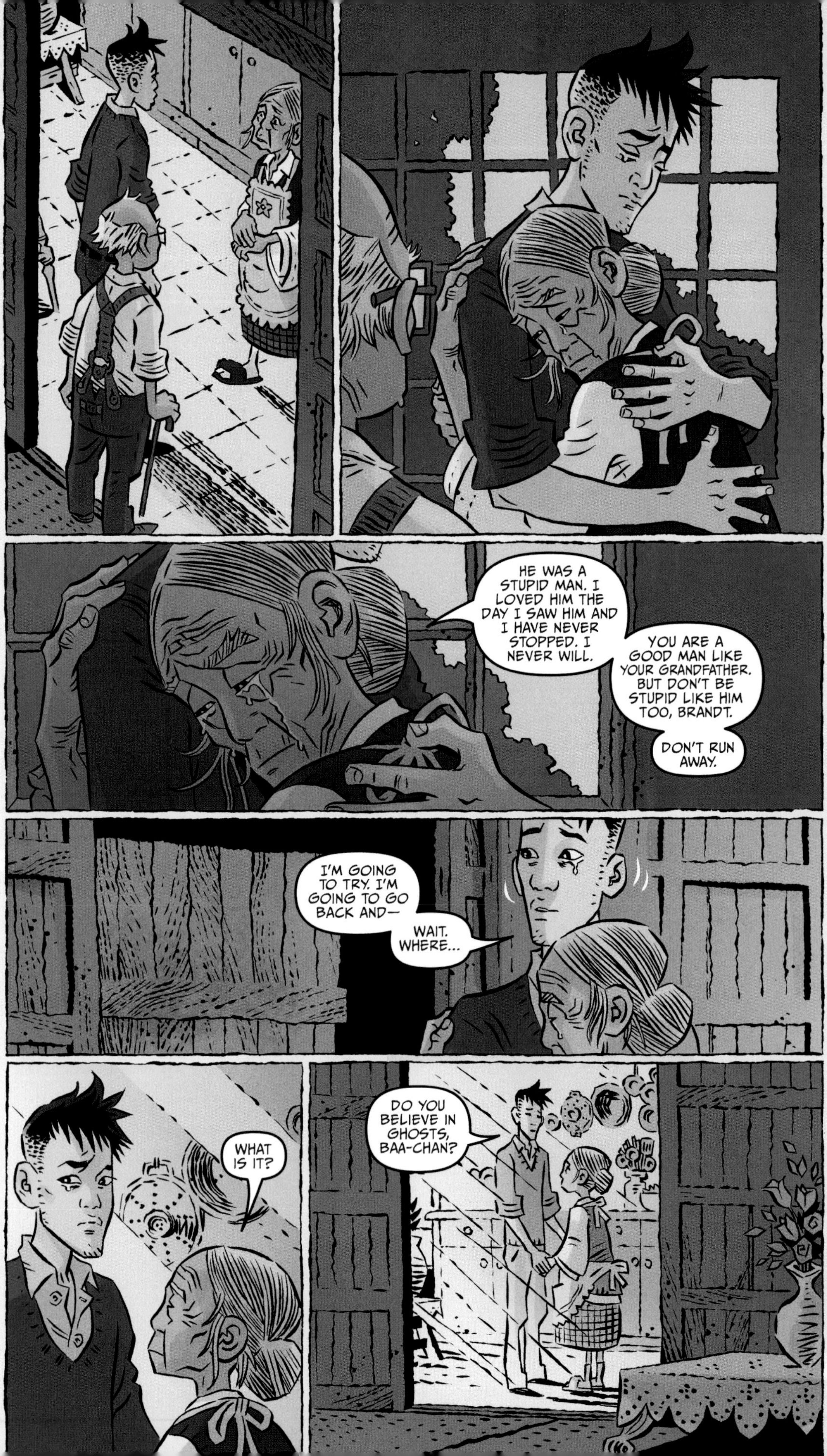
HE WAS A STUPID MAN. I LOVED HIM THE DAY I SAW HIM AND I HAVE NEVER STOPPED. I NEVER WILL.
YOU ARE A GOOD MAN LIKE YOUR GRANDFATHER. BUT DON'T BE STUPID LIKE HIM TOO, BRANDT.
DON'T RUN AWAY.
I'M GOING TO TRY. I'M GOING TO GO BACK AND—
WAIT. WHERE...
WHAT IS IT?
DO YOU BELIEVE IN GHOSTS, BAA-CHAN?

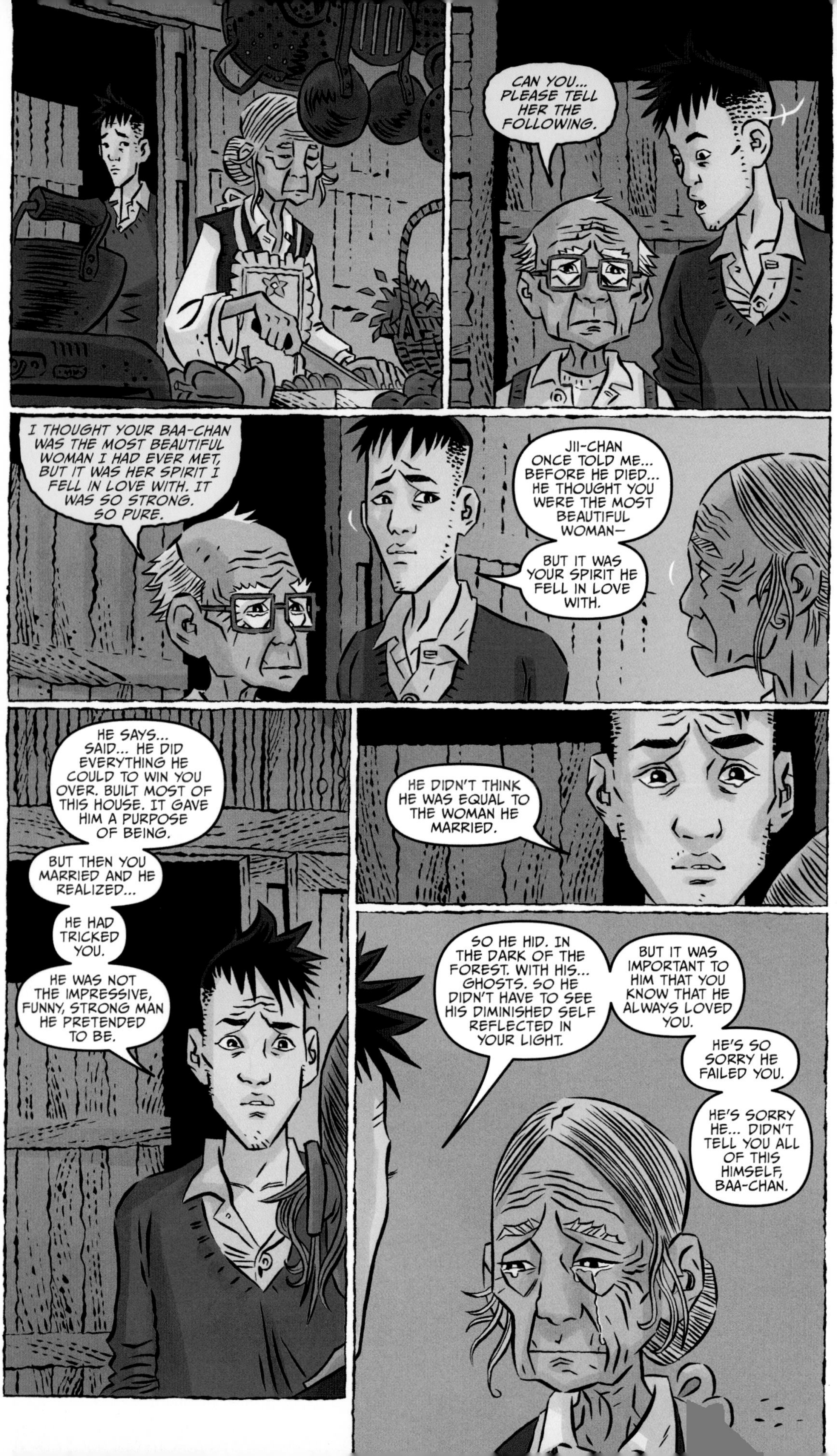
CAN YOU... PLEASE TELL HER THE FOLLOWING.
I THOUGHT YOUR BAA-CHAN WAS THE MOST BEAUTIFUL WOMAN I HAD EVER MET, BUT IT WAS HER SPIRIT I FELL IN LOVE WITH. IT WAS SO STRONG. SO PURE.
JII-CHAN ONCE TOLD ME... BEFORE HE DIED... HE THOUGHT YOU WERE THE MOST BEAUTIFUL WOMAN—
BUT IT WAS YOUR SPIRIT HE FELL IN LOVE WITH.
HE SAYS... SAID... HE DID EVERYTHING HE COULD TO WIN YOU OVER. BUILT MOST OF THIS HOUSE. IT GAVE HIM A PURPOSE OF BEING.
BUT THEN YOU MARRIED AND HE REALIZED...
HE HAD TRICKED YOU.
HE WAS NOT THE IMPRESSIVE, FUNNY, STRONG MAN HE PRETENDED TO BE.
HE DIDN'T THINK HE WAS EQUAL TO THE WOMAN HE MARRIED.
SO HE HID. IN THE DARK OF THE FOREST. WITH HIS... GHOSTS. SO HE DIDN'T HAVE TO SEE HIS DIMINISHED SELF REFLECTED IN YOUR LIGHT.
BUT IT WAS IMPORTANT TO HIM THAT YOU KNOW THAT HE ALWAYS LOVED YOU.
HE'S SO SORRY HE FAILED YOU.
HE'S SORRY HE... DIDN'T TELL YOU ALL OF THIS HIMSELF, BAA-CHAN.

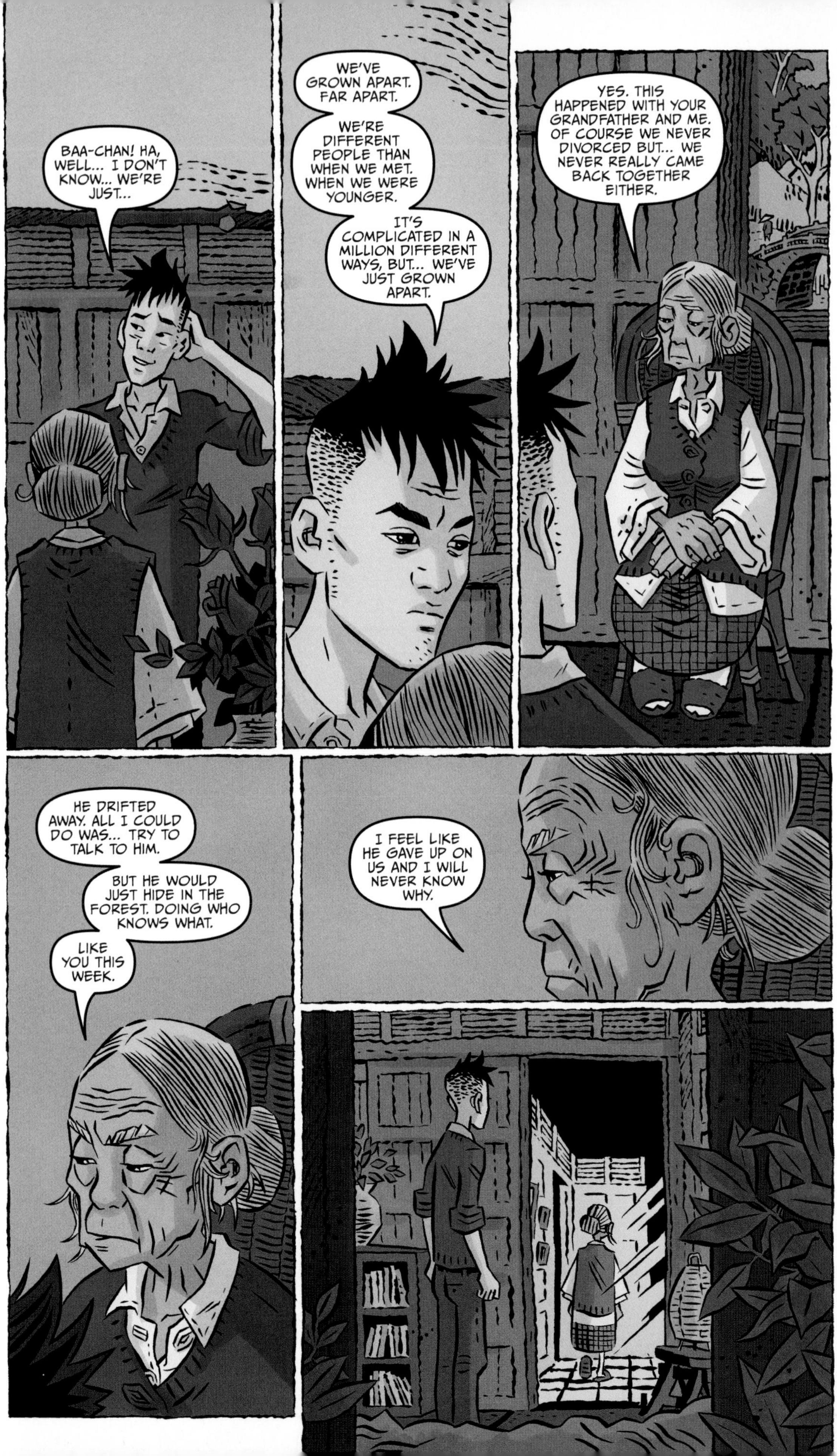
BAA-CHAN! HA, WELL... I DON'T KNOW... WE'RE JUST...
WE'VE GROWN APART. FAR APART.
WE'RE DIFFERENT PEOPLE THAN WHEN WE MET. WHEN WE WERE YOUNGER.
IT'S COMPLICATED IN A MILLION DIFFERENT WAYS, BUT... WE'VE JUST GROWN APART.
YES. THIS HAPPENED WITH YOUR GRANDFATHER AND ME. OF COURSE WE NEVER DIVORCED BUT... WE NEVER REALLY CAME BACK TOGETHER EITHER.
HE DRIFTED AWAY. ALL I COULD DO WAS... TRY TO TALK TO HIM.
BUT HE WOULD JUST HIDE IN THE FOREST. DOING WHO KNOWS WHAT.
LIKE YOU THIS WEEK.
I FEEL LIKE HE GAVE UP ON US AND I WILL NEVER KNOW WHY.

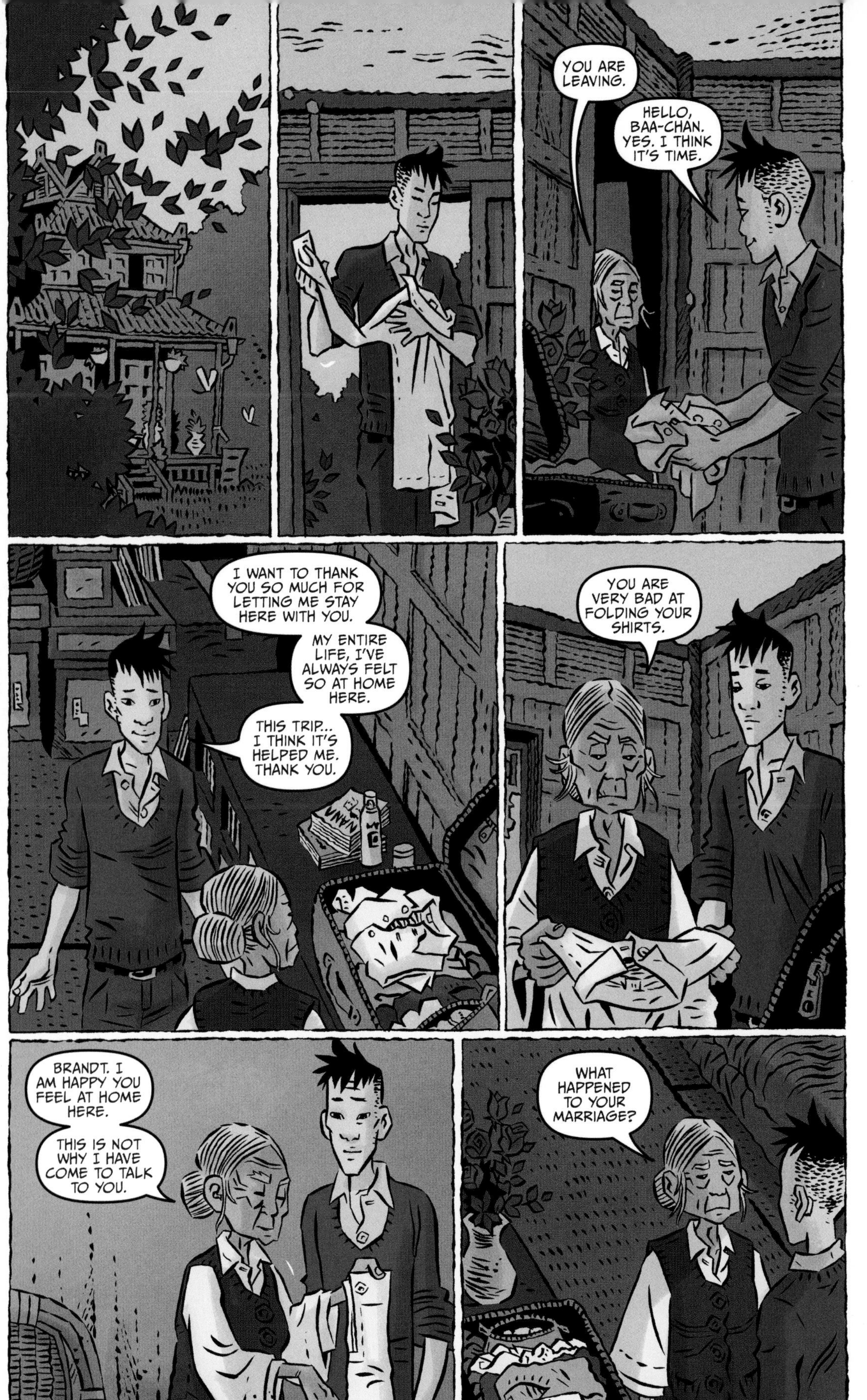
YOU ARE LEAVING.
HELLO, BAA-CHAN. YES. I THINK IT'S TIME.
I WANT TO THANK YOU SO MUCH FOR LETTING ME STAY HERE WITH YOU.
MY ENTIRE LIFE, I'VE ALWAYS FELT SO AT HOME HERE.
THIS TRIP... I THINK IT'S HELPED ME. THANK YOU.
YOU ARE VERY BAD AT FOLDING YOUR SHIRTS.
BRANDT. I AM HAPPY YOU FEEL AT HOME HERE.
THIS IS NOT WHY I HAVE COME TO TALK TO YOU.
WHAT HAPPENED TO YOUR MARRIAGE?

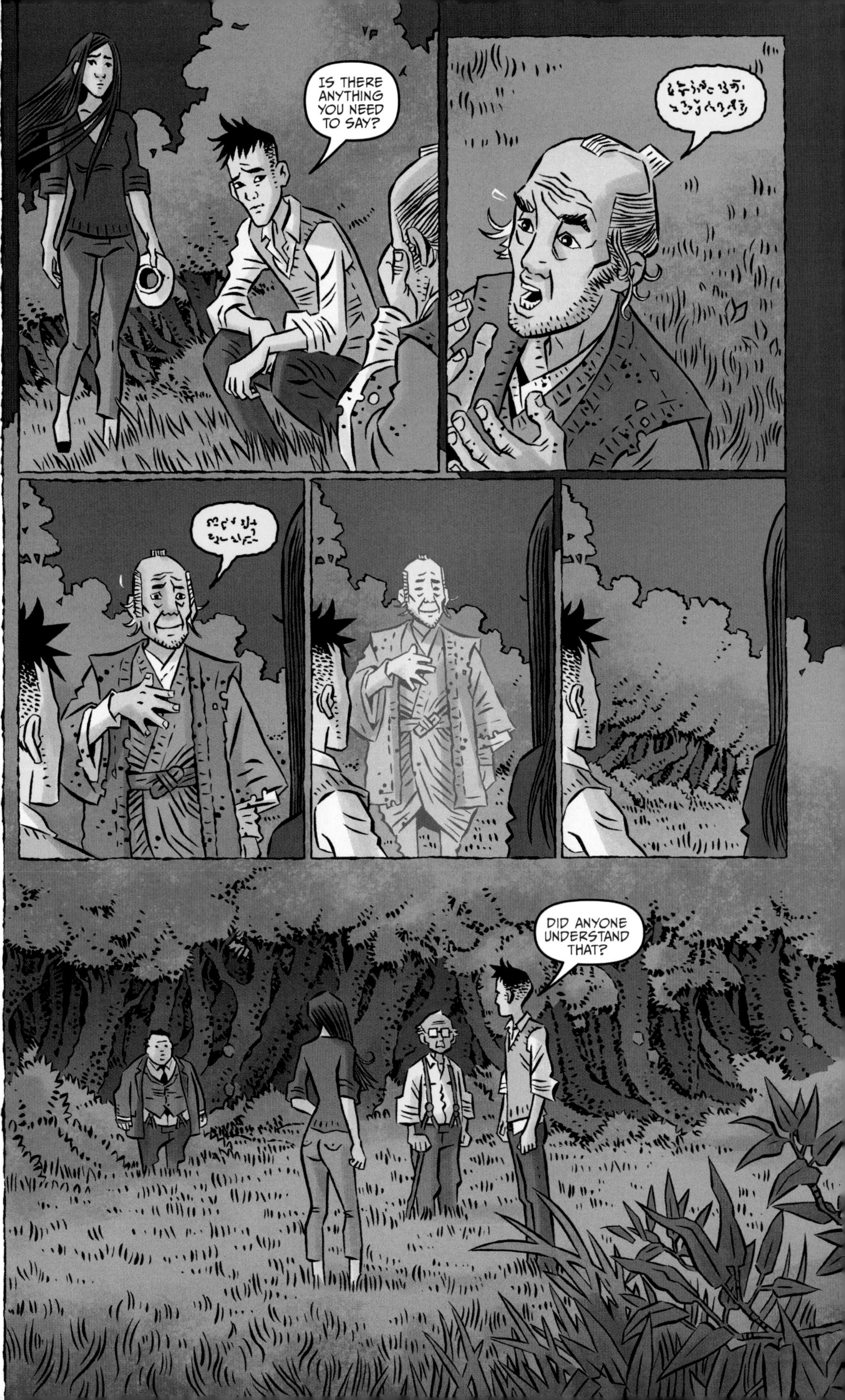
IS THERE ANYTHING YOU NEED TO SAY?
DID ANYONE UNDERSTAND THAT?

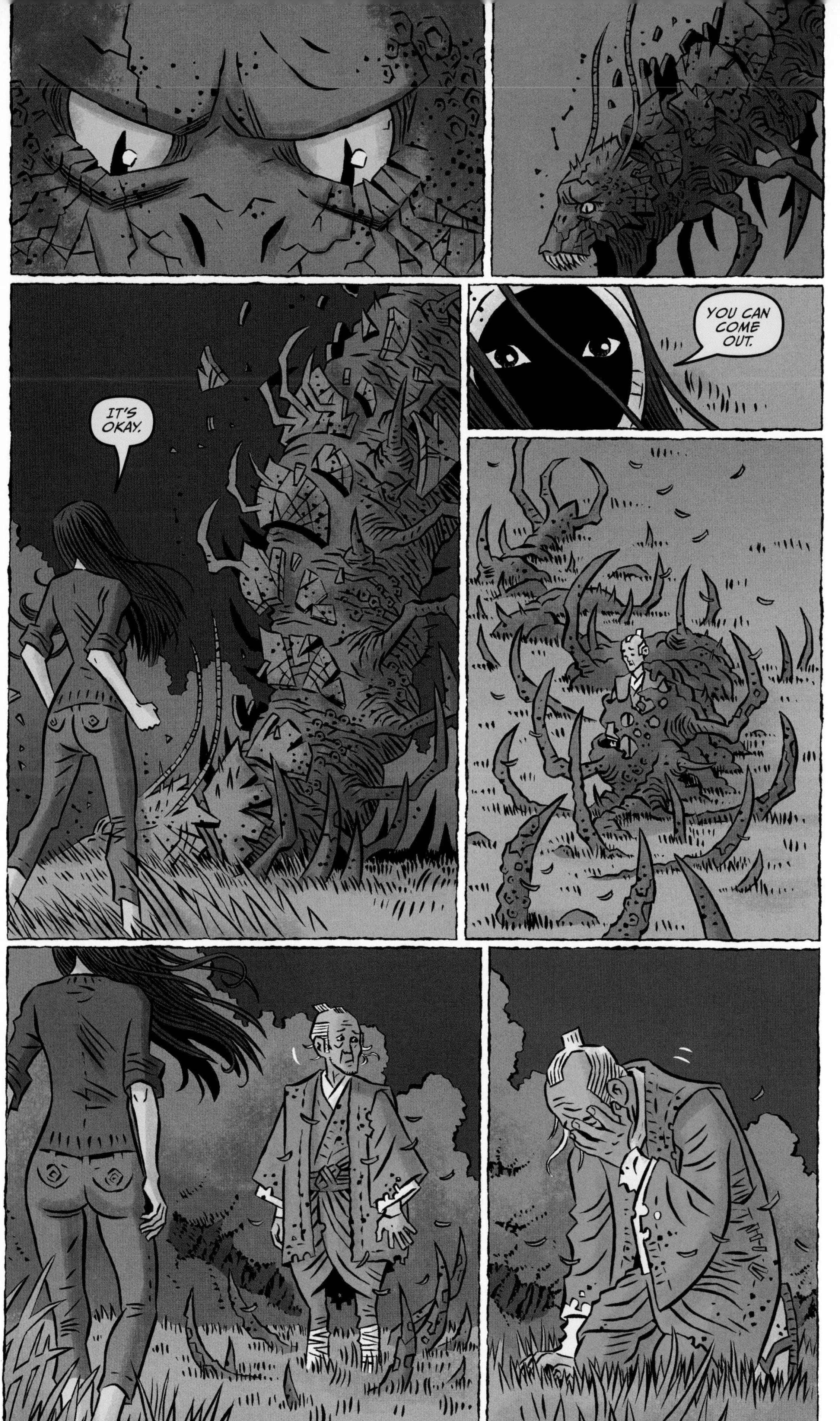
IT'S OKAY.
YOU CAN COME OUT.

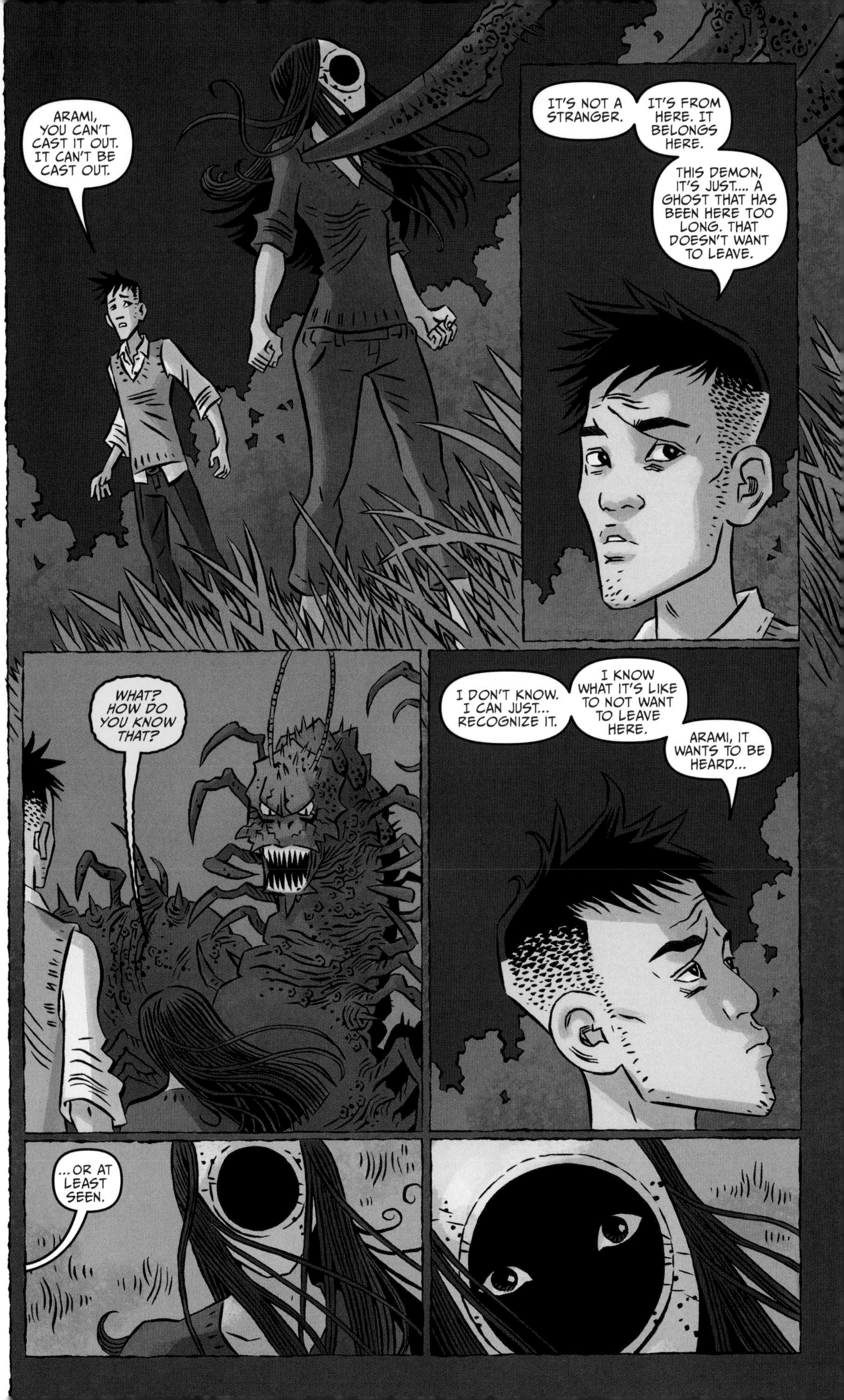
ARAMI, YOU CAN'T CAST IT OUT. IT CAN'T BE CAST OUT.
IT'S NOT A STRANGER.
IT'S FROM HERE. IT BELONGS HERE.
THIS DEMON, IT'S JUST.... A GHOST THAT HAS BEEN HERE TOO LONG. THAT DOESN'T WANT TO LEAVE.
WHAT? HOW DO YOU KNOW THAT?
I DON'T KNOW. I CAN JUST... RECOGNIZE IT.
I KNOW WHAT IT'S LIKE TO NOT WANT TO LEAVE HERE.
ARAMI, IT WANTS TO BE HEARD...
...OR AT LEAST SEEN.

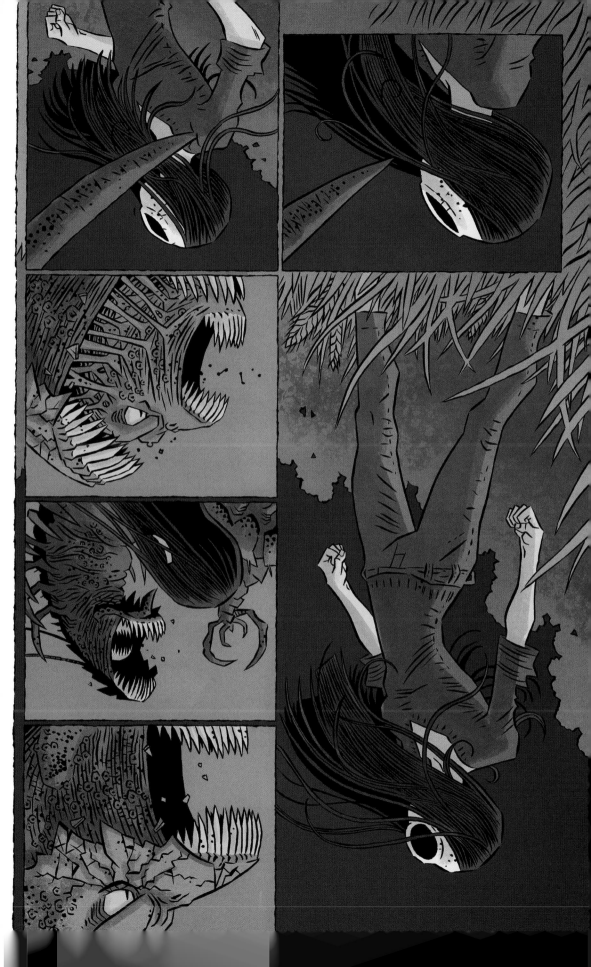

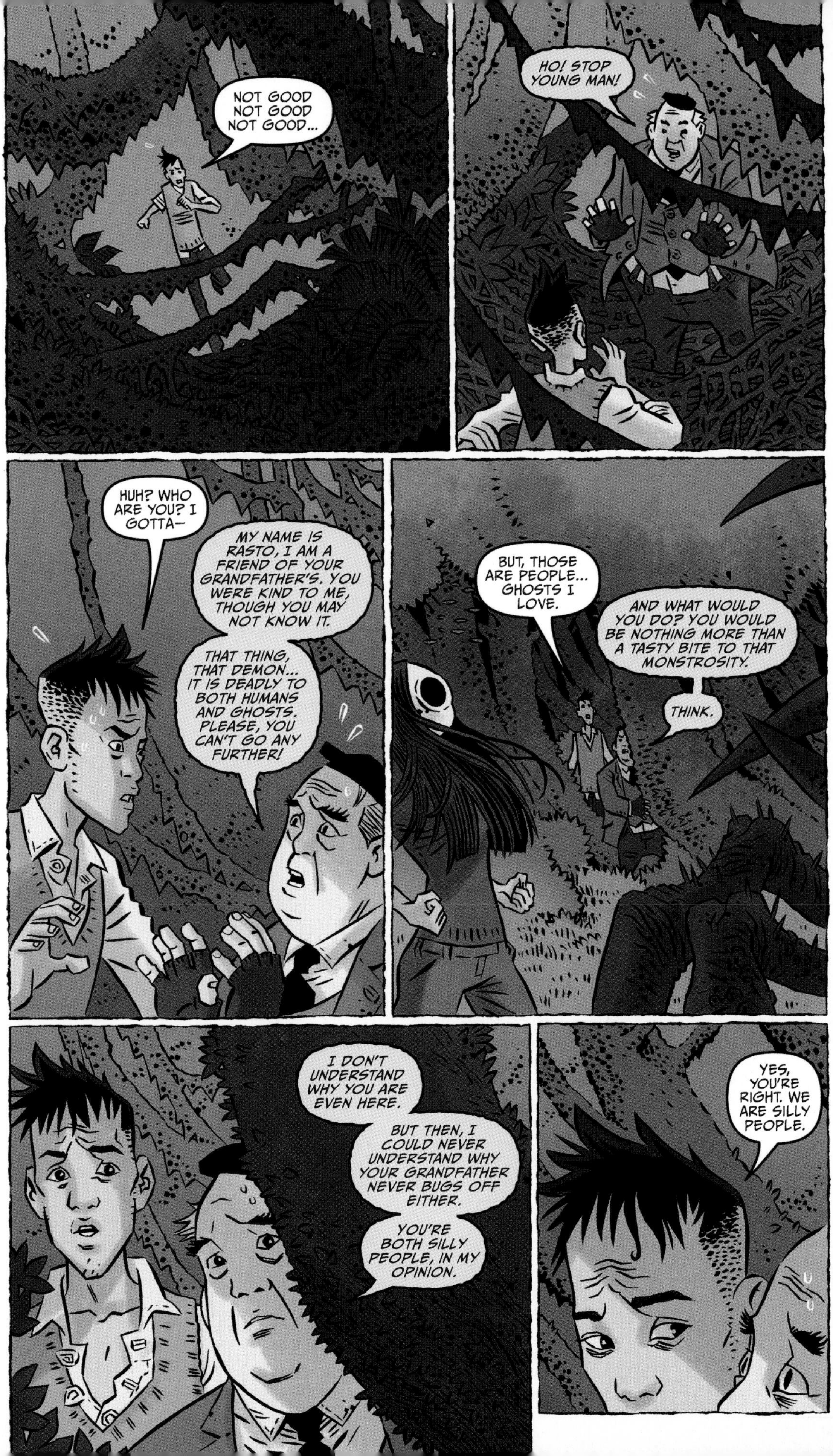
NOT GOOD NOT GOOD NOT GOOD...
HO! STOP YOUNG MAN!
HUH? WHO ARE YOU? I GOTTA—
MY NAME IS RASTO, I AM A FRIEND OF YOUR GRANDFATHER'S. YOU WERE KIND TO ME, THOUGH YOU MAY NOT KNOW IT.
THAT THING, THAT DEMON... IT IS DEADLY TO BOTH HUMANS AND GHOSTS. PLEASE, YOU CAN'T GO ANY FURTHER!
BUT, THOSE ARE PEOPLE... GHOSTS I LOVE.
AND WHAT WOULD YOU DO? YOU WOULD BE NOTHING MORE THAN A TASTY BITE TO THAT MONSTROSITY.
THINK.
I DON'T UNDERSTAND WHY YOU ARE EVEN HERE.
BUT THEN, I COULD NEVER UNDERSTAND WHY YOUR GRANDFATHER NEVER BUGS OFF EITHER.
YOU'RE BOTH SILLY PEOPLE, IN MY OPINION.
YES, YOU'RE RIGHT. WE ARE SILLY PEOPLE.

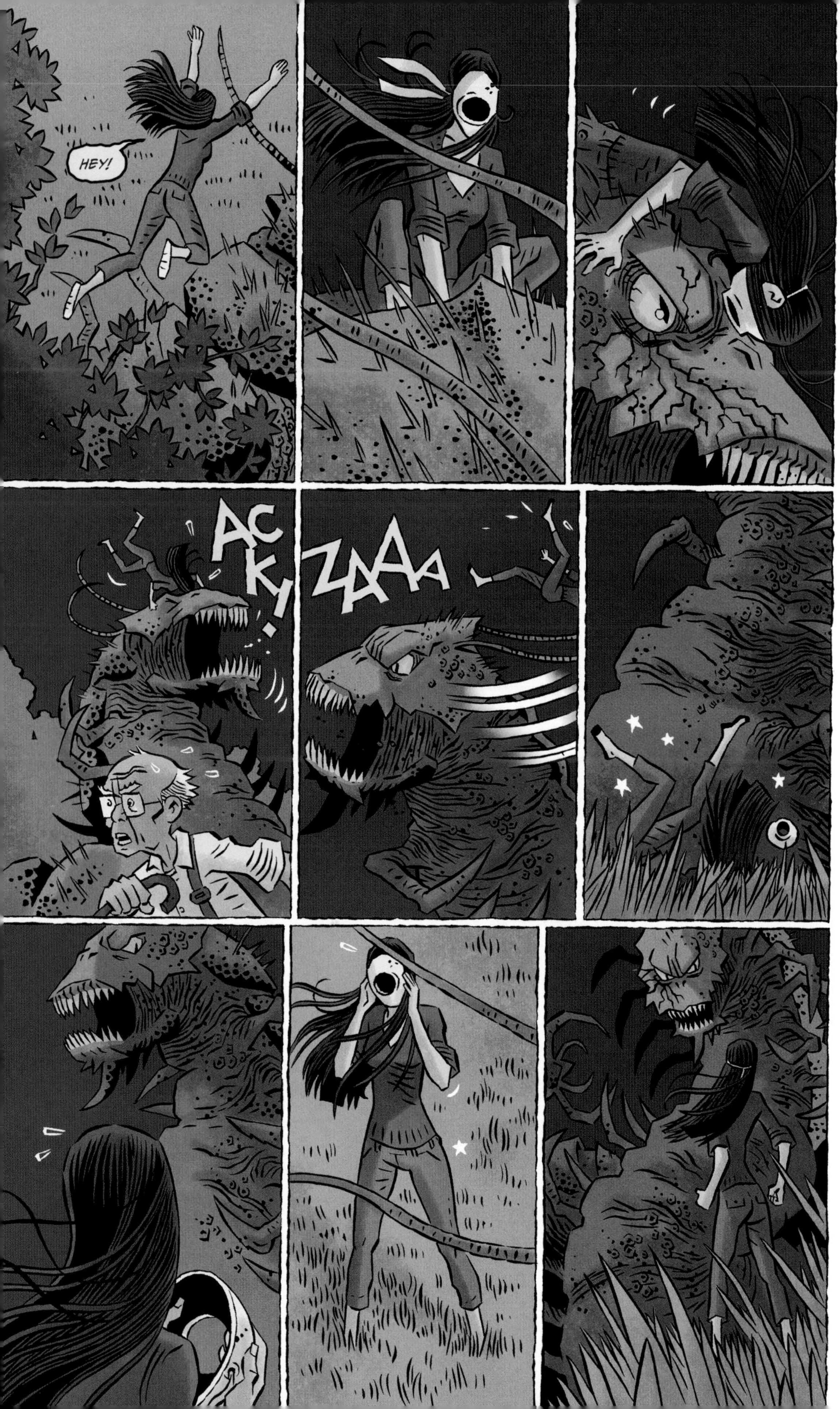
HEY!
ACK!
ZAAAA

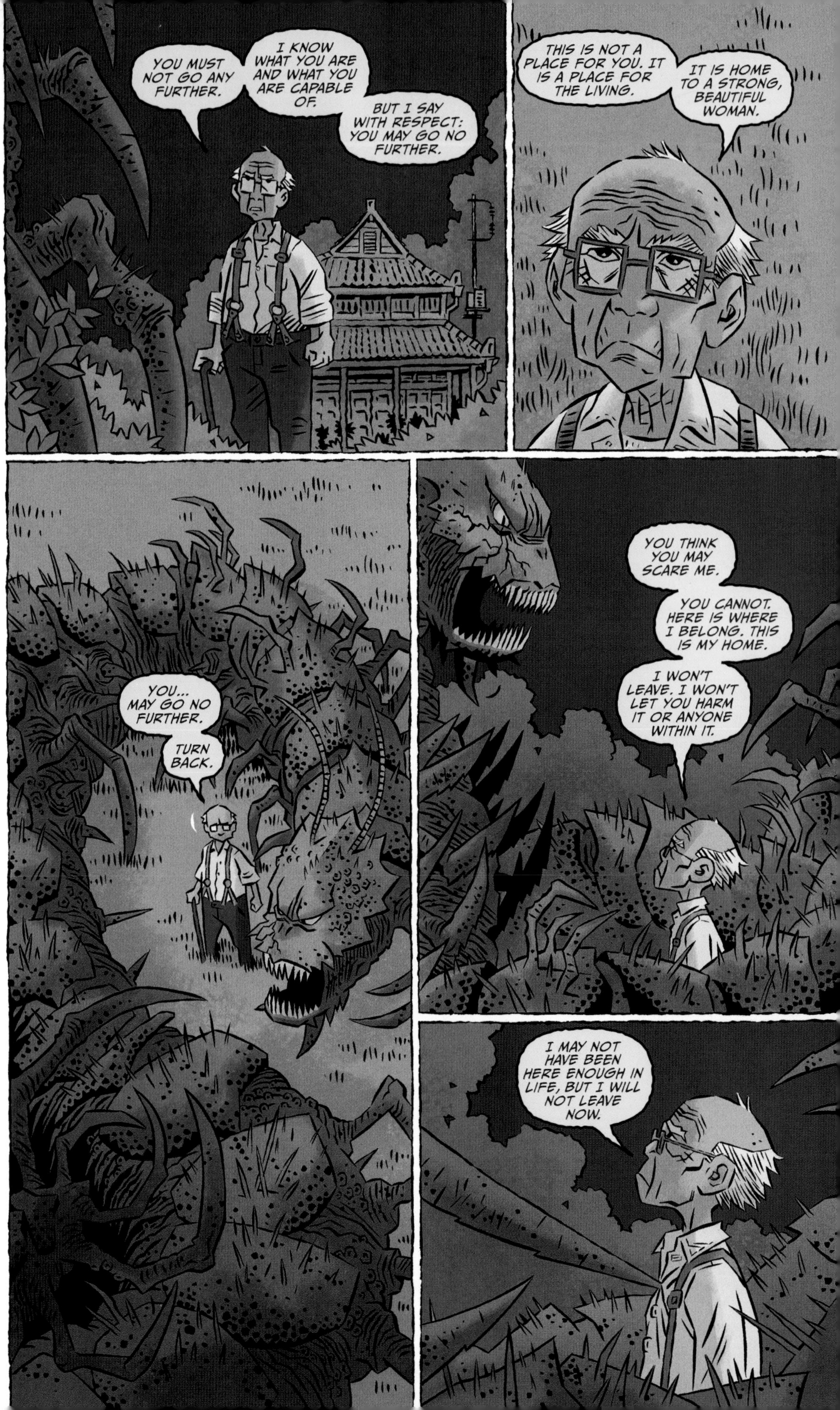
YOU MUST NOT GO ANY FURTHER.
I KNOW WHAT YOU ARE AND WHAT YOU ARE CAPABLE OF.
BUT I SAY WITH RESPECT: YOU MAY GO NO FURTHER.
THIS IS NOT A PLACE FOR YOU. IT IS A PLACE FOR THE LIVING.
IT IS HOME TO A STRONG, BEAUTIFUL WOMAN.
YOU... MAY GO NO FURTHER.
TURN BACK.
YOU THINK YOU MAY SCARE ME.
YOU CANNOT. HERE IS WHERE I BELONG. THIS IS MY HOME.
I WON'T LEAVE. I WON'T LET YOU HARM IT OR ANYONE WITHIN IT.
I MAY NOT HAVE BEEN HERE ENOUGH IN LIFE, BUT I WILL NOT LEAVE NOW.

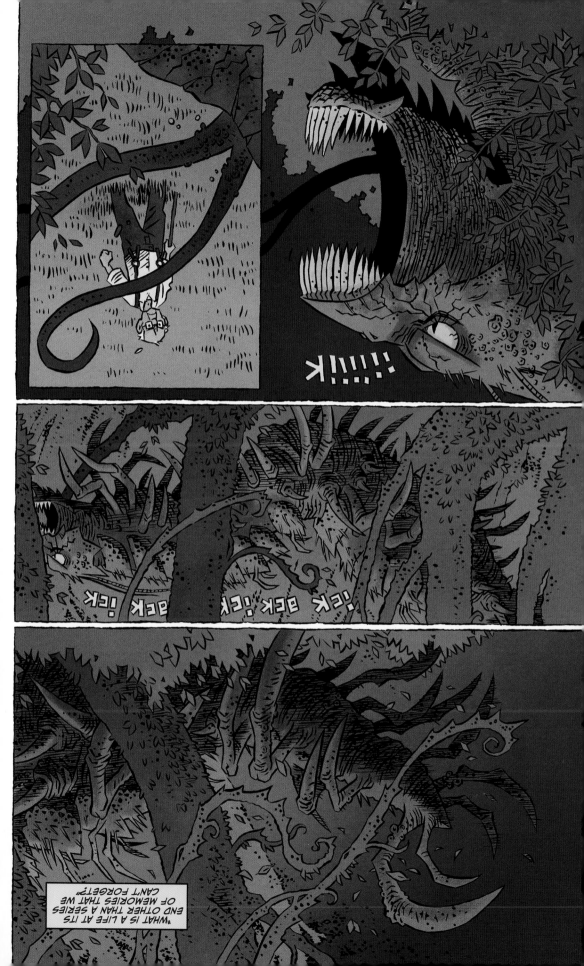

K!!!!!

iCK iCK iCK iCK iCK

"WHAT IS A LIFE AT ITS END OTHER THAN A SERIES OF MEMORIES THAT WE CAN'T FORGET?"

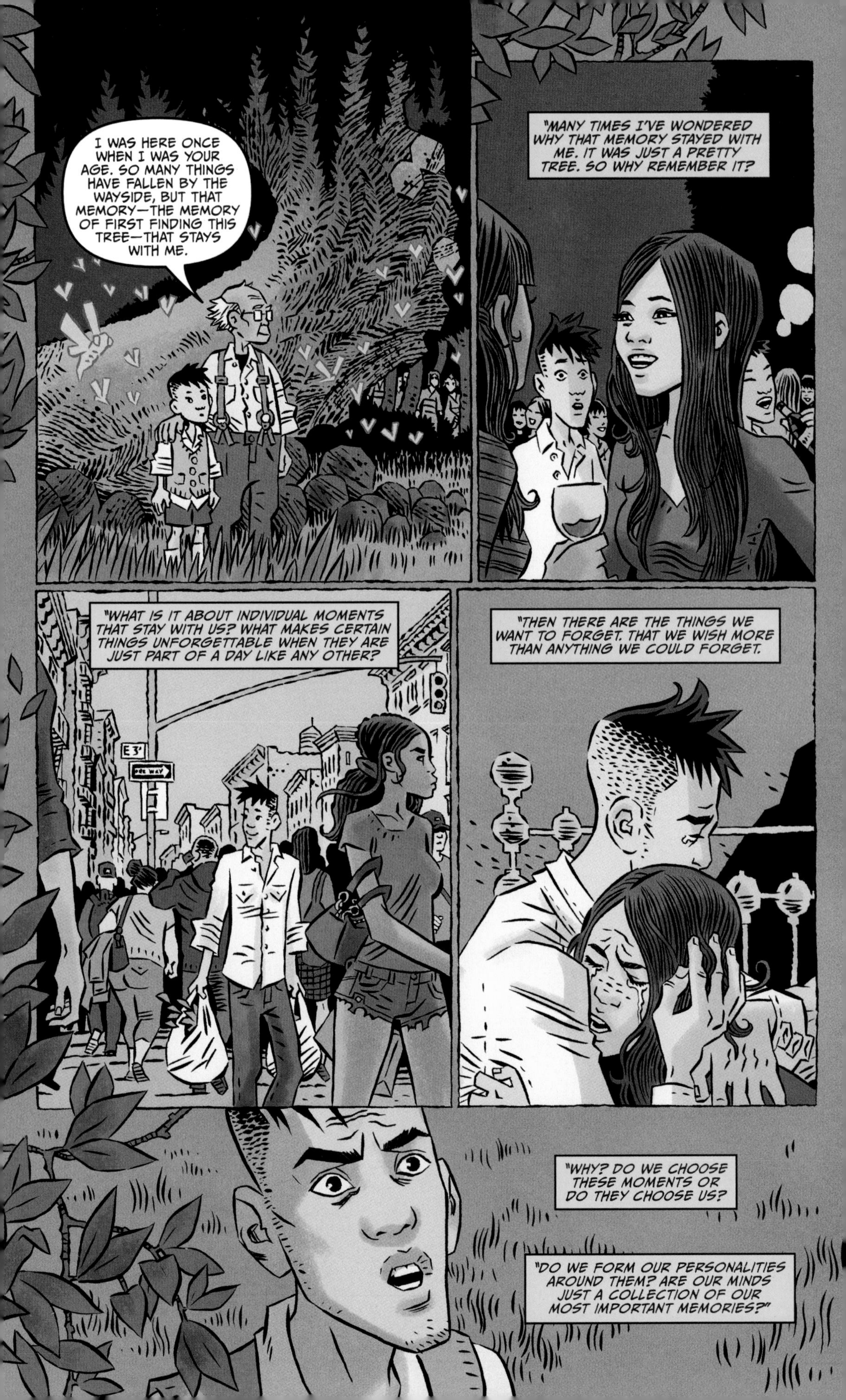
I WAS HERE ONCE WHEN I WAS YOUR AGE. SO MANY THINGS HAVE FALLEN BY THE WAYSIDE, BUT THAT MEMORY—THE MEMORY OF FIRST FINDING THIS TREE—THAT STAYS WITH ME.
"MANY TIMES I'VE WONDERED WHY THAT MEMORY STAYED WITH ME. IT WAS JUST A PRETTY TREE. SO WHY REMEMBER IT?
"WHAT IS IT ABOUT INDIVIDUAL MOMENTS THAT STAY WITH US? WHAT MAKES CERTAIN THINGS UNFORGETTABLE WHEN THEY ARE JUST PART OF A DAY LIKE ANY OTHER?
"THEN THERE ARE THE THINGS WE WANT TO FORGET. THAT WE WISH MORE THAN ANYTHING WE COULD FORGET.
"WHY? DO WE CHOOSE THESE MOMENTS OR DO THEY CHOOSE US?
"DO WE FORM OUR PERSONALITIES AROUND THEM? ARE OUR MINDS JUST A COLLECTION OF OUR MOST IMPORTANT MEMORIES?"